THE MEMORY
SNATCHER

A Doctor Collingsworth and Inspector Ninoska mystery

PASCAL INARD

Published by Happy Paw Prints, PO Box 2604, Cheltenham
3192, Australia
ISBN: 978-0-9874259-3-5

For Isabella, love of my life.

"Each book is Lazarus and you the reader, bid Lazarus to come forth. And it lives again, the dead words warmed by your glance."

Ray Bradbury

This book was written in Melbourne, Australia, on the land of the Wurundjeri people who have been custodians of this area for thousands of years.

The Wurundjeri are a people of the Indigenous Australian nation of the Woiwurrung language group, in the Kulin alliance, who occupy the Birrarung Valley, its tributaries and the present location of Melbourne.

I acknowledge the Traditional Owners of this land and pay respect to their Elders and families.

Chapter One

31st March 2046, Melbourne.

Doctor Stephen Collingsworth had the unenviable honour of being the first victim of the memory snatcher. That scoundrel could not have made a better choice; the doctor had hyperthymesia, a rare condition that allowed him to recall every detail of his life, from the most trivial, like the colour of the socks of the man who sat opposite him on the train to Ballarat where he worked, to the most complex, like the value of every parameter of the standard model of particle physics to the tenth decimal place.

The train pulled into Ballarat station, and Stephen made his way to the boarding area of the shuttle train that would take him directly to the Quantum Particle Transformer facility. It was placed completely underground, and the thirty square kilometres above it were some of the best protected in Australia.

The inauguration of the facility yesterday had been a success, but he couldn't get rid of the nagging feeling that something was wrong. It had started when he awoke that morning with a massive headache. He had blamed it on the glass of champagne that Bob Fultrow, school friend and Prime Minister of Australia, had made him drink, whispering something about the importance of public image.

But it wasn't just a feeling, there were signs that something *was* indeed wrong: his ponytail has doubled in length overnight, he had lost one kilo since last week, and the most disturbing one was the brown stain on the right pocket of his grey trench coat that wasn't there yesterday. His co-workers made fun of him for wearing it, but it was his insurance against Melbourne's capricious weather that was worsening every year. A forty-five-degree heat could turn into a ten-degree chill in a matter of minutes, and he didn't want to be caught out, so he wore it every day of the year, no matter what the weather forecast was.

Stephen touched the identification pad with his right index finger, and his DNA was matched against the security database to verify his profile. After the all clear was given, he exchanged his smartphone for a site-only tablet. As an additional security measure to ensure nothing could be leaked out, the area was in a cone of silence. No device that could communicate with the outside world was allowed inside. The researchers didn't mind, but to keep the technicians happy, a fitness centre complete with swimming pool and a relaxation room with the latest immersion games and cat videos had been included in the building.

Five minutes later, the shuttle arrived and Stephen entered the QPT facility. He was surprised that the decorations for the opening ceremony had already been taken down. He walked over to get a closer look at a new picture that had been hung next to his favourite, a representation of the Higgs boson. It represented a particle made up of eight purple strands shaped like an irregular infinity symbol arranged to form a sphere. According to the caption, the unitron was discovered at the Quantum Particle Transformer on the 15th of August 2045. How could the artist predict that Stephen was going to prove the existence of this new elementary particle, which was at the heart of his theory, in four months?

He walked briskly to his desk, looking around him for signs of other anomalies.

He sat down and consulted his schedule for the day. The first meeting was with the experimental team led by Andrew Frawson to prepare experiment Goanna at ten in the operation room. He didn't remember booking that one. It didn't make sense. The transformer wasn't ready to operate yet. A number of calibration tests were scheduled over the next week, and the entire team was mobilised to check the results. And only then could the fun begin.

Stephen scratched his head.

"Morning Stephen, how're you going?"

He looked up at Andrew; with the physique of a rugby player and the demeanour and blond hair of a surfer, you would never suspect that he was one of the brightest experimental physicists in the southern hemisphere, a worthy partner in Stephen's project to prove his universal theory.

"Ok, I guess."

"D-day at last! Aren't you excited?"

"I will be once we've run all the calibration tests and we can get Suzie going." Andrew had started calling the Transformer Suzie and the name had stuck. He hadn't given any clues as to whom he had named it after, but some suspect it was the name of his first and only love who had perished in the 2038 Queensland tsunami.

"Stop stalling, we're waiting for you! You told me yesterday morning that you'd worked out how to solve the issue with your model. You know, the Lagrangian renormalisation of the twenty-fifth constant. You were confident that you would be ready today to go through it with the team so that we could rerun experiment Goanna."

Stephen frowned.

"Hey, what's wrong? Did you come across another snag?"

"Were you dreaming? How could I have done anything yesterday, with Bob Fultrow and the media touring the place? We haven't even started calibrating Suzie, and my model has only got twenty-four constants, not twenty-five."

Andrew flinched. "Are you sure you're alright Stephen?"

"The champagne didn't agree with me, but apart from that, I'm fine. Why?"

"You sound like you're living in the past. You spoke about the celebration as if it was yesterday, and you're referring to your model and Suzie as they were then."

Beads of sweat formed on Stephen's forehead. "Wait, there's something I don't understand. You're telling me that Suzie is ready for an experiment, and you're waiting for me to adjust my model that has a twenty-fifth constant."

Andrew nodded; Stephen continued. "What is this constant?"

"You introduced it three months ago. Has your prodigious memory let you down?" Andrew asked.

"Just answer my questions, and then if I can, I'll answer yours."

"Alright, the twenty-fifth constant is the elliptical mass of the unitron."

"And what is this experiment you called Goanna? Is it to create a murkon?"

Andrew laughed. "That was nine months ago! Come on, you've got no excuse for forgetting that one, as usual you didn't drink a single drop of booze when we celebrated!"

Stephen considered Andrew's reply; the murkon was the particle that made up dark matter according to his theory. He had been waiting for the transformer to be built to prove its existence, but Andrew was saying that the experiment to observe it had already been successfully conducted.

It didn't make sense. Had he fallen into a parallel universe?

"So what is it?"

"As if you didn't know, it's to transform a W boson into an acceleron."

"My next question may sound silly, but please humour me. What is today's date?"

"March thirty-first."

"Of what year?"

"2046."

"Are you sure?"

Andrew smiled. "Well yesterday was the thirtieth, so unless the decimal numbering system was changed overnight, thirty-one comes after thirty."

"No, I meant the year."

"I celebrated my birthday last week, it was the big four-oh. Now let's see, according to my birth certificate, I was born in 2006—add forty and that makes 2046."

Stephen twirled his ponytail while he digested the information at hand. The picture in the reception area, the train running to an apparently future-dated timetable, Bob's seemingly premature election date announcement in the news and what Andrew had just said all correlated.

He had lost his memories of the last three hundred and seventy-four days.

Adrenaline flooded his body, making his stomach churn and his skin flush. He felt helpless. His infallible memory, the one thing in his life that he could always rely on no matter what, had let him down

Andrew put his hand on Stephen's back and said, "Mate, I think you've been working too hard. If I was you, I'd take the day off and rest. It's no drama, we'll reschedule the experiment."

The headache which had been slowly receding came back stronger than before. Stephen winced, took a deep breath and said, "I think you're right Andrew, I'm going to go home, and after a good night's sleep, whatever condition I have will have gone away."

As he spoke, he hoped that his words weren't just wishful thinking.

Stephen walked out and got on the shuttle train.

He recalled the morning's events one by one: he had woken up, as he always did, to the sound of cockatoos screeching and the neighbour's kids screaming that they didn't want to go to school, but the house was empty. On the trip to work, his smartphone had told him that he had finished reading a novel one year ago when he thought he was up to page 143, and that he had written a novel.

His good old iPhone 15 wasn't defective after all, a small consolation. He wasn't going to have to upgrade it for a model made by JCN, the company that had bought Apple. The JCN models predicted their owner's wishes and needs based on patterns of behaviour (very useful for a creature of habit like Stephen), and by measuring wirelessly their owner's biological variables: endorphins, adrenaline, blood sugar level and testosterone amongst others. There was no way Stephen was going to buy a single JCN product; he couldn't forgive what the corporation had done to his father.

Stephen felt relieved that his short-term memory was intact. But what about his long-term memory?

The value of Pi is 3.14159265358979323846264338327 9

He stopped at the forty-seventh digit and went straight to the last one he could remember: the 78675th digit is 4.

The capital city of Pakistan is Islamabad.

The currency of Botswana was the Pula before the formation of the United Republics of Africa.

His grandmother's maiden name was Gordon.

His grandfather watched the first man walk on the moon on the twentieth of July 1969; he was sixteen at the time. He met Stephen's grandmother at a concert of the Rolling Stones in Melbourne on the 17th of February 1973.

One year since his last memory.

All he knew so far about that period was that he had been successful in creating a murkon, and that he had introduced another constant in his model. But what else had happened? Where was his wife Cécile? Had she simply gone to work early today? Her down-under French fashion brand was doing very well, but she was anxious that her success wouldn't last in the fickle world of fashion and she often worked long hours.

At Ballarat station, Stephen got on the Melbourne train and sat in his usual seat. It was the first time he had travelled this early and the carriage was only half full.

The train started and Stephen looked out the window. He hadn't noticed before that the countryside had regained the colours that the four-year drought had drained out of it. Cattle were grazing in the fields again; it was amazing how quickly the recovery had been. Not that he usually paid much attention to the landscape, like most commuters who spent their time ingesting the information that their smartphones threw at them, or trying to get an extra half-hour of sleep.

He got tired of playing 'spot he difference' and called Cécile's number. It went to voicemail again; she was probably in a meeting. He dialled the number of her office; Juliette, Cécile's friend and associate, answered.

"Cécile Dubontant's office, how may I help you?"

"Hi Juliette, it's Stephen, I've been trying to reach Cécile all morning. Is she busy right now?"

"Maybe she is," Juliette replied drily. "Why are you suddenly trying to reach her?"

Stephen hesitated to tell Juliette that he hadn't seen Cécile for a year. "I was a bit worried, that's all."

"It's a bit late to worry about her. You should have done that a long time ago, instead of taking her for granted. But if you really want to know, I've never seen her better."

Stephen tried not to make his bewilderment apparent. "Can you ask her to call me?"

"Any particular reason why she should do that?"

"I have some news which may be of interest to her."

"I'll try, but don't hold your breath. She's moved on, and the less she hears about you, the better."

Juliette hung up.

That explained the empty bed and Filou missing. It was her cat; Stephen didn't see the point of owning a pet that was oblivious to the humans with whom it shared the house.

He closed his eyes to review what he had seen in the house before he left. Cécile's brushes and make-up were missing from the bathroom, and her painting was no longer hanging in the lounge room. Brighton beach, with its brightly coloured bathing sheds, painted with the brush strokes of an impressionist—Monet was her favourite.

Cécile had moved out, but why? What had happened in the past twelve months? And where was she living now?

Stephen called his best friend Mukassa, thinking he would have some answers.

"Hi Steve, how are you?" Mukassa continued without giving Stephen time to reply. "What did you think of our recording of *Birds of Fire* I sent you yesterday?"

Mukassa was a keyboard player in a jazz band and he had often said that he would love to play this song by the Mahavishnu Orchestra, a jazz band from the 1970s, but he had put that project on hold until he could find a violin player that could equal Jean-Luc Ponty.

"Oh, sorry. I didn't have time to listen to it. I had other things on my mind."

"Busy at work?"

"No, it's not that. I woke up this morning not remembering anything about the past twelve months."

"How is that possible? You don't remember anything?"

"Nothing, zip, nada, a complete blank. The last thing I remember is going to bed after the inauguration of the Transformer."

"How could that happen? Have you seen a doctor yet?"

"No, it took me a while to realise that I was no longer living in 2045; I'm on my way home now. I'm hoping it's temporary and I'll wake up tomorrow with all my memories."

"You and your extraordinary memory, you must have overworked yourself and exhausted it."

"Well, I can still remember every detail from the moment I woke up this morning, and everything before the inauguration of the Transformer. The only thing I've figured out is that Cécile moved out. I don't know why or when, and I can't reach her, she must've put a block on my number."

"I can answer some of your questions, but I can only go by what you told me."

"That'll be enough."

"You went through a bad patch last winter; something happened at work and it affected you really badly. You didn't tell me what it was, but you were tense and I hardly saw you. Not that I was seeing much of you before anyway, you were completely taken by your work. And then Cécile left you. You told me that it was very sudden, and that it was because you were neglecting her."

"When was that?"

"End of October I think."

She had left him six months ago, and she was already with someone else; at least that's what he thought Juliette meant when she said Cécile had moved on.

"How did I react to that?"

"Compared to the incident at work, rather well. I think by that time, you were so involved in fixing up whatever was wrong at work that nothing else mattered so much."

"What about Thibault and Félicie?"

"They moved with their mother and you see them every second week-end."

Stephen exhaled loudly; he had heard enough for the day.

He turned right and walked along Comer Street, with its stylish mansions. The value of the houses dropped every time the sea level announcement was released. Last year, a rise of three centimetres had resulted in a drop of ten percent in house prices on the west side of Brighton. The proximity of the beach that had made the suburb of Brighton so desirable was now its bane. Stephen would have joined the exodus and moved to Ballarat, if it wasn't for Cécile who wanted to stay in the fashion capital of Australia where she had her office, her friends and her clients. She preferred to wait to have her feet in the water before moving, even if she knew it was inevitable.

Stephen thought about what Mukassa had said. It didn't take much for Cécile to feel neglected. She needed to be reassured constantly—that she was a good wife, a good mother, a good fashion designer. The youngest of five children, she'd had scant attention from her parents, and needed to prove to the world that she was worthy of being loved. When Stephen's mind was totally consumed by the search for the key that would unlock the universe's mysteries, Cécile had a way of bringing him back to earth. It made Stephen's mind blink, and for a moment he reverted to his role of loving husband. But this time, his troubles at work had such a grip on him that there had been no room left for his wife's emotional needs.

Alone at home, with a headache that came and went, Stephen's hope that tomorrow he would be back to normal started to wane. He turned to his wall screen and asked for information on amnesia.

Amnesia is a deficit in memory caused by brain damage, disease or psychological trauma. Amnesia can also be caused temporarily by the use of various sedatives and hypnotic drugs. Memory can be either wholly or partially lost due to the extent of damage that was caused. There are two main types of amnesia: retrograde amnesia and anterograde amnesia. Retrograde amnesia is the inability to retrieve information that was acquired before a particular date, usually the date of an accident or operation. In some cases the memory loss can extend back decades, while in others the person may lose only a few months of memory.

"Tell me more about retrograde amnesia," Stephen said.

Retrograde amnesia is usually caused by head traumas or brain damage. Episodic memory which refers to one's life experience is more likely to be affected than semantic memory which refers to general knowledge about the world. The damage is usually caused by head trauma, cerebrovascular accident, stroke, tumour, hypoxia, encephalitis or chronic alcoholism. Retrograde amnesia can also occur without any anatomical damage to the brain. It often occurs due to a traumatic situation that individuals wish to avoid.

"If I had a stroke, I wouldn't have been able to go home." He rubbed his head and said, "If I was hit on the head, I would have a bump. A traumatic situation? That's very unlikely. So are sedatives and drugs." Stephen paused. "Unless my food or drink was spiked. I'll request a full security update of all the personnel tomorrow; there could be a traitor in our midst. What if our competitors knew that I was getting close and tried to neutralise me? A blood test will confirm that. Browser, what about treatments?"

Many forms of amnesia fix themselves without being treated, but there is no actual remedy for amnesia. To what extent the patient recovers, and how long the amnesia continues depends on the type and severity of the lesion. Improvements can occur with cognitive therapy in which amnesiacs develop the memory skills they have and try to regain some they have lost by finding which techniques help retrieve memories or create new retrieval paths.

Stephen started pacing the room, trying to clear his head but it only made him feel more anxious.

And why were his leg muscles painful?

Fatigue, muscle pain, weight loss and abdominal pain were all symptoms of Multiple Endocrine Neoplasia Type 1, a hereditary disease that had claimed his mother's life when a pancreatic tumour had spread to her liver. Stephen pressed the measurement button of his wireless Personal Health Assistant: five seconds later, the results were displayed. The interface of the prototype wasn't user-friendly because his father had been forced to stop the development of the device. It didn't indicate the normal values of the measurements, but Stephen had memorised them. His ACTH level was below the upper limit beyond which a medical consultation was deemed necessary. Still, there were things that weren't measured, like the levels of the thyroid hormones T3 and T4; it was time he got a full check-up.

He walked around the house, looking for something that would trigger a memory. He started with the lounge room; it was much the same as it was a year ago, minus Cécile's painting and her magazines which she used to pile up on the coffee table in front of the red leather sofa. In the corner a canvas half covered with paint in various shades of orange that vaguely evoked a sunset stood on an easel. It looked like Cécile had a bad day when she painted it. It was surprising she left it here. When she wasn't happy with one her creations, it ended up in the bin.

Maybe he'd had a full check-up in the last twelve months and he was on medications. He went upstairs and checked the medicine cabinet, but it was empty.

He sat on his bed to take stock of his situation. His memory had a big hole, but it was intact before and after. He could still remember Bob's speech at the QPT inauguration word for word.

"Ladies and gentlemen, good evening and welcome. It is an immense honour for me to open the Quantum Particle Transformer. This facility holds the key to a brighter and more prosperous future for our nation. The winds of change are blowing, and rather than resisting them, we have embraced them. We have hoisted the sails by building this installation, and it will carry Australia to a victory, the likes of which we have not seen since the America's cup in 1983. And in case you were wondering, we do have the equivalent of the revolutionary keel that helped us win us that race." Bob paused to let his words sink in. "And that's why there are some things that we can show you tonight and others that will remain secret. All the world needs to know is that we're on the road to finding a new source of energy, one that is unlimited and non-polluting. It will set us free and it will set the rest of the world free. Once they have bought it from us, that is." Bob waited for the cheering and applause to stop. "Yes, mark my words, thanks to this Quantum Particle Transformer and the team of researchers led by the brilliant doctor Stephen Collingsworth, Australia will lead the way to an energy revolution."

Stephen would have preferred that Bob dispense with the premature triumphalism, but Bob was counting on this event to turn the tide of his abysmal approval rating. It was Stephen's fault; he had used the argument that the generation of dark energy was a sure thing to convince Bob to commit the funds. When Bob was running for a second term, desperately looking for a new policy that would lead him to victory, Stephen had given him the answer. If there wasn't a market for the fuels that laid under its soil anymore, Australia was going to develop the technology to generate a new sort of energy. Stephen remembered his winning argument. "Consider this," he'd said. "68.3 per cent of the total mass-energy of the universe consists of dark energy, the primordial energy of the big bang, responsible for the expansion of the universe. It's incredibly powerful: it battles against gravity to expand the universe at a rate of 74.3 kilometres per second per megaparsec. If you give me the funds, I can build a facility that will find a way to transform ordinary quantum particles into accelerons, the mediators of dark energy."

More importantly for Stephen, it was going to prove his 'Theory of Everything', the single all-encompassing theoretical framework that was going to fully explain and link together all physical aspects of the universe.

The holy grail of physics, no less.

A simulation had followed the speech in which protons and neutrons had travelled at the speed of light. Stephen explained that particle colliders produced particles through the collision of other particles at high energy, but the QPT was different because it stopped the decay of the particles created and transformed them into other elementary particles. Andrew had developed an animation which showed the bosons being created; it looked pretty and wasn't fully accurate, but the media loved it.

A question and answer session had followed.

"Prime Minister, is this the right time to spend twenty billion dollars when we are in the middle of a recession, and Australia's credit rating is on the brink of being downgraded by three notches?"

"The return on investment is predicted to be phenomenal, and beyond the billions of dollars of revenue this will generate is the boost to Australia's status in the global energy market and scientific community. We will be seen as innovators and leaders. Australia has lived for far too long on the back of finite resources buried in its soil. Now it's over: after the Chinese closed all their coal power stations, we thought we would fall back on our feet by selling our uranium to fuel their nuclear power plants, and then vast deposits were discovered in the desert of Gobi. It's no coincidence that the Chinese Empire annexed Mongolia, apparently without any resistance from the Mongolians. The desert of Gobi also contains iron ore, so we're not going to have anything to sell to The Chinese Empire, nor to our other customers. They'll get their metals from the Chinese Empire at a much cheaper price. That's why I'm saying we are entering into a new era, an era of prosperity and renewed confidence on our ability to find creative solutions to our problems. We can do it and we will! After all, this is the country that gave the world the ultrasound, the bionic ear, the electronic pacemaker, the black box flight recorder, the refrigerator and, most importantly, vegemite."

The audience laughed.

"What do you say to your critics who say it's too little too late? If the Chinese are successful in developing teleportation, a lot of the energy problems we are facing will no longer exist."

"It's a very good question. Teleportation is a good concept, but the Chinese are years or even decades away from making it work on a large scale. The first test to transport a plastic pen one hundred metres required as much energy as a truck laden with thirty tonnes of goods to travel ten kilometres."

"Yes, but this facility requires its own nuclear power plant."

"It may seem ironic that you need energy to find how to generate a new type of energy, but it's a one-off investment. Don't forget that we are talking here about a new source of energy which will never run out."

"How safe is this research work?" another reported asked. "Do the scientists know what they're doing? What happens if they create a black hole that swallows this area and the city of Ballarat?"

Stephen had responded that safety was the utmost priority, and had given assurances about the technical safeguards that had been implemented. But he knew that the flat-earth believers, as he liked to call them, would continue to spread their doomsday messages. The riot police had been busy dealing with protesters during the construction of the Transformer, and Bob's office regularly received petitions asking for its closure.

Stephen had been relieved when the ceremony had finished, but he hadn't expected waking up a year later with his memories and his family gone.

The house was an empty shell now that his wife and children had moved out with all their belongings. Stephen was not a materialist. His most treasured possession was his memory. He had never had to do anything to develop it. It was a gift bestowed to him by nature, the prize he had won in the lottery of life.

He remembered everything he saw, heard, smelt, tasted or touched. Most hyperthymesiacs (not that there were many of them) were overwhelmed by the uncontrollable stream of memories and found their condition a burden, but Stephen had learnt to control it. He only retrieved memories that were useful or pleasurable, like the taste of a Tarte Tatin Cécile had made two weeks ago (he wished she would make it more often). When his parents had realised that Stephen was gifted, they used his talent to find their car in the parking lot and participate in the Pi memorisation competition where Stephen had set a new record.

He had been fascinated with the workings of the brain, and the components of this marvellous machine that were involved in memory. His answer to the 'what will you be when you grow up' question customarily asked to children his age had been without hesitation 'neurologist'. But when his curious mind turned to the question of what the universe was made of, he saw that it still kept many secrets. The standard model of particle physics developed in the 1970s fell short of explaining everything: it didn't contain any viable dark matter particles, incorporate the full theory of gravitation nor did it account for the accelerating expansion of the universe.

Where others had failed in defining a 'Theory of Everything', Stephen was going to succeed. He was sure of that, failure was not an option, and he would stop anyone from stealing his work. He didn't want to end up like his father, self-destructing slowly and painfully in front of his family after his work had been diverted to a futile use when he'd had high hopes for what it could do.

How close to proving his theory was he now? The answer was somewhere in his brain, but it was useless if he couldn't retrieve it. Retrieval was as important as storage, everyone knew that.

The only time his memory had been deficient was in his university days when he had his first taste of alcohol at a party; he came home, staggering, at five AM and the next day had been hell. He had been unable to recall anything he had said, done, seen or heard after his third glass of whisky. That was the last time he had drunk any alcohol, until the inauguration of the Transformer, which in his mind was still yesterday.

He didn't mind being called a party pooper; he wasn't concerned about his public image like Bob was. It wasn't as bad as visiting Cécile's relatives in Normandy where refusing to drink the aperitif, the white wine and the home-made Calvados that accompanied every meal was taken as an offence. To make up for it, he forced himself to finish the dishes that were invariably drowned in cream and butter. He used his Personal Health Assistant to confirm on the spot that these infringements to his diet hadn't affected his cholesterol level.

That night, Stephen's sleep was hijacked by the fear that he was going to wake up in 2047, and the more he tossed and turned in bed, the more he thought about the fact that sleep improved the consolidation of information and that the functioning of memory, even one like his, depended on getting sufficient sleep.

Chapter Two

1st April 2046, Melbourne.

The memory snatcher had quite a feast on Stephen's memories, but it was hungry for more, and it was looking for something with less formulas and numbers. The memories of inspector Ninoska Kristayeno of the Melbourne homicide squad were just what it was looking for: Ninoska wasn't good at remembering dates and numbers. She relied on her team to remind her of appointments she had forgotten to put in her smartphone, but she never forgot a face or a place. Like the doctor, her job was to resolve mysteries, so her memories made a hearty meal.

Ninoska walked into the Victoria Police building in Lonsdale street like she did every morning. Only something was bothering her, a feeling that things weren't as they should be. She took a nicotine chewing-gum out of her pocket. They had been supposed to help smokers quit their habit when smoking was banned, but she had become addicted to them. It annoyed the hell out of her boss, chief-inspector Claude "head-butter" Soucleau, and that was a sufficient reason not to give them up. But the nicotine only amplified her malaise.

She had noticed a scar on her left cheek when she was braiding her hair, but she had no recollection of what had caused it. She felt like she had a hangover, which didn't make sense. She only drank three vodkas last night, barely anything; the only hangover she'd had in her life was after her fiancé Hubertus had been killed, and the vodka had failed to calm her anger and drown her sorrow.

She climbed the stairs to the first floor, home of the Melbourne homicide squad. A young Asian woman with short black hair turned her head as Ninoska walked in and said, "Nino, big chief was here a minute ago looking for you." Ninoska had never seen her before. Who was she and how did she know her? Claude could wait; she never started her day without looking at her note board.

There were notes that she didn't remember making on the case of the serial killer who murders a woman every year on the first of May. The photos of a trade union official were no longer there; who had taken them down?

Another mystery. She wiped her forehead and sighed.

Ninoska walked into Claude's office without knocking, figuring that by claiming to have an open door policy, it meant that knocking was redundant.

The only hair on Claude Soucleau's head was above his lips, a thick salt-and-pepper moustache. Very little was known about his background in the French police force and his reasons for coming to Australia. But he liked to talk about his days at the Castelnaudry rugby club, where he was a redoubtable front-row forward player, and about his mother's cassoulet that after years of searching for the right ingredients he had managed to reproduce here.

He went straight to the point. "What is that new lead you hinted at yesterday? Is it promising? In case you forgot, we only have a month before the next victim."

"What do you mean a month? The first of May is seven months away!"

"Have you lost your mind or are you trying to buy some time? On my calendar, April is just before May. If your new lead is a dud, just say so and stop beating around—"

"But we're not in April yet!"

"Yesterday was the thirty-first of March, so..." He paused. "I get it. It's an April fools' joke. *Un poisson d'Avril, bien sur!* Well done Nino, you nearly had me!"

But the joke was on Ninoska. She recalled the day before, the twentieth of September 2045, her father's seventieth birthday. His five children and his wife were gathered around him. A black forest cake, his favourite. Ninoska could tell he was in pain. She was the only one with a razor-sharp intuition; it never failed and was the most efficient weapon in her arsenal. He was good at dissimulating, a skill he had mastered in his youth when he was an amateur actor. She hadn't been able to speak to him about it; he wasn't alone for one minute, his family laughing at his jokes like it was the first time they had heard them.

Claude kept speaking, but his words weren't registering. Ninoska's heart was beating louder and faster, questions whirling around in her head. Where had those six months gone? How much progress had she made on the case? Had her father's health deteriorated? The answer to the last question was in her bones and she didn't like it one bit.

"Hello there, Earth to Sputnik! Are you receiving?"

"Please excuse me, I think I've lost something important on my way to your office."

Ninoska turned around and exited Claude's office. She walked faster and faster down the corridor. She saw the woman who had greeted her.

"Ninoska, what's wrong? You look like you've seen a ghost."

"Just going for a run to clear my mind."

There was nothing unusual about that. It was what she did during her lunch break whenever she was stuck in a difficult case.

She ran out of the police building, and up Lonsdale Street, faster and faster than she had ever run, as if she was running away from an enemy, as if her life depended on it.

But she wasn't; she was running from a nightmare. It had to be a nightmare. This could not be happening to her; it was impossible. You don't wake up one morning with your memories missing.

She ran up Exhibition Street. The slow traffic allowed her to ignore the traffic lights, but drivers still honked their horns for good measure. She accelerated, thinking that the faster she ran, the quicker she would wake up and find everything was as it should be.

She stopped at the fountain in front of the Melbourne exhibition building and collapsed.

Cool water on her face. Where did it come from? Where was she? She opened her eyes, saw branches adorned with orange leaves. She closed them and opened them again to see two men staring at her, unshaven and smelling of cheap wine.

"I think she's OK, she's opening her eyes."

"Don't you think we should call an ambulance?"

"Yeah, and why not the cops while you're at it? It'll mean no end of trouble."

"She looks familiar. I'm sure I've seen her somewhere."

Ninoska opened her mouth to speak but no sound came out.

"She must be thirsty, give her a swig of your bottle."

"Why mine? I'm gonna run out of grog. Give her some water instead."

"I don't wanna hang around. It'll wake her up quicker than you can say Wangaratta Wahine."

Ninoska felt a warm liquid trickling down her throat. She sat up and coughed.

"*Vot zhopa*! That's bloody awful!"

"Told you!" the older of the two men said.

Ninoska remembered waking up feeling hung over, speaking to Claude, running. It felt all too real, and yet it couldn't be.

"What's today's date?" she asked.

"How the hell should I know?"

She rubbed her eyes and looked around her. The orange leaves, it couldn't be spring. So it was true, six months of her life had vanished.

"Do you at least know the year?"

"Is this a test or something? Are you trying to trick us?"

"2046, the soccer world cup will be on in a few weeks," the younger man said.

Ninoska got up and looked at him.

"Bazza, it's you, I thought I recognised your ugly voice."

"Inspector Ninoska, long time no see." Bazza turned to the other man who was preparing to run away. "Cool it mate, she's alright. Give her a bit of info 'bout what's going on and she'll turn a blind eye." He turned back to her. "Seeing you like that was so unexpected. I kept thinking it couldn't be you."

I've had my share of unexpected today myself, Ninoska thought.

Ninoska walked away, and thought about what she was going to do next.

Claude had spoken about a new lead that she had hinted at yesterday, but unless she had shared it with her team, it was as good as gone.

She had a bad feeling about her father, and she didn't want to tell her mother that she had lost her memories; she would worry too much. She called her brother.

"Vlad, I have a bit of a problem and I need your help. This is going to sound weird, but I've lost—Vlad, are you there?"

Why did he hang up? Maybe he thinks I'm playing a joke on him.

Ninoska called again, but he didn't answer. She called her sister Katrina.

"Katrina, it's me Nino. I have a bit of a problem and I need your help. This is going to sound weird, but I've lost my memories of the last six months."

"What do you mean?"

"The last thing I remember is going to bed after Papa's birthday party."

"That was six months ago! How can you suddenly lose your memory? Have you been sampling confiscated drugs or something?"

She was going to complain that her sister had a low opinion of her, but stopped herself. If the murderer got wind that she was getting on his trail, he could have drugged her. She didn't know how, but it was a plausible explanation.

"No I didn't; I don't know how it happened but I'm going to find out. Tell me how Mama and Papa are going."

"*Bohze moi*, you really have lost your mind! You really don't remember?"

"That's what I keep telling you. Wha... What happened?"

"Papa passed away on the twenty-fifth of January."

Ninoska swallowed hard, trying to repress her tears, before asking, "But how?"

"Pancreatic cancer; when the doctor diagnosed him, it was too late, he only had three months."

In between sobs, Ninoska said, "I didn't have time to say goodbye."

"What are you talking about, you did! You don't remember it, but you did."

Ninoska composed herself. "Did you check the bouquets at the funeral?"

"You did that Ninoska; there was only one that had an odd number of flowers and you quickly removed it."

"And How's Mama?"

"It's changed her, she's serene now. It took her a while to admit it, but she's relieved. All those years living in the fear the mafia would come here to get him."

"Anything else I should know?"

"I'm expecting."

The news was bitter sweet; a new life was a reason for celebration, but Ninoska had to live alone with the sorrow of her loss that nothing could take away.

"How's Vlad? I tried calling him, but—"

"Don't mention that *podonok*'s name."

"What did he do to you?"

"Not to me, but to the whole family. He made up a false will in which Papa left everything to him. It was so obvious that it was a fake, but we still had to go to court over it. I hope I never see him again."

"What about the scar on my cheek, did I tell you how I got it?"

"You made up a story about tripping in your apartment and landing on some sharp object. You didn't fool me. I know you don't talk about your work because you don't want Mama to worry."

Katrina didn't know that there was one person to whom Ninoska spoke about her job. Her father was proud of Ninoska; he didn't say it in front of anyone, because he knew that his wife disapproved of Ninoska's choice and she held him responsible for it.

"What are you going to do now?" Katrina asked.

"See a doctor, there's got to be a cure for this amnesia."

"Guys, you need to help me fill the gaps," Ninoska said to her team after she had come back and explained that she had lost her memories of the past six months. "The last thing I remember is interrogating Sinead O'Donnell."

"We checked his alibi for the murder; it's solid," Alex said. "We handed him over to the sexual crime unit; they suspect he has something to do with the rape of three teenage girls last year."

"Have we had any other leads?"

"We've confirmed that all the victims are linked to the RAAF in one way or another."

"But we dismissed that idea, because the third victim was a pharmacist happily married to an accountant; she had nothing to do with the RAAF. It was just a coincidence that both the first and the second victims were RAAF wives."

"Remember how the Chief of Defence Forces said she was the niece of a close friend when we asked him why he was at her funeral? You asked us to check, and it took us a while, but in the end we found that the relationship to the victim was of a different nature." Alex paused and waited for Ninoska's reaction.

"Well, what was it? I'm not in the mood for riddles."

"She was his mistress."

"How did you find out?"

Alex smiled. "Air Marshal Battler wasn't a very good liar. The victim's father was an only child, so was her mother. But why would he lie? He was obviously covering up something. We checked the records at the pharmacy where she worked;

Air Marshal Battler was a regular customer—Viagra amongst other things. And then there were transfers of money to her account. At that stage Claude made us stop, but we had enough evidence."

"The killer visibly has a bone to pick with RAAF men and he's killing their wives and mistresses."

"We started by making a list of neo-pacifists and other anarchists," Yoshimi said. She had joined the squad three months ago and according to Alex, fancied Ninoska. It was his way of coping with rejection; he thought he was so irresistible that any woman who didn't succumb to his charms was a lesbian.

"Did anything come out of it?"

"The list is long. We've started with those that already have a criminal record."

"Anything major?"

"Usually arrested for violent behaviour during demonstrations."

"Why do these guys call themselves pacifists? I thought they were supposed to be non-violent."

"They're a tough crowd to deal with. They refuse to answer questions, hurl abuse at us—"

"It's good training for you Yoshimi."

Yoshimi ignored Ninoska's comment and continued.

"Then you wondered if the killer could be someone inside the RAAF, so you asked us to look at RAAF personnel with post-traumatic stress disorder, but the RAAF psychiatrist refused to give you the list. Then you started digging for any crimes that had been committed by RAAF personnel. You had a connection inside the RAAF police that gave you a tip."

Ninoska blushed; Fred Picoll, one of her ex-lovers, was an RAAF cop; she hoped that she hadn't done anything that she regretted. But now that she had lost that memory, there was nothing to regret.

"He told you about a scandal at the RAAF Darwin base where women pilots were being abused. It had been covered up at the highest level. He gave you the list of the perpetrators, and we went through it, but none of the victims of the serial killer were related to either the victims of the abuse or the perpetrators."

"Is that all?"

"Yes, and you were about to give up on that idea when I found something of interest in the news archive. An incident involving an RAAF pilot that happened exactly one year before the first murder."

"Interesting; I had been wondering why the first two murders were committed on the first of May. If we'd found the body of the third victim in time, we would have had the exact date, but the coroner did say it was around that date. What was it?"

"The bombing of the Ishawar."

Ninoska's blank stare prompted Yoshimi to elaborate.

"On the first of May four years ago, The Ishawar, a ship from Indonesia with three hundred people on board fleeing their submerged island approached Australian territorial waters. The ship sank and no survivors were found. The event wouldn't have made the news if it hadn't been for a Greenpeace drone that was flying close to the ship and filming everything. The sinking of the ship wasn't caused by a typhoon; it was bombed by an RAAF plane. It was just before sunrise, but there was enough light to identify the plane. No media outlet accepted to publish the video, so Greenpeace put it on social networks around the world and it went viral. The RAAF made a statement that the pilot did not act on orders, and an investigation subsequently revealed that he was a member of The White Australia Resistance gang which claimed responsibility for the bombing. He was sentenced to life imprisonment for manslaughter. We thought the WAR gang was avenging his imprisonment. It was impossible to get a list of gang members, so you went to the Sunbury high security jail to see the pilot of the plane, but you were denied access because of the security risk."

"How can there be a security risk in speaking to him?"

"You tried to argue with the prison manager, but he ended up calling his security guards to calm you down. You escalated the situation to Claude who called the minister of justice, but that didn't work. Your request to the high court for a warrant wasn't a success either."

"*Vot zhopa!*"

"Claude asked you to give up and turn your attention to friends and relatives of Indonesian refugees because he thought it could be someone who didn't believe the official story. We started compiling a list, but last week you said that you had found something really big and if your suspicions were correct, the fallout would be enormous."

"Did I tell you what sort of fallout?"

"You said you couldn't tell me more in the office. We went for a drink and you said you had stumbled on something big that involved a senior politician. You were going to gather some more info before telling me more."

"Have I spoken to anyone else about this?" She asked her team.

They shook their heads.

Ninoska paced between two desks. "Interesting coincidence isn't it. Just after I find something potentially compromising, I lose my memory."

Alex shrugged. "What do we do now?"

"Put together a list of senior politicians who live in and around Melbourne, see if any of them, or their relatives, have been the subject of any investigations. Can I count on your discretion?"

Ninoska didn't want Claude to know; the last case involving a senior politician had ended in a disaster. This time, she needed to be more careful.

She accepted a call from Greta Heimer, a member of Ninoska's roller derby team the Titanic Terminatresses.

"Nino where are you? We're waiting for you for the warm-up."

"What warm-up?"

"Are you having me on? We're playing the Tigress Warriors in the final tonight!"

Ninoska stopped herself from telling Greta about her memory loss; she didn't want the team to know that she had lost a part of her mind. They needed their captain to be strong. "I had a meeting with the boss that ran over time; you know what it's like. I'm on my way now."

"Well hurry up then!"

Nino searched "Roller Derby Final"; just as well, it was at the Titanic Terminatresses' home stadium in the Docklands. She would be there in ten minutes. Playing in the final—they had done well this season. A rush of adrenaline filled her body as she recalled the last match they had played against the Tigress Warriors. Time for pay back, they couldn't afford to lose. They were going to be hard to beat, but Ninoska was ready. She relegated her memory loss to the back of her mind to focus on the up-coming battle, and ran to the stadium.

Chapter Three

"Hurry, Amanda's waiting for you," Andrew said when Stephen arrived at the Transformer facility.

Stephen took the lift to level -1, where the administrative department was located; Amanda's assistant let him in as soon as he walked in, a sign that Amanda was in a hurry to see him.

Short hair dyed black, thick-framed glasses, a sharp angular plain face; Amanda had erased all traces of her femininity. The world of scientific research in Australia remained a male-dominated one, and Amanda had worked twice as hard as her male counterparts to get to her position.

She looked at him with icy eyes and waited. Stephen had never let himself be intimidated by Amanda; he had a powerful friend he could count on to back him up.

"Have Super-mnesiac-man's powers suddenly deserted him?" Amanda asked with a wry smile.

"Not completely, I can remember everything that happened yesterday and—"

"But nothing of the past year?"

"No, it's inaccessible for the moment. I picked up my blood test results before coming to work which is why I'm late. There were no traces of hypnotic drugs and my vitamin B1 levels were OK, which rules out Korsakoff's syndrome. It was unlikely anyway because I'm neither malnourished nor alcoholic. The doctor has referred me to Ballarat University's neurology department to get a full brain scan."

"When are you going?"

"In two days."

Amanda let out a sigh. "This couldn't have happened at a worst possible time. You told me that you'd fixed your model and that you were ready to rerun experiment Goanna. I promised Bob I would have results next week so that he could make an announcement. You're really stretching your friendship with him, you know; he's depending on us to win a second term. When a politician is in election mode, they don't consider their friends. The Australian people need some good news to cheer them up, otherwise they'll vote for the opposition, no matter how bad it is. The only other thing that could do the trick is Australia winning the FIFA world cup, and what are the odds of that?"

"But I heard the election was in November, it gives us just over seven months."

Amanda pounded her fist on the desk. "You know as well as I do that the experiment was only the first step. We have to put together a working prototype to prove that dark energy can be generated for a fraction of the cost of nuclear energy. There's a shitload of work to do, Stephen."

Stephen's ears turned red.

"Can you fix your model by next week?"

"Even if I work on the week-end, I doubt I can make up a year's worth of work in seven days."

"Haven't you got any notes?"

"Well, no it's all in my head—or rather it was."

"What about Andrew, was he across what you were doing?"

"He was, but I'd made some material changes which I was due to communicate to him yesterday."

"Talk about bad timing; so what are you planning to do now?"

"I'm looking for clues that will trigger a reminiscence; I'm going to go through my computation and simulation results and speak to the team about the progress made during the year—"

"Progress, yes that's I want, a daily progress report. I want to see signs of progress, not 'I did this' or 'I did that'."

Amanda got up, signalling the meeting had ended. Stephen got up and made his way to level -3 where his desk was located.

He requested the results of all the computations he had made in the past year on the QPT's one peta-qubit supercomputer in reverse chronological order to save time. When he looked at the latest one, dated thirtieth of March at nine PM, he saw that he had tested the formulas of his model using different vales of eM_u, the twenty-fifth constant. Adding the elliptical mass of the unitron was not the only change he had made. He had modified the unified gauge symmetry, but why?

He was looking at pieces of his work of the past year as though it was for the first time. He closed his eyes and waited.

A big blank stared at him.

He heard a voice behind him say, "Stephen, I heard about your memory loss; are you feeling better now?"

He opened his eyes and turned around. Satish looked at him with concern. Short and stout with wiry hair, he was the operations manager.

"Same as yesterday; I'm trying to put the pieces together. There's one thing I don't understand. Both Amanda and Andrew said that we were going to rerun experiment Goanna. What happened the first time?"

"It's ... complicated."

"I think I can handle complicated things, it's my job isn't it?"

Satish cleared his throat. "We finished preparing experiment Goanna two weeks behind schedule. On the fifteenth of August, we were ready. I remember that day very well. Everyone was excited; we checked the transformation chamber again and—"

"That's OK, Satish; I don't need all the details. Just fast forward to the experiment."

"When it started, everything was going well, and then suddenly, the transformation chamber imploded."

Stephen's eye widened. "Did you find out why?"

"No, we were never able to look inside. It was as big as a tennis ball—from the outside of course; we don't know what the inside was like. It remained at a temperature of -234 degrees. Eventually we moved it to a safe storage area. The only information we had was the recording that was made by the detectors. When you first watched it, you deduced that there was a problem with the parameters Andrew used for the experiment, but Andrew was convinced there was a gap in your model, something that hadn't been taken into account. The unitron's mass was measured as zero, but if it didn't have a mass, where did the energy come from? The two of you had a big row, it got quite ugly.

"I had to intervene to stop Andrew from smashing your face. The next two months were very painful. You and Andrew stopped talking to each other, and each team was blaming the other team; not much work got done. Amanda didn't do a great job managing the crisis. You know her, not exactly a people person. Yelling and threatening didn't achieve anything."

Stephen rubbed his eyes. "This feels weird, like you're talking about someone else, another Stephen, a man I don't know."

"You didn't act like the Stephen we know, so you're right, it was another man. There were days when you came in and didn't speak to anyone; you just sat at your desk, lost in your thoughts. When you did speak, it was to criticise or complain; you were on edge and took everything we said against you. We gave up trying to make conversation with you. And then there were days when you didn't show up. I called you, but you never answered. I was worried you might do something foolish, so I asked my cousin Bala who lives in Brighton to check if you were OK."

"Thanks for looking out for me Satish."

"That was the least I could do; I asked you to consult a doctor but you refused. You said there was nothing wrong." Satish took a sip from his glass of water and continued. "The turning point was when Judy from HR got her friend Tracy Van Der Berk to come in to run a creativity workshop."

"What on earth for?"

"It's a workshop she runs in corporations to lift the productivity of employees by developing their creativity. We didn't have a choice; we had to go. Amanda thought it was a great idea. She had high hopes that it would energise the team. We all did as we were told, dragging our feet, complaining about the waste of time and money, but we ended up having a great time over the two days."

Stephen winced. "What did you do?"

"We doodled with crayons, made up a fairy tale, built a tower with matchsticks and string and had a joke telling session. Amanda had some great ones, but I didn't get the one about the elephant, Andrew had to explain to me what—"

"Did it make any difference?"

"Not really, we all went back to our routines, but it had an effect on you that was imperceptible to most people. But not to me, because I was watching you. I saw your eyes sparkle; I could tell that your mind was in motion. In December, while our minds were on Christmas and the usual parties, you made a breakthrough. Your hypothesis was that the unitron had a mass, but it was elliptical and could not be measured using existing technologies. When Andrew heard this, he was very excited; he came to see you and said that your idea was brilliant. He was going to design a detector that would be able to measure the elliptical mass. I remember that day well; it was three days before Christmas when Andrew and you reconciled."

The idea seemed preposterous; where did he get it from? Did the creativity workshop loosen his mind? And yet Andrew was on board, had he gone crazy too? His eyes wandered in the distance, looking for a clue.

"Stephen, are you listening?"

"Sorry, yeah; it's a lot to take in. I feel like I'm listening to someone else's theory. But go on, Amanda's on my back. I need to know as much as possible."

"After the Christmas break, you started making changes to your model by introducing eM_u, the twenty-fifth constant. You were convinced it was the missing piece that was going to resolve the inconsistencies. Two days ago, you said that you were expecting to finish the changes to your model and we prepared Suzie to rerun the experiment."

"What about the elliptical mass detector?"

"It was ready. Andrew was waiting for you to give him the value of eM_u."

Stephen tilted his head and poked his tongue into his cheek. He got up abruptly. "Still nothing! Show me the recording of the first Goanna experiment."

Satish started the playback.

Stephen reviewed the experiment on the monitors that showed in slow motion the photons travelling at four times the speed of light and colliding in a burst of white light that turned orange and then faded to darkness. A new particle appeared, then a second, a third, a fourth and a fifth.

"Pause here Satish. Are they..." Stephen stopped. He knew the answer, but he wanted to hear it from someone else to convince himself that he wasn't dreaming.

"Yes, they're unitrons."

He wanted to see them in action. "Continue."

The four unitrons spun around the middle unitron and then it swapped places with one of the four others. The group of unitrons danced together in perfect harmony to a melody that only they could perceive, a universal tune for universal particles.

If the unitron was what he thought, the next step was to find out how to transform it into an acceleron rather than a photon or any of the other energy-mediating particles.

The unitrons' dance became more and more frenetic until they were undistinguishable in a purple blur.

"This is where we trigger the particle transformer." Satish said.

A small luminous spot appeared in the middle, and then all the monitors went black.

"That's it," Satish said. All the lights went out, the collapse of the transformation chamber triggered a short-circuit, and the emergency generator switched on. The silence was such that you could hear a pen drop."

"A pin, the expression is 'you could hear a pin drop'."

"That as well, yes."

Stephen wiped his forehead. "Thanks Satish. That was fascinating, but it still felt like it was the first time I'd watched it."

"What are you going to do now?"

"Continue my search for clues on the past year."

Satish smiled. "Good luck Sherlock."

Stephen put three tomatoes, an onion, a zucchini, an eggplant, thyme and basil leaves in the auto-cuisinator, added some olive oil and selected ratatouille.

He wondered where else he could look for clues. If he was like a normal person, he would have recorded his appointments and reminders in his calendar, but his schedule was in his head; he had no need to being reminded of anything. His exceptional memory was an asset in normal circumstances, but now it was a liability.

He asked his smartphone to open his bank statements, hoping they could fill in some of the blanks.

"First of April, Glein Eira Council, three thousand seven hundred and twenty-two dollars. Twenty-second of April, Enercon, eight-hundred and—"

"Skip the bills."

"Third of July, TTE, four thousand and—"

"Wait, what's TTE?"

"Total Travel Experience."

Why go on a trip when he was busy at work?

"Where did I go?"

"Vladivostok, and you spent three days there."

His previous job was at the International Hyper-Speed Collider in Vladivostok. But why would he have gone back?

"Was there a message from the IHSC?"

"Message received on the second of July: *Dear Stephen, we regret to inform you that Sergei Kroushnavost has passed away; the funeral service will be held at Pokrov church.*"

Sergei was not only the leading physicist at the IHSC, he was Stephen's mentor.

Stephen had met him when he had given a lecture at Melbourne University. Sergei said that no physicist had succeeded in formulating the theory of everything, but he was convinced that someone in that lecture theatre would succeed. Stephen had invited Sergei for a drink after the lecture to find out more about the challenge that he was going to embark on. Sergei spoke with passion of his quest and had finished the evening by giving Stephen some advice: "believe in yourself and don't let anyone convince you that you are doomed to fail. I'm convinced you'll go far, young man."

The two men kept in touch, and when Sergei offered Stephen a position at the newly opened IHSC, he accepted without hesitation. It was the opportunity of a lifetime, and Vladivostok was a four-hour flight from Melbourne, allowing him to spend the weekends at home.

His adjustment to the standard model to incorporate the existence of gravitons was proven to be correct, but it wasn't enough to overcome the other limitations of the standard model. It still couldn't account for dark matter and dark energy. So he developed a new theory, and left the facility when he realised that it couldn't validate his new model.

Sergei had been the first to hear Stephen's theory of everything; he hadn't said anything, but Stephen could see the approbation in his eyes and the recognition of the long road that lay ahead. It didn't matter how sound your theory looked on paper, it had to be proven to work. Sergei had passed away knowing that one of his protégés was on the way to accomplishing the dream of his lifetime.

How had Sergei's death affected him? It had come shortly before the failed experiment. Death was a mystery to Stephen, but not one that he could solve. There was an abundance of beliefs, superstitions and hypotheses, but none of them could be proven. It was only when he was confronted with a loss that he thought about it.

Stephen had read about men and women who had a Near Death Experience. They had been clinically dead for a few minutes, and had come back to describe what they had experienced: they floated above their lifeless bodies, seeing what the medical team was doing to revive them, their life flashed before their eyes, they went through a tunnel with a light at the end, and an ethereal being welcomed them and asked them what they had done with their lives. Like many scientists, Stephen believed that Near Death Experiences were hallucinations provoked by a chemical imbalance in the brain and that the nearly dead had merely seen what they believed in. He rejected the argument that if Christians, Buddhist and atheists had the same experience, this could be a proof that God existed and that men had a life after their life on earth.

Enough brooding, it was time to continue digging for information.

"Next bill."

"October 6th, Tracy Van Der Berk, three hundred and fifty four dollars."

Tracy Van Der Berk, the creativity consultant who ran the workshop—but it was organised by HR, why would he have paid for it?

"October 20th, Tracy Van Der Berk, three hundred and fifty four dollars."

Again? He must have consulted her after the workshop, but why? Was he so desperate that he paid someone to help him recover his creativity?

"October 31st, Tracy Van Der Berk, three hundred and fifty four dollars.

One thing was certain, Tracy had found a way of creating money.

"November 1st, Melbourne Art Supplies, two hundred and seventeen dollars."

That explained the canvas; Tracy must have advised him to try painting—it certainly hadn't been a success.

All very interesting, but the bells of his memory were still silent.

"Mukassa is here," the security system announced.

"Let him in."

Mukassa walked in and his big smile, denim jacket, thick gold bracelet and black jeans revealed to Stephen that he hadn't changed since he last saw him. He gave Stephen his traditional bear-hug.

"Stevo, how are you going? Have you recovered yet?"

"No, I'm trawling through my past in search of something that will unlock my memory, but so far nothing's worked."

"I've been thinking about it; you came to see me just before last Christmas. You looked like you'd recovered from whatever was troubling you. When I told you that I had one of my off-moments and couldn't find the inspiration to write a song, you suggested composing a piece about the elementary particles. I thought it was too technical, but you described the symmetry and harmony that exists in your world. The orbit of the electron, the spin of the fermions and their antiparticles, the red, blue and green colour charges of the quarks.

"I didn't understand everything, but it didn't matter. I went home and wrote *The Antilepton groove*."

Mukassa uploaded his piece of music to Stephen's sound system. The soft sound of a xylophone started Mukassa's composition; it was followed by what sounded by crystal glasses being gently struck. A saxophone played long notes and bongo drums and a violin joined while the tempo increased until the song reached its cruising speed. The instrumental piece finished with a dialogue between a piano and a saxophone.

Stephen opened his eyes. "It's beautiful, at the end I could picture the quarks interacting with the photons. When did you find a violin player? He's superb."

"You don't remember that either? It was thanks to you, he's a cousin of your colleague Andrew."

"I'm glad Alter-Stephen could help."

Mukassa looked at Stephen quizzically.

"It feels like everything I did was done by someone else."

Mukassa smiled. "So if you committed a crime, you could say that your alter ego did it."

"Now you're scaring me, I can't be sure I haven't done something horrible. The memory loss could be my mind's way of coping with it."

"I can't imagine you doing anything terrible. You went through a bad patch, but you were fine the last time I saw you."

"Unless I have schizophrenia."

"Stop imagining the worst; you're probably burnt out. Just take a break."

That wasn't an option, but he didn't tell his friend why. After all, he was the one who had put himself in a situation where he was under pressure. Andrew had warned him about mixing science and politics, and Stephen had replied that if it wasn't for politics, they would have nothing. He would still be at the IHSC, in a state of continuous frustration at not being able to prove his model. He wouldn't have been the only one; many of his confrères had developed theories that couldn't be proven with existing technologies.

It was a well-known fact that Ballarat University was encased in an eco-dome, but it required imagination to believe it, for the semi-permeable membrane that the dome was made of was invisible. It only let in the water and heat that the organisms inside it needed, and it stored the excess for the times when there weren't enough. The result was a constant daytime temperature of 26 degrees Celsius and green grass all year round. The drawback was that it was designed to withstand winds of one hundred and twenty kilometres an hour, but meteorologists had predicted that hurricanes were going to be more frequent and reach one hundred and eighty kilometres an hour within the next five years.

Stephen walked towards the neurology wing where he had an appointment for a brain scan.

Professor Trevor Luong was a renowned neurologist. If something could be done to retrieve Stephen's memories, he was the one who could do it. Stephen remembered reading about the professor and the intricate maps of the brain that had been produced using the full brain scanner that he had invented. It was Stephen's last hope, he had no plan B.

The professor greeted Stephen warmly. "This university was supposed to be self-sustainable, and an exception was made for the brain scanner. I rely on your facility's power plant, and I have to schedule my scans when you're not conducting experiments. But I understand that will be a thing of the past when you find out how to generate dark energy. How are you progressing?" He put his hand on his mouth. "I'm sorry, you haven't come here to talk shop, but your GP has prescribed a brain scan." He looked at his notes and said, "Hmm, a memory loss with no apparent physical or psychological trauma."

"Yes, I woke up one morning having lost all memories of the past year."

"And since then, no memories have come back?"

"I've tried a few triggers, but I feel like I'm hearing about someone else's life."

"Let's have a look."

The professor got up and Stephen followed him to a side door. The professor invited Stephen to sit down in what looked like a dentist's chair.

Stephen looked around him; the room was bare, except for a giant monitor behind the chair he was sitting in.

"You're going to wear a helmet with sensors and the scanner's magnetic field is going to excite the water molecules in your brain. The antennas will pick up the resulting signals which will be converted into a map of your brain. It's painless, although you will feel a bit of tingling in your head. I'll scan all the areas of your brain that are involved in memory, which is most of them. Behind the scenes is a DNA nano-computer. All its components are based on artificial DNA: the circuits, the molecular switches and motors, and the memory storage. Ten years ago, scanning a whole brain would have taken forty-eight hours, and required one tonne of DNA to store the data. That's why it was never done, until I managed to compress it to two kilos of DNA and thirty minutes. That was the first generation of my brain scanner. Today, with the second generation, the scan takes three minutes. Do you realise what this means? Three minutes to scan one hundred thousand kilometres of white matter, enough to circle the earth four times! These fibres form millions of pathways that carry information from one part of the brain to the other at the speed of light. Despite his advances in technology, man has not been able to build a machine with one tenth of the complexity of the human brain."

Enough with the presentation, when is he going to start the scanner?

"One day, Stephen, it will be possible, mark my words. This is a stepping stone to reaching that goal. I am compiling a detailed map of the brain, and my computer is enriching its knowledge with every scan, comparing new data with past acquisitions."

"I hope my brain scan will help advance your understanding."

The hint to get on with it was too subtle; the professor kept going.

"And all this was possible with the bare minimum funding because all the money went to build your facility. Don't get me wrong, I think that finding new sources of energy is worthwhile. My colleagues in the Chinese empire are no better off; their government is spending a trillion dollars on teleportation research."

"Is the scanner ready?"

"Of course it is; sorry, it's not often I have a patient with whom I can converse in scientific matters." He turned to the monitor and said, "Ready to scan."

The light went off, and Stephen felt something warm on his head. At first, his head tingled, and soon after it felt like someone was hitting him with a mallet. The thumping stopped and he saw the date *March 31.* He didn't know where it came from; his eyelids were closed, the word just appeared. The film of that day streamed in front of him in six dimensions, one for each of his senses and one for his emotions. His discussions with Andrew, Mukassa and Juliette, his realisation that he had lost his memories, nothing was missing.

12th February 2046—darkness, cold, pure and absolute. He had never 'seen' darkness like that. But sight was irrelevant when there was nothing to see, like a black hole had swallowed everything inside his mind. The void was suffocating him. He would have given anything to see something, or to hear something. His body was tense, his nerves were taut. He wanted to yell 'Stop' to the professor, but no sound came out; he was paralysed. It was like trying to get out of a nightmare.

25th December 2045—more darkness. Christmas day with no memories of gifts given and received or lunch with family.

Can't you see there's nothing? Skip it, skip it!

As if the professor had heard, the next date appeared: *9th September 2045*—still nothing.

Go to the 21st of March!

20th March 2045—the darkness was replaced by a scene in Amanda's office: Bob Fultrow's protocol officer read Bob's speech and Amanda nodded. In the professor's lab Stephen breathed a sigh of relief.

22nd March 2045—the darkness came back.

21st March 2045—the inauguration day flashed in a blur, as if in eight times fast forward speed.

The lights were switched back on, and the chair swivelled around. Stephen took his head in his hands; he rubbed his temples with his fingers. His throat was parched and he felt queasy.

"Care for a lemon squash?"

Stephen nodded; he wanted to get up but felt too weak.

The professor came back with two cans and gave one to Stephen. The cold, sweet and tangy liquid refreshed him.

When the professor saw that Stephen was coming to, he made a gesture and the monitor came alive. A three-dimensional map of Stephen's brain appeared. It rotated slowly at three-hundred and sixty degrees, showing it from every angle. The image zoomed to reveal a network of wires arranged in a grid. There were coloured lights travelling on the wires in every direction.

"Your memory processing capacity is impressive; I haven't seen anything like it, and it's going to take me a couple of days to fully comprehend what makes it tick. The scanner had to adjust its magnetic field to cope with the intensity of the signals your brain was emitting. I hope it wasn't too painful."

"I've had visits to the dentist that were more pleasant."

"This is all for a good cause though."

"So what did you find?"

"To map the exact areas of the brain where specific memories are stored, I use triggers like dates or words. I can follow the path that is being followed to retrieve the memory associated with the trigger. Your brain signals were exceptionally strong, so the images were as clear as a movie."

The professor made another gesture and the map of the brain was replaced by Stephen's conversation with Andrew. Stephen's memory was on display; if he had any secrets buried in his memory, they wouldn't be secret any more. A wave of panic ran through him; had the scanner stolen his memories of the 31st of March? No, they were still there. He fast forwarded from the morning to the evening: nothing was missing.

"Don't worry Stephen, this recording will be stored securely; I am the only one who has access. No one else but me can operate the scanner. And by the way it can't read your thoughts—I'm not there yet; your facial expressions gave away your discomfort. But this is astonishing; I've never seen a memory as clear as yours."

"So far, you've only demonstrated what I already knew about my memory."

The professor's eyes squinted. "Where it gets interesting is when I trigger memories of last year. Look at what happened when I tried to make you recall the 12th of

48

February 2046. This is the retrieval signal that immediately follows the recognition signal. Of course, what you're seeing is in slow motion. Look, it knows exactly where to go, to the place where the memories for that particular day are stored."

The monitor went black.

"And there's nothing; the memories have been erased completely. When I scan an amnesiac's brain, I can find where his lost memories are. Of course it's a lot harder than flashing a trigger word, because the pathway has been destroyed. I have to search his entire brain, which can be a long process; I'm getting better at it, although the end result is hazy at the best of times. The functioning of the memory relies on the ability to find the information, but it's always there. When we say we forget, it doesn't mean we've lost a part of our memory, it means we've lost the ability to retrieve it. Unless there's drastic damage to the brain, and I don't see any. The white matter is intact but empty. I'm sorry, I have no explanation. Your condition is going to require more investigation."

"But how did my memories get deleted?"

"I don't know. If you compare your brain to a computer hard drive, all the files containing your memories of the past year have been wiped out. There is no backup or even a recycle bin that you could use to recover your files.

"Homo sapiens used to depend on his memory for survival; it was used in the pursuit of progress. Books were used to share our knowledge, our intelligence, our ideas, and our memories. Then came computers and the Internet. Nowadays Homo sapiens hardly uses his memory; if he wants to know anything, he uses his smartphone. It reminds him of anything he needs to be reminded of. I predict that our technological advances are going to lead to an evolution in man's brain. I am seeing it already; our memory is being underutilised, and the incidences of Alzheimer's disease have been steadily increasing since the start of our century. You probably thought you were safe, with your prodigious memory... "

Stephen tuned out. He didn't know what to think any more. What he had heard and seen today had only made matters worse.

He was tired. He just wanted to go home and sleep, wake up and find another way of resuming his work. He couldn't rely on his memory, that much was clear, but he hadn't lost his mind and he could put it to good use. Who else but him could find how to generate dark energy?

The sun scorched the earth and its inhabitants; a bush turkey had found shade under a bush near a watering hole. An emu walked toward the turkey which squatted down and doubled up his wings in such a way as to look as if he had no wings.

The turkey opened its beak and said, "Dinewan, the other birds will think that I'm the cleverest bird when they see what I can do without my wings, and they'll make me king instead of you."

The emu walked away and crossed the plain until he saw another emu; he said, "Birrahgnooloo, the Goomble-gubbon said that he would become king because of the many things he can do without his wings."

"He should never be allowed to reign in our stead; we are taller than him and if he thinks he can be king because he has no wings, we can get rid of ours and our kingship will be saved."

She picked up a stone tomahawk and she cut off his wings; he did the same to her wings.

He ran to the watering hole and said to the turkey, "Goomble-gubbon, look. I've cut off my wings, and now I'm just like you. There's no way you can become king now!"

The turkey laughed, jumped up and danced around, spreading his wings out and flapping them "Dinewan, the birds will surely now make me king as they would not want a king that had no wings and that was so easily taken in."

The emu ran after the turkey, but it flew away.

A wail filled the air and woke up Stephen.

The neighbours must have had a baby last year. He (or she?) kept crying; it was time to install the triple-glazed windows that Stephen had kept putting off.

The emu losing its wings was the dreamtime story Tanami had shared with him. The emu was his totem animal, handed down from his father. Was there a link with, eM_u, the twenty-fifth constant of his model? It seemed too much of a coincidence. He hadn't seen Tanami since he had been looking for a potential site for the Quantum Particle Transformer facility. The Aboriginal shaman had warned him against building it on the sacred lands of the Keyeet Balug clan of his tribe, the Wada Wurring, at the foot of Mount Buninyong, an extinct volcano west of Ballarat.

Tanami had explained that during the dreamtime, a parallel time stream that was more real than reality itself, spirits had created the world. When they had finished their arduous task, they had changed into landscape features and stars. The dreamtime was an infinite spiritual cycle, so the spirits lived on for ever in whatever form they had chosen. As dreamtime spirits lived on Earth and in the dreamtime at the same time, Stephen had compared them to quantum particles that can occupy simultaneous positions in spacetime.

Daramulum was a very important spirit who had transformed himself into Mount Buninyong. Not only was he the son of Baiame, the creator god and sky father, and his emu wife Birrahgnooloo, he was also the protector of the shamans and he looked after the weather. You didn't want to upset Daramulum, Tanami had said, the changes in the climate showed how grumpy he already was.

Stephen had been captivated by Tanami's explanations, they seemed logical in a strange way. How could you argue with a man whose people had lived on this land for more than sixty thousand years? They had a story for everything, from the patterns of the seasons to the position of the stars. They were one with the earth; it was a part of them. They had no need for a written language, for the stories of the dreamtime had been handed down over thousands of generations.

Stephen had found another site north of Ballarat, pleading the case of the aboriginal people to the board of directors who had accepted.

Today was Saturday, and he didn't want to stay pacing around at home like a lion in a cage. He booked a car at Ballarat station.

Stephen parked at the foot of Mount Buninyong, and spotted the track where he'd been walking when he met Tanami. The place was deserted; you had to be crazy to come here in this heat. The eucalypts gave no shade; their trunks were charcoal black and green shoots were sprouting— survivors of a bush fire. Acacias had grown back swiftly, their flowers filling the air with their delicate scent. Coming here on an impulse wasn't the best idea he'd had; he didn't know if Tanami was going to be there this time, but a bit of exercise could be beneficial for his mind.

After walking a hundred metres, he stopped and opened his backpack to get a drink bottle. The song of the cicadas grew louder. It sounded like an army of them were behind him ready to attack. He turned his head and saw Tanami.

The old man (his age was a mystery) showed no surprise, as if he had arranged this meeting. He was calm, his eyes looking straight through Stephen; you couldn't lie or keep a secret from Tanami. His bright eyes, large ears and broad nose gave him the advantage of perceiving his environment in a precise way that no technology could surpass.

"I wish you wouldn't creep up on me like that," Stephen said.

"You're in trouble; Kirrinjawa did that to you."

"Did what?"

"Your memory's gone; you're like a kookaburra with a broken wing."

Tanami put his hand on Stephen's shoulder and his face grimaced, showing what Stephen thought was fear.

"My people, do you know how they survived? By remembering where water holes are, where the lair of the wombat is, where the Akudjura tree is. Our land is our home; we move all the time, we have no computer, no GPS, but we have our memory. Not just memories of our land, but memories of dreamtime, of our ancestors' spirits. It gets passed on from generation to generation. These days, the young ones, they drink, they take drugs, they forget. It's sad, Stephen, but I don't cry. I do something about it. I go and look for young ones, and I talk to them. If they reject me, I continue until I find one who listens to me. And then, I take him walkabout, I teach him about the ways of his people. His soul starts to wake up and shine. A little flame at first and then it grows. When I'm gone, he'll pass the flame of our spirit to the next generation."

Stephen didn't know where Tanami was going with this, but he knew better than to interrupt. Besides, he said something about Kirrinjawa doing this to him, what was it?

"Stephen, you remember everything; you could survive in the bush, like us. But now you're wounded because Kirrinjawa took your memory."

"Who is this Kirrinjawa?"

"Evil spirit. If you try to get back what he took from you, he'll hurt you. Beware Stephen, he has great powers, and what he has done to you, he'll do to others."

"But why did he do that?"

"He feeds off people's memories, and now that he's woken up from his long sleep, he's very hungry."

"How can we stop him?"

"I need to ask Birrahgnooloo."

Stephen didn't know what to make of Tanami's story, but when he was in his presence, his rationality was on pause. Tanami made the extraordinary seem quite ordinary. Kirrinjawa must have had quite a feast with Stephen's memories.

"What will happen if he finds you?"

"If he takes my memory, I'm as good as dead, but Daramulum protects me."

"Kirrinjawa didn't take all my memory; do you think he can come back to get the rest?"

Tanami looked for an answer in the sky. "Nah, he wants other people's memories now."

Tanami's explanations gave him little comfort; if the rest of his memories were safe, there was no way he was going to get back the ones that were the most valuable.

"Tell me Tanami, did you see me during the last year?"

"Nah, you were too busy."

"I made a change to my model, I introduced a new constant the eM_u, or elliptical mass of the unitron. I don't know how I got this idea, but I wondered whether there was a link to you."

Tanami smiled. "Ah, maybe it was Birrahgnooloo's way of thanking you for saving her son. I don't understand your model Stephen, but if you put emu, it must be good."

It was Stephen's turn to smile. Who needed a Quantum Particle Transformer when a model could be validated by powerful ancestor spirits? "Thanks, Tanami."

"Take care, brother."

As he drove away, he resumed thinking rational thoughts. His encounter with Tanami had left him unsettled. How could he have known that Stephen had lost his memories? He couldn't imagine how anyone, let alone an evil spirit, could have taken his memories, and for what reason.

Chapter Four

6th of April 2046, Ballarat.

A close win, 215 to 190, but a win was a win. The Tigress Warrior's ferocious blocking had been no match for the Titanic Terminatresses' strategic moves. Ninoska's team had effectively dismantled walls at key moments, and narrowly avoided the penalty box. But the score could have been higher, Greta had said, if Ninoska had remembered the tactics they had been discussing for the past two weeks.

The week-end was spent celebrating, and on Monday Ninoska was sitting in the chair in Professor Trevor Luong's scanner room; the light went off and she felt something warm tickling her head. Soon after, she felt like her head was being hit by a truncheon, not that she had ever been on the receiving end. The thumping stopped and she saw the date *April 1.*

Dribs of that day flashed in random order: calling Katrina, running through the streets of Melbourne, realising that she had lost her memories.

12th February 2046—a thick and heavy implacable darkness, suffocating her. She wanted to escape from it, but she couldn't move. She was trapped. She lost the notion of time, like it had stopped.

The same thing happened for the 22nd of September and the 1st of November.

20th September 2045—her father's birthday celebration; the last time she saw him alive, or rather the last time she remembered seeing him alive, which was the same thing as far as she was concerned. She wanted to cry, but something was stopping her. And then the torture stopped, whatever had been on her head was no longer there. Ninoska sighed loudly and accepted the can of lemon squash the professor gave to her. He waited until he saw she was well enough to hear what he had to say.

"Ninoska, I've made a complete scan of your brain, and the good news is there's no physical damage. Your white matter is intact."

"And the bad news?"

"When I flashed the trigger dates, it was to scan your memory. You remember the first of April and the 20th of September, but nothing in between."

It was as if her privacy had been violated. "You mean you saw inside my memory?"

"This scanner is very rudimentary; I only saw blobs of colours."

The images on the monitor were as he described them. "I flashed three random dates within the period you have forgotten, and it showed that your memories had been erased completely."

"Erased, but how?"

"I don't know, this is going to require more investigation, this is the first time I've seen such a case."

"Could it be a drug?"

"The results of the blood tests were negative, and the scanner hasn't detected any foreign substances. If a drug that erased memories did exist, it would leave traces, either in the brain itself or in the blood."

Ninoska got up from the chair, still dizzy, but all she wanted was to go home to think about what she had heard. Something didn't feel right, but she didn't know what.

The north Carlton cemetery had become a familiar place to Ninoska after her fiancé was buried in the Orthodox section; a non-practising Lutheran, he had happily converted to his betrothed's religion where he found the manifestations of God's love that the Lutheran church had deprived him of.

And now it was the resting place of her father.

A brave and generous man.

When he had refused the generous bribes offered by the Russian mafia in exchange for his silence, they had threatened his family. He hadn't backed down; he had sent his wife and children to safety in Australia, and after his testimony had resulted in the prosecution of the godfather of the Solntsevskaya Bratva, he had joined his family, changed his name and started a new life as the proprietor of Dimitri's Deli. Ninoska was twelve at the time, and had told her new school friends that her father was a KGB agent in hiding. Later, when she had learnt that he was the only police inspector to stand up to the mafia when all his colleagues and superiors were buying luxury cars with dirty money, and that if they had stayed her mother would have been the first victim, she had realised how brave her father was and how much danger they had been in.

Ninoska's last memory of her father was one of a happy man, but it was tainted by a premonition that had been confirmed.

"Papa, do you think we are cursed? You were a brave man standing up to the mafia, and when they threatened your family, you were not blinded by your pride, you put our safety first. We thought we would have a better life here, and in many ways it was true. But I lost my fiancé, and now not only I've lost you but also my memories of the last time I saw you."

Ninoska paused; she didn't want to talk about Vlad, even if her father already knew about it. When she was a little girl, her Babushka had told her that the rain was the tears of angels and the spirits of the departed, who cried because of the meanness of the living. How her father must have cried when he saw what his son had done.

"But my most precious memories of you are still deep in my heart where they cannot be taken away from me. You've always loved me no matter what; when I behaved like a tomboy and Katrina would laugh at me, you comforted me. I remember when I had a tantrum because I wanted to go boar hunting with you. Mama said it wasn't a girl's place, but you saw in my eyes how important it was and when we went, you showed me how to load the rifle. How proud I was when you shot a boar; I felt I had played a role in it.

"I treasure the memories of Babushka. Underneath her toughness, there was an unlimited fountain of love. I'm sure she was as proud of her son as I am of my father. I remember the stories she used to tell me: wicked Baba Yaga, Masha and the bear, the snow girl and Zhuchka. And her cooking, my mouth waters whenever I think of the gingerbread she made with the honey I helped her to collect, not like the ones made in factories with condensed milk."

Ninoska let her tears drop on the tombstone.

"I remember the day I announced to you I was going to the police academy. I was afraid of how you and Mama would react. She was upset because she was scared for me, but you hugged me and said to me that you knew I would be a great policewoman. You told me to take care because they didn't have the mafia here like we did back home, but there were some nasty gangs out there. I know you and Mama prayed for my protection, but there's something I never told you.

"I was investigating the murder of a man. His apartment was ransacked, but none of his valuables were missing, so it wasn't a robbery that had turned bad. The man was a public servant in the State Treasury and didn't deal in drugs, gamble, or had known enemies, but he deposited large sums of cash in his bank account every month. Turns out he was blackmailing the Premier of Victoria because he had evidence of large-scale corruption. Claude ordered me to drop the case, but I didn't. I wanted to stand up for the truth, like you had done, Papa. I didn't let myself be intimidated. I knew you would have done the same thing, but I didn't want to tell you until the Premier was behind bars. So I kept going, to find the evidence that the Premier had commissioned the murder. One night, I was with one of my squad members and we got ambushed; the bullet that was meant for me got him instead. I was shattered; a man had lost his life because of me. There was no way I was going to continue on this case, but I didn't want to leave the force. I didn't want to disappoint you. I was afraid Claude would sack me for insubordination, but he let me stay in exchange for my silence.

"Papa, I hope you will forgive me; please help me find the serial killer. I've lost a precious lead, but it was connected to a senior politician and I may have to drop this case too."

Ninoska got up, wiped the tears from her face and looked around her.

We are just passing on this earth. When life takes away our loved ones, we have to stay here until our time is up and we are reunited.

She had lost the two men in her life, and her memories. It wasn't a coincidence. It could only be the evil eye, and there was only one cure for it, to find a witch-doctor. Her babushka had told her about a *babka* who could whisper away any illness or misfortune, the best one in the country. She was renowned for curing patients with terminal diseases.

Ninoska couldn't tell her mother or her sister; they would worry too much. Ninoska's family had lived twenty years with the fear that the mafia was going to find them in Australia and carry out their revenge. But the family left Russia a long time ago; surely the mafia would have forgotten about them. They had better things to do. During that time the criminal organisation had become richer and more powerful. It was rumoured that it had been involved in the formation of the Russian Imperium, some even suggesting that the emperor was a member himself.

Joyful memories of her mother country rose up to her consciousness, like champagne bubbles. Snowball fights with Katrina and Vlad, holidays at her babushka's farm where she let the children milk the cows, the smell of mandarins filling the house on New Year's Day, the taste of pancakes at *Maslenitsa*.

But her memories were those of a child; she would see things differently now, and twenty years was a long time; Ninoska wondered how much her country had changed.

Her decision was made; it was a long shot, but it was worth trying. The *babka* was her only hope; the professor, a renowned specialist in the field of neurology, had no clue how to cure her.

If the *babka* was still alive.

Maybe she had a daughter and had passed down her knowledge and her powers. Ninoska's babushka had said that she lived in a small village, with the bare necessities. She didn't accept any payment for her services, only gifts. She had no means of communicating to the outside world; she was only known by word of mouth.

Ninoska gripped her armrests and clenched her teeth; she waited for the plane to finish its approach to a terminal at Pulkovo airport, Saint Petersburg, to open her eyes.

Ninoska exited the plane and made her way to the border security control gate. The line was slow; she heard her fellow Russian passengers make jokes about customs officers, the same sort she'd had to put up with at school about police inspectors. She got so sick of hearing that they worked in groups of three because one could count, another one could read and the third one was pleased to be in the company of smart people, that when the family had moved to another suburb of Moscow, she had told her new schoolmates that her father was an accountant.

The officer looked at her passport; Ninoska smiled, hoping there was nothing that would betray her real identity, as she suspected the border security service was one of many the mafia controlled directly or through bribes.

"You have an Australian passport, but a Russian name," the officer said.

Kristayeno was a name his father had made up; she hoped there was no one else by that name.

"I was born in Australia but my father was Russian."

He stared at her. "You look familiar."

Ninoska lowered her head; the man looked like he was in his fifties; could he remember her family fleeing Russia twenty years ago?

"It must be a coincidence."

"Are you visiting family?"

"Yes, I'm going to visit the birth place of my father."

"Where's that?"

Ninoska began to sweat; she wasn't used to being interrogated.

"Ust' Yandoma."

"Never heard of it."

"It's a small village in the Karelia region, near Petrozavodsk."

The officer chuckled. "Good luck trying to get there."

"Why's that?"

"Don't you read the news? There was a Roscosmos launch base in the Karelia region. They had built a spaceship that was going to reach Jupiter in one month. It disappeared before it took off from Earth, and so did the blueprints and the crew. It was as though it had never existed. All sorts of theories have been put forward to explain the disappearance; the most popular one is that it fell through a wormhole created by aliens. The region's a desert now; only a few die-hards have stayed behind. You'd have to be a fool to go there."

The officer gave her back her passport and motioned the next person in the line to come forward.

Ninoska sat down; it came back to her, she had heard about the vanishing spaceship, but she hadn't paid attention. Space travel was a waste of money, what did they expect to find on Jupiter anyway?

Her time was counted; she had lied to Claude about a funeral of a close family member she had to attend in Russia, and she had been given three days of leave on the condition that she would make up for it when she came back. She had chosen a night flight from Melbourne to save time, but she hadn't slept one minute. It was going to take her six hours to travel the four hundred kilometres to Petrozavodsk. That left her one day to find the *babka*.

She wasn't afraid of being considered a fool; she trusted her intuition. Hadn't Ivan the Fool defeated the Dragon Serpent and got the Tzar's daughter's hand in her favourite fairy tale? He had listened to his inner voice telling him to take the road straight ahead when he had been at a crossroads, despite the dangers he knew laid ahead.

She got up and went to the car hire counter. It was a good thing the officer had told her about the situation in the Karelia region; she told the clerk that she was going to travel to Finland, a popular destination now that it was part of the Imperium.

She located her Lada in the car park and took the E105 highway to Petrozavodsk.

The road to Petrozavodsk traversed empty villages; fields that Ninoska guessed had been cultivated or used as pasture now grew wild. There were no signs of human activity, but there were plenty of birds and deers.

Ninoska's heart sunk. The joy she had felt on setting foot on Russian soil was replaced by despair. It was like going to see an old friend and finding she had passed away.

She kept driving, clinging to the hope that the *babka* had stayed when everyone around her had abandoned their home.

A black car was following her; she slowed down to let it overtake her, but it stayed behind. If the mafia had spotted her, it would be very easy to fake an accident. She had thought about bringing a gun; the Imperium (no doubt thanks to the mafia) had followed the way of the Federation of American Nations and had allowed everybody to own firearms, but try explaining to the border security officer why she felt the need to bring a gun to visit her father's village.

Ninoska kept driving, trying to ignore the black car as best she could.

The small town of Lodejnoje was the last one before entering the Karelia region. Ninoska stopped at a petrol station; the black car kept driving on.

She bought some water and some biscuits that were two years past their use-by date. Her attempts at making small talk were received by grunts from the woman dressed in black.

The time was two PM and she was half-way to her destination. There was no time to lose. Ninoska didn't want to be driving at night, but she hadn't thought about where she was going to sleep. She hadn't really thought about anything other than finding the *babka*.

The lack of sleep was starting to take its toll; Ninoska opened the car window to let the fresh air keep her awake.

Adrenaline rushed through her body as she heard the unmistakable sound of two gunshots. She looked at her rear-vision mirror, glanced to the left and then to the right. Then she saw the black car parked on the edge of a forest.

Hunters, she thought.

She drove through Petrozavodsk at thirty kilometres an hour above the speed limit, but there was no one to notice. After the inhabitants had left, looters had stripped the town bare, taking windows, doors, roof tiles and anything else that could be reused or sold.

Twenty minutes later, the navigation system ordered Ninoska to make a right-hand turn onto a dirt road. She slowed down and zigzagged to avoid the potholes.

The village, if you could call it that, consisted of a dozen wooden houses, in various stages of decay. The roof had collapsed on many of them; fences around houses had been torn down leaving scattered posts. The demise of Ust' Yandoma dated well before the exodus of the nearby city.

Ninoska broke the silence that filled the air by asking if anyone was there. She was about to turn back and make her way back to civilisation when she spotted a sign of life in a field at the edge of the village.

A cow.

Had it been left to fend for itself by the last inhabitants of the village? Cows couldn't survive by themselves for so long. She walked to the closest house; the door was not locked. She stepped inside. A mixture of odours filled her nose: juniper, mould, wood smoke. She instinctively took off her shoes, like she always did when she entered someone's house; she only dispensed with this custom when she was on duty.

A hen was pecking at the floor; Ninoska's eyes accustomed themselves to the darkness. A young lady dressed in white was sitting on an armchair; her blue eyes sparkled like her voice.

"Ninoska, here you are; I've been waiting for you. I know what you're looking for; I am the one you seek."

Was she the *babka*'s daughter?

"I know what you're thinking, but I have no descendants; rather, I have found the elixir of eternal youth, but that's not what you're after. You've come a long way and you have a brave and pure heart. Few are those who come this far, they let their fear of the unknown be their master; they are not worthy."

She smiled and continued. "You want me to cure you of a mysterious ailment. You want me to whisper away the evil eye. But it is not what you think. Illness comes from the spirits of nature, and those who master the spirits can bring on diseases. But there is something unnatural that has taken from you what is most precious. I only know the secrets of nature; what it takes away, I can return. I can make these

66

things right, but I cannot do anything for you. All I can give you are words of encouragement."

The *babka* paused and looked at Ninoska in the eyes.

"You will know many trials, but you will succeed. Believe in yourself and listen to your inner voice; it is the voice of truth. Don't believe everything you are told. A man with long hair has the key that will uncover what is hidden from you."

Ninoska didn't know what to say; she put the box of *Kozinaki* she had brought on the table to thank the *babka* and left.

On the road back, the *babka*'s words echoed inside her mind. She smiled to herself. If she believed everything she was told, she would be out of a job. What did the *babka* really know about her? She didn't know a man with long hair; she didn't find men with long hair attractive. And what was the *babka* referring to when she spoke about something unnatural? If she subscribed to the theory that aliens had stolen the Jupiter spaceship, did she believe they had taken her memories too? Ninoska shook her head. If that was the case, the babka wouldn't live here.

Ninoska's head hurt; she had travelled fifteen thousand kilometres for nothing.

Something about her visit to the professor came back to her. An alarm bell had sounded inside her at something he had said. It wasn't what he had said, but the way he had said it. She had ignored it at the time, but now she had to put her mind at rest.

Chapter Five

Ninoska took a taxi from the airport to Ballarat University when she arrived in Melbourne the next day.

"Do you have an appointment with professor Luong?" the secretary asked.

"No, but I need to speak to him urgently."

"I'm sorry, he only consults during appointments; the next available—"

Ninoska showed her police card. "This isn't for a medical consultation; I need to ask the professor some questions relating to an investigation."

"Oh I see. He's currently performing a scan; he shouldn't be too long."

Ninoska had told Claude she had a new lead. It was true in a way; if she could find how her memories had been erased, it could lead her to who had done this. It was a shortcut of sorts; she wouldn't have to recover her lost memories if the memory eraser and the serial killer were one and the same. There was only one flaw in her theory: how could a serial killer have the equipment to *erase* memories?

A man with a braided multi-coloured beard and a purple top hat walked out of the scanner room. He had angry eyes and slurred his words as he said goodbye to the professor.

What a weirdo, but where have I seen him before?

"Miss Kristayeno, I'm afraid you're a little early, I haven't finished analysing your results."

Ninoska showed her police card. "Today I'm on official business. Where can we talk?"

The professor took a step back and tried an unconvincing smile. He cleared his throat and said, "Why don't you step in my office," as he directed her to the right.

Ninoska walked into his office and stayed standing while the professor sat in his chair. She always found it gave her the edge; she liked to look down on the people she questioned.

"Professor, I am now talking to you as an inspector; I'm on the case of a serial killer who is due to strike again in a month."

"How does this concern me?"

"As you know, I have lost my memories of the last six months; it just happens that the day before I lost my memory, I had found a new lead in this case. It just seems too much of a coincidence and I have a feeling you're not telling me everything you know."

The professor stiffened. "What makes you say that inspector?"

"Yesterday you said that it was the first time you'd seen memories erased like mine were. Professor, what's made me successful in my job is my intuition, so when it tells me that someone is lying, I listen to it rather than the person who is speaking to me."

The professor pursed his lips and rubbed his chin. He looked like he was considering his options. Ninoska crossed her arms and waited for him to speak.

"I'm sorry but I can't tell you anything more. I am bound to respect my patients' privacy."

"I thought you might say that; it's the standard response for doctors. In any other circumstance, you would be in your right, but in this case, failure to cooperate would be seen as an obstruction to justice. Plus, if there have been other cases, there could be a threat to public health. If the memory loss was caused by a virus, the health authorities would need to get involved; we could have a code orange or—"

"Alright, you've made your point. There are two other cases that I know of. My last patient was Jimmy Yarrawallah; you may have heard of him, he's the lead singer of Flash Forward."

"The man who just walked out as I came in? I thought he looked familiar. And the other?"

"Another public figure, Doctor Stephen Collingsworth."

"What does he do?"

"He's a physicist who works at the Quantum Particle Transformer, not far from here."

"Not your run-of-the-mill celebrity."

"He was on TV a year ago, when Bob Fultrow inaugurated the Quantum Particle Transformer."

Ninoska took notes while the professor was speaking. "Have you found anything in common in these two, I mean three cases?" She was in it as much as the others were.

"No, the scanner shows that the memories have been erased, but for different time periods. A year in the case of Stephen, three months in the case of Jimmy, six months in your case."

"Anything significant about the periods that have been erased?"

"Stephen's lost period starts after the inauguration of the Quantum Particle Transformer, Jimmy's is the day after his wedding. You didn't tell me whether anything special happened on the 20th of September."

"It was my father's seventieth birthday. I sensed that he was in pain, and he died four months later."

"I'm sorry to hear that," the professor said in a voice that was starting to be more compassionate. "It confirms that the lost time periods start the day after events that have a high

70

emotional weight. Emotions play an important role in memory retention; the stronger the emotion, the stronger the memory."

"You said you had never seen cases where memories had been erased, but what about amnesiacs?"

"Amnesiacs never lose their memories; they only lose the ability to retrieve them. The memories are still there, but amnesiacs don't know where they are."

"Isn't there a cure?"

"There are many cases of spontaneous recovery, but outside of that, no cure has been found yet. It will be the next stage of my research; today I can locate an amnesiac's lost memories. Tomorrow I will be able to regenerate the pathways that have been destroyed."

"That doesn't help me though, does it?"

"No because it's the opposite; the pathways are still there but the memories aren't."

"But what is the cause professor?"

"So far I've ruled out drugs and viruses; there are no traces of either of them. I don't know what else could have caused the losses; I need more time to investigate the brain scans."

"Never mind if you can't explain the how, I'm going to try to find out who is behind this."

The professor raised his eyebrows. "I don't see how anyone could erase memories, and in such a precise way."

"But it has to be someone; I can't see the connection between the victims yet, but something tells me there is one; they're not random people."

"But what would be the motive?"

"In my case, it's clear; someone is trying to stop me from finding the killer, which means I was getting close. As for the others, I'm going to visit them to find out."

Stephen opened the door; Ninoska recognised him from the footage of the inauguration of the Quantum Particle Transformer she had viewed before coming. He wasn't exactly the same man: he had dark circles under his eyes and looked ten kilos lighter. The sparkle in his eyes was gone, had he lost it at the same time as his memories? His long hair reminded her of what the *babka* had said, but she couldn't see how a man like him was going to help her.

She hadn't waited to get a security clearance to see him at the Quantum Particle Transformer; she had preferred to see him at home that evening.

"Doctor Stephen Collingsworth? I'm Inspector Ninoska Kristayeno."

"Come in Inspector," Stephen replied. "What can I do for you?"

Ninoska looked around Stephen's living room. Minimalist furniture, no decorations, although there were signs that a frame had been taken down from the wall.

Ninoska didn't see any reason not to tell him that she was a victim as much as he was. "I'm in the homicide squad, but that's not the reason I'm here today. The crime I'm investigating is of a different nature. In fact so different that it's not recognised by the laws of this country or indeed any other country. The law makers are going to have some catching up to do."

Stephen looked at her quizzically.

"I am conducting an investigation into the deletion of memories that have so far affected three people so far, you and me included."

Stephen's eyes widened.

"Are you saying you're treating this as a crime?"

"Yes, it's my conviction that someone is erasing memories deliberately and that he is targeting his victims specifically."

"But why?"

"I was hoping you could help me to answer that question."

"How?"

"By telling me what has been erased."

"A whole year of my memories."

"Can you be more specific?"

Stephen hesitated.

"You must promise not divulge this information to anyone that doesn't need to know."

"This *is* a criminal investigation, but it hasn't been made public.'"

"I've been working on a new model of particle physics, predicated on the existence of a universal particle that mediates all types of energy in the universe. I've called this particle a unitron; it's a bit like a stem cell that differentiates into all types of cells in our body, except it transforms itself into the different energy-mediating particles; for example a photon, which is the quantum of light and all other forms of electromagnetic radiation. The Quantum Particle Transformer is able to trigger this transformation, and I was approaching my goal of creating accelerons which are the particles that mediate dark energy, before I lost an entire year worth of work. It's a major setback; Bob Fultrow was counting on it to win the next election."

"I saw the inauguration of the Transformer, and so did the rest of the world. Your competitors would no doubt benefit from your loss."

"I'm the only one working in this field. It's ground-breaking research that requires very expensive and sophisticated equipment. The Quantum Particle Transformer is unique; there's no one that could replicate it."

"What about other states?"

"The Chinese Empire is working on teleportation, the Federation of American Nations is broke, and the European Union is struggling to stay united. That leaves the Russian Imperium. I went there during the year that's been robbed from my memories. I attended the funeral of my mentor, Sergei Kroushnavost. He was the leading physicist at the International Hyper-Speed Collider in Vladivostok. But I don't know who his successor is. For all I know, he could have connections with the Russian mafia."

Ninoska wrinkled her forehead.

"You're not Russian are you?" Stephen asked. "I'm sorry, I didn't mean to imply anything about the corruption of the Russian—"

"It's worse than you can imagine. The Russian mafia's the reason my family came here."

"Could the Russian mafia want to erase your memory if you had evidence against them?"

"If I did, they wouldn't have gone to the trouble of erasing my memory; they would have just killed me. But the case I'm working on has nothing to do with them."

"You said you were in the homicide squad."

"I'm investigating a serial killer. He's killed a woman every year in the past three years, every time at the same date. The first of May, date of the bombing of an Indonesian refugee boat."

"What if the Russian mafia was involved in people smuggling? The bombing of the boat wouldn't be good for their business."

"It's not their traditional turf, but even if they were expanding their operations, they wouldn't wait for the first of May every year to strike. It's not their modus operandi."

"So the serial killer would have benefited from your memory loss, but I can't imagine what he would have gained from mine."

"Whoever is erasing memories is being commissioned to do it. In your case by a rival, in mine by the serial killer. The only thing I haven't figured out is how a crook would have found the means to erase memories. It's impossible according to the experts. But I trust my intuition; it has a good track record, it has never failed me. Unless you have a better explanation."

A good track record, but not perfect, Ninoska thought. There had been that case of a mother who had murdered her own son, and Ninoska had gone on two false leads before acknowledging that the unthinkable had indeed occurred.

"An aboriginal shaman I met at Mount Buninyong was convinced that my memories were stolen by an evil spirit named Kirrinjawa. He feeds off people's memories, and apparently he's very hungry."

The so-called *babka* had said that whatever had caused the memory loss was unnatural; were evil spirits in that category?

"Interesting, and did he have a spell to ward off this evil spirit?"

Stephen laughed. "No he didn't, and if it was an evil spirit, how would you arrest it?"

Ninoska scowled at him.

"You said there were three victims, who is the third one?"

"I'm afraid I can't share that with you."

"You don't have to give a name, an occupation will do. Is he a scientist, a police person, or—"

"No, it's classified information, I can't tell you anything."

"And how are you going to find this memory eraser?"

"That's my job, don't worry about that. I'm like a hunting dog; when I'm on a trail, I follow it to the end. It's only a matter of time before I find the evidence I need."

Ninoska handed Stephen her card. "If you find out anything out of the ordinary that happened during the time that you lost your memories, call me on this number.

Jimmy Yarrawallah wasn't in the phone directory; he didn't want to be pestered by his fans. The professor had given her his address, a PO Box in Apollo Bay, a little village on the Great Ocean Road. Ninoska had sent Yoshimi to watch the post office to see who was picking up the mail. Officially she was watching a suspect in the case of the serial killer; Ninoska didn't want Claude to know that she was using her team to track down the memory eraser, but she was convinced he would lead her to the serial killer. While Ninoska was questioning Stephen, Yoshimi had sent her the GPS coordinates with a message: 'The mail was picked up by Evangelista Charez, I'm sure it was her. They live in a tree house in the Otway forest.'

A bloody tree house, am I going to have to climb up to see him?

Ninoska was afraid of heights, but no one in the squad knew that. When she couldn't delegate an outing that involved heights, she relied on her Xanax to stop the panic attack that she knew she was going to have.

Yoshimi had assumed Ninoska knew who Evangelista Charez was. She didn't have a criminal record, could she be a celebrity? She searched the Internet and found that

Evangelista Charez was a top model who became famous working with the French fashion designer Cécile Dubontant; she stopped her career when she became Jimmy Yarrawallah's partner.

No wonder Ninoska had never heard of Evangelista. She didn't know the meaning of fashion; she was happy in her jeans and her rock band T-shirts that her grandfather collected when he worked as a concert promoter. Her favourite was the 1998 Rolling Stones Bridges to Babylon tour when they played at the Luzhniki Stadium in Moscow; Mick Jagger had autographed the back of the T-shirt.

Ninoska clicked Cécile Dubontant's name; she was married to Doctor Stephen Collingsworth. An interesting connection that Ninoska filed in her mind to look at later.

Ninoska had listened to an audio transcription of Jimmy's file on the way to his house; he had been arrested at the building site of the QPT for violence against a police officer during a demonstration. The protesters were convinced the QPT was going to create a black hole that was going to engulf all of Ballarat and probably most of Victoria. They must have been disappointed their predictions hadn't come true.

Another interesting connection. Jimmy had a motive for erasing Stephen's memory, but did the memory erasing machine (is there was such a thing) backfire against him? And why would he have erased Ninoska's memory? Unless he was the serial killer; after all, his views against all sorts of authority were conveyed through his songs. If he was on the list of neo-pacifists that the squad had compiled, Ninoska made a mental note to ask Alex if he had checked Jimmy's alibi.

She had to tread carefully; he wasn't going to be cooperative if he knew she was in the police.

Ninoska drove up the forest track until it stopped at a gate in the middle of a wire fence; she got out of her car and looked around. The trail went downhill; she guessed that Jimmy's house was at the bottom of the hill.

Ninoska spotted a koala on a branch looking at her.

It must be a survivor. I thought koalas had vanished in Victoria.

"Hello, is anyone there?" Ninoska yelled.

She didn't wait for an answer, she opened the gate and followed the path which turned to the right to reveal a walkway attached at the halfway mark of the hundred-metre tall gum trees. Ninoska's heart accelerated and her vision started to blur. She took a box of Xanax in her denim jacket and swallowed the pink pill with water from a plastic bottle that she always carried with her. She waited for the pill to calm her down to continue on the walkway. She breathed slowly and steadily. She would be fine, as long as she didn't look down.

Down, even the word made her feel sick. The wind made the walkway shudder; Ninoska walked faster to shorten her ordeal, but she stopped when she heard the sound of a didgeridoo. It came from above, as if someone was on a branch playing. She saw a long wooden pipe floating in the air. It had a funnel at one end, where the wind was rushing in.

What is this place?

She continued walking until she reached a house built between two trees, fifty metres off the ground. Above the roof a wind turbine was spinning its blades. As she approached the door she heard a voice yell "This is private property, go away."

"I saw you at the lab this morning. I think we may have something in common."

"What do you want?"

"I've lost my memories just like you have. Together we may be able to find who's behind this and get our memories back."

"Come in then, but make it quick."

She walked into the lounge room where multi-coloured bean bags were strewn around. In the corner, Evangelista Charez was painting on a canvas what Ninoska guessed to be a life-size portrait of her partner in the aboriginal style: the background was ochre, the outline of the body and the bones were white and there were red and yellow dots forming the shapes of the eyes, the mouth, the nose and beard.

"She's a real artist, she paints with her heart," Jimmy said. "Our creative souls have been brought together to bring harmony to this corrupt world."

Ninoska continued looking around and saw Jimmy's tools of his trade: a flute, a saxophone, bongo drums and a guitar.

"So it seems the black hole factory has claimed another victim; how many more before they shut it down? I tried to stop them; I knew something like this was gonna happen."

"Sorry, I don't follow you."

"Don't you realise? My memory and yours, they're gone. Swallowed by a black hole that the Quantum Particle Transmuter made while we were sleeping." He showed her a piece of paper, with some yellow stains. "Here, sign this petition. Now that you're here, I have proof that the whole country is in danger. We're the first two victims, but there's gonna be plenty more."

Ninoska signed, wondering whether he really believed what he was saying.

"And how much of your memory was swallowed by the black hole?"

"I didn't realise it straight away. I was working on my new repertoire, and one morning Evangelista told me to get ready because the other musos were waiting at the studio. I didn't know what she was talking about; I had only written one song, so why go to the studio? She looked at me strange and asked me if I was OK. I did have a headache that morning. Zook doesn't usually do that to me; I didn't remember taking that much the previous night. She pushed back the studio session to the next day. My headache was gone, but I still only remembered one song. Evangelista said I had written ten! And there was no way she could have made so much progress on her painting in one day. What I thought was yesterday was three months ago."

He wiped his forehead and continued.

"Three months of my life gone! Nine songs, a gig with Rancid Joe, ninety nights of love-making. Evangelista hummed the tunes of the songs I had written, but I didn't feel a connection. I freaked out, I can tell you. I thought it might have been the zook, but Evangelista drank some as well and she wasn't affected."

"What is zook, some sort of drug?"

"No, it's all natural. I make it myself with herbs, flowers and roots. My father is a shaman, he handed me the recipe. Aborigines take it during their corroborees, they say it opens the gate to the dreamtime; it doesn't work for me like it does for my father because I'm only half aborigine, but I take it to give me inspiration to write my songs. I can see ideas that no one has had yet."

"I always take zook before I paint," Evangelista added. "It gives me endless creativity. With what I see, I could even write a novel or invent something."

"Jimmy, do you have any enemies?"

"Not everyone likes my music, and life would be boring if everyone did. But enemies, no. My music brings people together in peace and harmony. I get on with everyone."

"Even the police?"

"They're the puppets of our fascist government. Damn Bob Fultrow, he's the one who got the Quantum Particle Transmuter built." His eyes lit up. "It makes sense now. He can do whatever he wants; all he has to do is erase our memories before the next election. We'll have forgotten all the evil stuff he did; he'll rewrite the news and no one will be the wiser. That man is more devious than I thought." He turned towards Evangelista. "Babe, we've got to do something. This lady and I have been guinea pigs. Now that it works, he's gonna unleash his weapon on the whole populace."

Ninoska was going to say that man who was directing the experiments had lost his memories himself, but Jimmy would probably see that as another proof that the Quantum Particle Transformer was responsible for the loss of his memories.

But why would someone go to the trouble of erasing Jimmy's memories? Was it a rival musician jealous of Jimmy's success?

"And what memories have *you* lost?" Evangelista asked.

Ninoska remembered an article she had read in the professor's waiting room. "I'm an architect; I was working on self-sustainable villages that could be built anywhere, even in the remotest deserts."

"That's a terrible loss. Jimmy, we must alert the media."

"Are you kidding?" Jimmy said "They're puppets too. Bob will make sure this is kept under wraps. It's only a question of time before he makes his next move."

"So what are we going to do?"

"Don't worry babe, I'll think of a plan. But in the meantime, you're going to write down everything that's in

81

that beautiful head of yours. You've got to have a backup if the same thing should happen to you."

"I don't need a backup. I know that everything that happens to us is also recorded in the cells of our body. Our brain isn't the only source of memory; our cellular memory is a bio-computer far more powerful and reliable than we think. I told you to go to the Holy Holistic Healer so he could do a reading of your cells, but you didn't want to."

"If he's so holy, why does he charge six hundred bucks a consultation?"

Ninoska turned to Evangelista. "I was just thinking, on the day before Jimmy lost his memory, were you with him?"

"I sure was."

"Did anything unusual happen? Did he fall or eat anything he doesn't usually eat?"

"No, we had a very creative day; I was painting, he was working on 'Legends of the sparkling sea'—I'm sure it'll be a hit."

Jimmy shrugged. "Yeah, If I remember it."

"Don't complain, I've done my best to sing it to you!"

"But I told you, I'm not getting the right vibes; I can't do anything with it."

Ninoska let the couple continue their discussion without her.

"Ninoska, I don't know what you're up to," Claude said, "but time's running out. Do I have to remind you that the killer is going to strike again in twenty-one days?"

Ninoska was standing in Claude's office, arms crossed. "I know that, but just give me a couple more days."

"How's that going to help?"

"If I find who's erased my memories, I'll find the killer. I'm convinced he knew I was too close and hired someone to erase my memories."

"Erased your memories, you're not serious, are you?"

Ninoska glowered at him.

"Alright, I'll give you the benefit of the doubt. It won't be the last time and in the past you've always come up with the goods. I'll give you forty-eight hours, not one second more. You can have Yoshimi. Alex will continue investigating friends and relatives of Indonesian refugees. But on one condition, you stay away from senior politicians."

Ninoska was going to say something to defend herself, but Claude continued.

"I heard that you told your team you had found a clue leading to a senior politician. Now let me be clear on this:

a) The idea that a senior politician would be involved in the murder of RAAF wives is so preposterous that I'm going to pretend I never heard this.

b) Even if there was a remote link, and so remote we're talking about light years here, there's no way he would have found a way to erase memories. Granted, it would be a useful tool for politicians, but this is the stuff of science-fiction."

Ninoska thought about the Australian Security Intelligence Organisation. "But suppose ASIO or the army had found a way to do this?"

"I hadn't finished, I was up to c), and I've saved the most important one for the end."

"Alright, you don't need to remind me about the time I stuffed up with a senior politician."

Ninoska rummaged through her notes, looking for something out of the ordinary. Something that would lead her to the memory eraser. If he was capable of erasing memories, she wondered what other powers he had. She didn't know what sort of adversary she was dealing with, and it gave him the edge on her.

She tried to swallow, but she felt her internal plumbing contract; her body was rebelling. A white shape moving outside caught her eye; she turned her head and saw a cockatoo on the windowsill. The large bird tapped on the window, it had probably seen Alex's half-eaten sandwich on his desk. Ninoska ran towards the window and shooed away the cockatoo.

"Relax Ninoska, it wasn't going to break the window," Yoshimi said.

"But it was a very bad omen. It means someone in this room is going to die. There's no one else here, so if it's not you, it can only be me."

"Stop it, that's crazy, where did you get that idea?"

"My father, the last time I saw him, there was a bird on the windowsill. And then he died."

"I'm sorry about your father, but that doesn't prove anything. We're all going to die one day, bird or no bird."

Ninoska saw that she wasn't going to convince her colleague. She went back to her desk and continued searching. There was nothing other than what her team had told her. She hadn't written anything on her new lead, it was lost.

She flipped through her diary, not expecting anything interesting. Planned activities were sparse, a few roller derby matches, an appointment with the dentist—not what she particularly wanted to remember. February the twelfth, creativity workshop. What made her go to that?

"Yoshimi, do you remember me saying anything about going to a creativity workshop?"

Yoshimi raised her head. "What a joke that was. We all went, even Claude. It was his idea. He raved about how Tracy Van Der Berk had helped lots of famous people boost their creativity. You asked what that had to do with our job, that we weren't bloody artists." Yoshimi had imitated Ninoska's accent, but Ninoska let it go. "He said that we didn't have a choice. We needed to improve our ability to see things differently, to find new ways of solving problems. Our performance was below par according to him, but when we got there we saw why he had insisted, he couldn't keep his eyes off Tracy. He was always the first to answer her questions or volunteer for role plays. It was stinking hot that day and she just wore a very light dress with no bra, it was quite a sight."

"Alex must've enjoyed himself."

"Not really, he was jealous of Claude."

"And where was the creativity in that?"

"I don't know, but in the end it was a fun day. We built a tower with matchsticks, made up a fairy tale." Yoshimi chuckled. "We had to play roles that were completely opposite to our personalities and Claude ended up being the damsel in distress."

"I wish I was there."

"But you were."

Ninoska raised her voice. "Don't you get it? I don't remember anything of the past six months. People tell me I did this, I said that, I was there, but to me it's like someone else had done those things."

Ninoska saw remorse in Yoshimi's eyes. "Sorry, I'm on edge. I'm getting nowhere with this." She looked at her watch. "And now I've only got forty-seven hours to find whoever or whatever erased my memory. I would've moved on if it wasn't for the fact that two other people have lost their memories. The thing is, there's nothing in common between the three of us. The memories that have been wiped out are so different. The first one was doctor Collingsworth, a physicist working on a new source of energy. Next, Jimmy Yarrawallah, a singer working on his new songs and then an inspector who had just found a new lead in a difficult case."

"The three of you had things that were in progress, and possibly very close to finishing."

"That's true, Stephen said that the experiment he was about to conduct was going to lead to a breakthrough in his research."

"You're all leaders in your domains; I think you're right, it can't be a coincidence. The eraser certainly knows how to pick his victims. I bet that the next one will be someone important and well-known. He's not going to delete the memories of a cleaner or a waitress."

"That doesn't narrow the list of victims very much, does it?"

Yoshimi looked up and bit her lips. A tear reflected the afternoon sunlight that had sneaked in between two buildings.

"Hey, what's the matter?"

Yoshimi lowered her head and muttered, "Nothing, just a stupid thought I had about the memory eraser."

"It doesn't matter how stupid you think it is; I won't use it against you."

Yoshimi looked at Ninoska. "For a moment I wished I was going to be the next victim."

Ninoska raised her eyebrows.

"There's something I can't get out of my head. I wish I could forget it, but it haunts me. I've tried to toughen myself up, but it's too powerful. I thought joining the police would channel my anger, but it still burns inside me."

Ninoska motioned her to sit down, and did the same.

Yoshimi cleared her throat; she was struggling not to break down in tears.

"When I was twelve, two men burst through the living room windows while we were eating. They demanded that we hand over all our valuables. I was terrified, I couldn't stop crying. One of the men yelled at me to stop; when my dad saw that he was going to slap me, he got up and said that if they laid one finger on me, there would be hell to pay. The man didn't like that, he plunged his knife into my dad's chest. I saw my dad collapse, blood spilling on the floor."

Ninoska took Yoshimi's hand and held it.

"But that wasn't the worst part. I was in shock, but just as I stopped crying, my mum rushed to my dad's side. She told them that she would give them anything they wanted if they spared me. They laughed at her, but we couldn't see their faces, they were covered with balaclavas. Mum told them where her jewels and her purse were. While they were grabbing everything they could, I was huddled in my mother's arms. When they finished, we thought they were going to go, but the other man looked at us. He grabbed me and pushed me away. He ripped my mother's clothes. The only thing that stopped him from raping my mother was the sound of the police siren. Our neighbour had heard the commotion and called triple zero."

"Did the police catch them?"

"No, they never found them; we couldn't identify them. Our neighbour noted the rego, but it was a stolen car; they just dumped it on the side of the road. I remember everything, the stinking man's smell, and my mother's cries. It's horrible. I can't get it out of my head."

Ninoska could see Yoshimi was struggling not to burst into tears. "Yoshimi, it's OK if you cry. We're allowed to have feelings you know, even when we're on the job."

Yoshimi stood up. "If I hadn't cried, my dad would still be alive. I've never allowed myself to cry since that day." She paused. "I had to be strong to help my mum. She told me I was the only reason she didn't commit suicide. From that day, I knew what I was going to be when I grew up. I knew my father would be proud of me, that even if the man who killed him wasn't brought to justice, I would be getting rid of some other vermin. And who knows? Maybe one day I can join the cold case team and find those bastards."

"They wouldn't let you work on that case; it's personal and you would lose your objectivity. Imagine if you did find them, what would stop you shooting them? I know the cold case inspector; I can ask him if anything's come up. So even if that memory is painful, you don't want to lose it. There might be a detail in there that will lead to your parents' aggressors."

Ninoska knew how Yoshimi felt; she had been refused permission to work on the case of her fiancé's death, but she had taken matters into her own hands, investigating members of the snuffers' gang who she suspected had avenged the death of their leader in a shoot-out with Ninoska's squad. She had arrested two of them with no evidence and had let them go when Claude had found out.

"But there are other memories that are useless," Yoshimi said, "like my first boyfriend for example. I've pushed him out of my head, but whenever I hear the song *Don't go breaking my heart*, I feel like vomiting. He sang it when I dumped him, and he's a really awful singer."

They looked at each other and both laughed. An uncontrollable, hysterical fit of laughter that filled them with joy and released their tension. When one of them stopped laughing, the other stopped. But then they looked at each other and burst out laughing again.

Alex walked in the room. "Hey, care to share the joke? It must be a whopper."

"Sorry Alex, it's just an in-joke, you wouldn't understand," Ninoska said. She turned to Yoshimi. "I've just thought of something. My informers might have tipped me off on this new lead I had just before I lost my memory." She put her hand on her temple. "It can't be Bazza; I saw him a couple of days ago and he said that he hadn't seen me for a long time. What about Fongers and Crinky? Let's go, Yoshimi."

"Where are we going?"

"To Paddy's in Footscray, that's where they usually hang out. You better dress down to go there. Do you have anything with stains or holes?"

Yoshimi shook her head.

"The cupboard behind you has everything you need."

Ninoska's informants were her 'B team'. In exchange for a blind eye to their petty drug operations, she got information, lots of it. What at first glance didn't seem relevant could prove to be valuable; she never dismissed anything they gave her—if there was something happening, they had their eyes and ears open.

Ninoska saw that Yoshimi was looking around her, not sure how to conduct herself in this urban jungle. At this time of day, shop windows were shut behind rusty iron curtains covered in graffiti. An emaciated young woman asked them if they wanted any blue stuff, the code word for Nedeax, a drug that induced out of body experiences similar to those claimed by people who'd had a Near Death Experience, minus the angelic being who asked you what you had done with your life. Instead the drug consumer saw an evil being who promised him eternal life if he killed someone. Across the road, a black man was being punched by a group of bikies.

"Don't look at them," Ninoska said. "Remember we're not on a peace-keeping mission. Ah, there's our destination, on the corner."

Paddy's pub had been there since 1845, handed down from father to son (all named Paddy) for ten generations. As they approached, the sound of raucous laughter and conversations grew louder and the smell of sweat and beer reached Yoshimi's nostrils, making her wonder if her father's killer was there, enjoying a beer.

"Relax Yoshimi, act as if you were a regular. You don't want to be the white crow in *that* crowd."

"I never thought acting was going to be part of my duties when I joined the force."

"You have to be a chameleon, to blend in any environment. You'll get the hang of it pretty quickly if you want to survive."

The two policewomen entered the pub and when straight to the bar, oblivious to the pairs of eyes assessing them.

"Ninoska, you're looking hot tonight, what's your friend's name?" The barman asked.

"Cut out your bullshit Wayne, and give us two vodkas. Your reserve of course, not the rotgut you serve to your regulars."

The barman retrieved a key from his pocket and opened a cabinet where his best bottles were stored. He smiled and poured the transparent liquid into two shot glasses. Ninoska sculled her glass and Yoshimi imitated her, dissimulating her discomfort as best she could.

"Have you seen Fongers and Crinky?" Ninoska asked.

"Yeah Crinky's here, but I haven't seen Fongers for a while."

Ninoska surveyed the room; she recognised a few of the regulars. She walked towards a man wearing black jeans and a black tank top. His outfit matched his eyes, dark yet piercing; he reminded Ninoska of a crow.

"Well if it isn't young inspector Ninoska. What brings you to the house of fun this time?" Crinky asked as he walked towards her, leaving his drinking companions.

"I wanted to talk to you about that tip you gave me about ten days ago."

"Did Wayne spike your drink or something? I haven't seen you for yonks. It must've been Fongers. The last time I saw him, he mentioned he had a hot tip for you, but he wouldn't say what it was."

"And you haven't seen him since?"

"No, I got worried and I asked the boss of the Burning Cross. He said Fongers hadn't turned up for work since last week; I asked his mates, but it was the same story. He just vanished; I hope he didn't get into trouble over something he told you."

"I'll check the other coppers to see if they picked him up, but I doubt it. I've given strict orders to leave him alone—unless he did something really bad, but I would've been told."

"What was his tip about anyway?"

"It was something about the case I'm working on, the serial killer who strikes at the same date every year."

"Come on inspector, you can tell me what it was."

"The less people know about this the better; if someone got rid of Fongers because he knew too much, he could do the same to you."

Crinky finished his drink and said, "Yeah, sure."

"Call me if he does turn up, and one more thing: have you heard of any hitmen using new methods?"

"Like what?"

"Erasing memories."

"I didn't think that was possible, although I can see a big market for that. Imagine if you could erase memories of witnesses. Much cleaner than disposing of them."

Ninoska wanted to drink one for the road but decided against it; she had doubts about Yoshimi's capacity to hold her liquor. The two women walked back to the train station, Yoshimi's relief to leave the place was palpable.

"If someone went to the trouble of eliminating Fongers, he must've been onto something really big." Ninoska said.

"What are you going to do now?"

"Buggered if I know."

Chapter Six

10th April 2046, Melbourne.

Zyv'Oom closed his eyes and tuned his cortex to the frequency of Hive Commander Tanqu'Oom's mind.

"Zyv'Oom unit reporting on status of operation Terra Tena. Savant Pin Chuei's memory field successfully removed from its container. What shall I do with it?"

Tanqu'Oom projected his thoughts into Zyv'Oom's mind. Their intensity was overbearing, Zyv'Oom knew he was going to have to rest his mind for ten standard time units after the call to recover.

"Follow the standard procedure. Keep it in a safe place; it will be analysed when you bring it back. Have you finished scanning the noosphere?"

"Yes. All units involved in teleportation research have been dealt with. There are other units who think about it, but they are harmless. They have no knowledge that would enable them to come close to developing it."

Zyv'Oom had entered the planet Earth's noosphere, the thinking layer of the planet where all mental interactions took place. Such a concept was new to the Terrans, who understood the idea of the biosphere, but struggled with the noosphere, although they did have an electronic version of it they called 'Internet'. The first time he had been there, he had seen the thoughts of the Terrans, but many of them were alien to him. Some devoted their lives to killing and destruction, other just thought about it. Then there were those who had benevolent thoughts one minute and maleficent thoughts the next. Homo Erraticus, that's what they should be called. No wonder the Ooms' Chief Risk Officer had assessed the Terrans' advances in teleportation as a severe threat. They were a primitive people and that's what made them dangerous. Once they mastered teleportation, the next step was going to be wormhole travel. The potential for havoc was enormous; their progress had to be stopped and that's why Zyv'Oom had been sent to Planet Earth to steal the memories of all the humans who were working in this field.

In his second visit to the noosphere, he hadn't let himself be distracted. He had focussed on the notion of teleportation before entering, and he had spotted all the minds that were working on it. Some were close to a breakthrough, others less so but the orders had been to deal with all of them.

It had been surprisingly easy to steal the Terrans' memories. They didn't have any defences against external mind alteration, because they didn't believe it could be done. The orders were to minimise harm and leave no trace. His victims woke up having lost all memory of their project but with all their other memories intact. They attributed their memory loss and their headache to any number of factors: alcohol, shock, vitamin B1 deficiency. None of them suspected that their memories could have been stolen.

"Zyv'Oom unit, you are to stay for thirty more Earth days; keep monitoring the noosphere in case other savants continue the work of your victims. Your next target is dark energy. Recent monitoring of Terran communications has revealed signs that they are close to mastering it. It is equally as dangerous to the equilibrium of the universes as teleportation. Terrans must be stopped. And make sure you remain undetected. Next communication in fifteen Earth days."

Another thirty days; it wasn't much. Just when Zyv'Oom was beginning to feel an attachment to this planet. He had been warned against this and had been ordered to keep his psionic shield up at all times. Mind contamination would mean staying in quarantine for an undetermined period of time, but the temptation of experiencing human feelings had been too strong. He had been briefed on their propensity to attach themselves emotionally to other human beings or objects, which was the cause of much of the violence they were renowned for. But there was more to it, otherwise why didn't human eradicate those feelings? Twenty-five earth centuries ago, a delegation from planet Zorg had visited Earth and had bestowed their knowledge on a man called Gautama Siddhartha. He had understood the danger of attachment and had conveyed a path of enlightenment to his followers. They had called him Buddha, the enlightened one, but after his death, his teachings had been distorted to the point of non-recognition. So-called Buddhists worshipped gold effigies of the man, the biggest one weighing five Earth tons. Zorgians had concluded that the minds of Terrans had not been sufficiently advanced to understand Zorgian concepts. They had tried again with a man called Jesus; the results had not been conclusive and direct action had taken the place of education.

Zyv'Oom had seen how preoccupied Terrans were with what they called love, which he understood to mean emotional attachment. It seemed dangerous, but incredibly valuable, judging by the great lengths Terrans went to get it.

95

Life on planet Zorg seemed bland in comparison to life on planet Earth. The Ooms had settled on planet Zorg after their home planet had been destroyed, and they had attained complete mastery of their environment, their minds and their bodies. Diseases had been eliminated, Ooms were protected from painful thoughts and emotions using mind control techniques, and natural disasters were unheard of. The only threat to their existence came from other planets and the Exo-Planetary Threat Suppression Hive (EPTSH) monitored alien life forms and sent their elite squads to deal with the risks they posed before they became threats.

Life on planet Earth was everything he had dreamed of, dangerous and unexpected, but he hadn't been prepared to see such beauty. The colours, there were so many of them; they were blinding at first for a being who only knew five hundred shades of grey. The sights, smells and sounds had awakened something in him; he had fought against it at first, and then he had let his psionic guard down and had seen what the humans meant by 'harmony' and 'beauty'. Now he wanted to taste, feel, see and hear as much as he could in the time he had left. It was his last chance.

Ooms do not have a word for 'temptation' in their language, because there is nothing worthy of temptation on their planet. How then could Zyv'Oom deal with it? He thought his psionic shield was sufficient defence, but it only worked if he willed it to work. And now he was blind to the consequences; at best, a few months in a decontamination camp, at worst he would be a threat to his planet, a threat that would have to be eliminated, like all the others.

Stephen stopped reading the novel he had written. His thoughts raced around as he tested an idea he had about the implication of his writing. He looked up 'Noosphere':

> In the writings of Vladimir Vernadsky and Teilhard de Chardin, the noosphere is the sphere of human thoughts and consciousness that sits above the biosphere. The word derives from the Greek *nous* (mind) and *sphaira* (sphere), in lexical analogy to atmosphere and biosphere.

It was something that Sergei had spoken about, but Stephen had dismissed this esoteric concept.

He looked up planet Zorg and smiled at the definition:

> Australian slang. Imaginary far distant planet used to explain odd or weird behaviour as in 'I asked him to put the red wine in the fridge and he looked at me like I was from planet Zorg.'

Oom wasn't a word, but an acronym with many meanings:

- Out of Memory
- Order of Magnitude
- Object-Oriented Methods

Stephen stopped at Order of Merit. It was clear he had taken the name of the aliens and their planet and the noosphere from the real world, but what about the idea of a memory thief? He looked up 'memory thief', 'memory snatcher' and 'memory stealer' but nothing came up, it was an original idea.

What a strange coincidence.

I went to a creativity workshop that triggered an idea that I turned into a novel, albeit incomplete, then what I wrote happened. Except I thought my memories were erased and in the novel, memories are stolen to be analysed.

But there's no way to find out if aliens did steal the memories of the Chinese scientists researching teleportation, they would never admit it. But I have an advantage over them; I know how they lost their memories.

The aliens are right about one thing: Terrans have made a mess of their own planet and they would probably do the same to other planets if they had the chance.

This is all too far-fetched, am I going crazy?

Or could it be a premonition?

Even more far-fetched, unless...

If Sergei was right and the noosphere does exist, when the aliens entered the noosphere, I 'saw' them and I wrote down what happened. Another reason for the aliens to steal my memories. They removed the evidence of their visit. Except they forgot to erase my novel. A surprising oversight from such advanced beings who have the technology to travel to our planet undetected, enter our noosphere and steal our memories.

If they think Terrans were close to generating dark energy and that it's a threat, it means that my model is correct and that dark energy could be used to travel to other galaxies.

Maybe they use dark energy themselves...

Could this be a confirmation that there *was* highly intelligent life on other planets, something that Stephen had always believed in, from the first time he had set eyes on the stars?

That Russian police inspector had lost her memory too, but what possible threat could she be to life in other galaxies? Unless she had seen something during her investigation on the serial killer. She had also mentioned that there was a third victim, but who was he, another scientist? He got up and went to the kitchen to make a tisane, as he did whenever he had a problem to solve.

He sipped the pungent liquid and closed his eyes. He had an idea on how to get the information he needed.

He made a video call to Ninoska.

"Inspector, I've gathered some information that led me to a hypothesis on our memory losses, but to confirm it I need to know who the third victim is."

"I told you, I'm not allowed to share information with the public about a current case."

"You do want to solve this case, don't you?"

Ninoska paused. "Alright, he's a well-known musician."

"Come on, who is it?"

"Jimmy Yarrawallah, lead singer of Flash Forward."

"I know who he is, that band is my daughter's favourite."

Stephen thought about how he could fit this information with his hypothesis. *Zyv'Oom could have wanted to take with him the memories of Jimmy Yarrawallah, to create music himself and bring a bit of joy to Planet Zorg.*

Ninoska told Stephen about her visit to Jimmy's house in the trees.

"The reference to the dreamtime is interesting."

Ninoska looked puzzled.

"Have you ever thought that the ancestor spirits that the aborigines see in the dreamtime were aliens?"

"No, I can't say I have."

"Many unexplained events in humanity's history could have involved beings from other galaxies. Consider this, there are hundreds of thousands of galaxies. Rather than thinking about the probability of there being life in one of those galaxies, I prefer thinking that it's extremely unlikely that not one of those is populated."

"But how does it help me solve this case?"

"Let me finish, please. Let's say we accept the presence of life in other galaxies. Then we assume they are much more advanced than we are, because they've been around for longer than we have. Advanced to the point that they can travel easily from one galaxy to another, undetected. They visit our planet, help us along the way. A few humans see them but of course they don't recognise them for what they are. Take Jesus for examples and his miracles, they could very well be manifestations of extra-terrestrial powers."

Ninoska lowered her head and made a sign of the cross.

"And the ascension, could it not be Jesus being hoisted up to a spaceship? You see, these aliens are not only more advanced technologically but also morally, they don't know violence and war. They tried to teach us how to live in harmony, several times through Jesus, Buddha and others. After those dismal failures, they gave up; I mean, there haven't been any new prophets for centuries. But they are still monitoring our progress and have intervened because our technological advances are threatening the peace of the universe."

"And that's your hypothesis, is it? That green men have erased your memory because your research was going to provoke an intergalactic war. Look I may not have gone to university like you have, but I'm not a fool. If I was, I couldn't do this job. It requires a lot more intelligence than you think."

Stephen shook his head. "That's not what I meant at all."

"Your hypothesis doesn't stack up anyway. Why would they have erased my memory?"

"Because you saw something they didn't want you to see."

For a brief moment, Ninoska seemed affected by this. "And Jimmy, did he see them too? That's hardly likely, he spends most of his time in his tree house, composing songs and playing."

"I thought about that; what if they were more advanced technologically and morally but less artistically—it would be impossible to be advanced in every domain. For example, they would have the technology not just to erase memories, but to steal them, but their civilisation would not know music, painting or sculpture. They would have stolen his memories to study earth music; they might do the same to other artists. Have there been other victims?"

"No the professor would have told me. But let's pretend for one minute that you were right, what would you expect me to do about it? The time my boss gave me to pursue the memory thief is going to expire in twelve hours. I don't have any evidence to put forward to him that would persuade him to give me more time, and I'm certainly not going to mention your crackpot idea. So that's the end of the line for me. Tomorrow I'm going to go back to the case of the serial killer; I have to pick it up where I left it six months ago; one my informers has disappeared and the killer's going to strike again in three weeks."

Stephen pondered this. "All I'm asking of you is to let me know if there are any new developments."

"And how are you planning to find E.T.?"

"Don't worry inspector, you'll be the first to know if I find anything."

Stephen had the Prime Minister's personal number. He rarely used it and knew that he was taking a risk. Bob was exasperated about the lack of progress and he had communicated his infuriation through his official channels. He didn't have the time (or was it the courage?) to do it personally. Stephen had the element of surprise on his side; Bob would not be expecting him to call.

"Bob, it's Steven."

"Doctor Collingsworth, what can I do for you?"

This was not a good sign. "Have you had any reports from IETLIA lately?"

"No, I've never heard from them since the base was open, but no news is good news. I have other things to worry about, as you very well know."

The International Extra Terrestrial Life Intelligence Agency had been created ten years ago by the governments of the Russian Imperium, the European Union, the Federation of American Nations and Australia to monitor signs of Extra Terrestrial life and to prepare for any threats alien life could pose to Earth, after a spaceship bound for Jupiter mysteriously disappeared before it took off from Earth. A year later, an American team of scientists working on wormhole travel disappeared. Alien intervention had been suspected and faced with a common enemy, the most powerful states had come together, except for the Chinese Empire, which as usual had preferred to do its own thing. Very little was known about IETLIA; the location of its bases and the identity of its personnel were closely guarded secrets.

If there had been alien activity, the IETLIA would be the only place capable of detecting it. But if Bob hadn't had a report from them, it didn't mean there had been no alien activity, just that no activity had been detected.

"Could I contact the base to check if any unusual activity has been detected?"

"How is that going to help you deliver an unlimited source of energy?"

If Stephen told him about his hypothesis, it would not go down well. "Bob, you have to trust me, in the name of our friendship."

"Don't give me that, you know I can't afford to let my friendships interfere with my work. It's a question of survival. In case you forgot, if you don't deliver I'll lose my job in a few months. And don't count on still having yours. Anyway they won't divulge this sort of information over the phone. Communications with the outside world are strictly limited, to protect the knowledge of its operations from any alien beings already on Earth under human guise."

"So how would they raise the alarm if an incident occurred?"

"I would get an encrypted message that could only be decoded with my DNA sequence."

"Isn't there a way you can get information?"

"Visitors are allowed but only under limited conditions; for a start, they need a security clearance from myself, and remain under close supervision at all times while they're there."

"Couldn't you give me one? What have you got to lose?"

Bob didn't answer straight away; Stephen wondered if he had pushed his request too far.

"Alright, but don't call me again unless it's to announce me the good news. Make your way to RAAF Base Curtin and your pass to the IETLIA facility will be there."

"Is that where it is?"

"The security guys have done their job very well, I don't even know the exact location myself, just that you have to take a helicopter at the base to get there."

Stephen boarded the flight from Perth to Derby, also known as RAAF base Curtin, as it was used both as a civil and military airport. He had followed the instructions to dress like a tourist and leave his trench coat behind. The orders were to avoid attracting attention, as tourists were the only ones to go to Derby; they went to see the giant baobabs and the horizontal falls that were the main attractions.

After the plane had reached its cruising altitude, Stephen looked at the red and barren earth underneath.

It's a miracle any life survives down there. Maybe there are planets like that, populated by life forms that don't need water. What if water was deadly for them, like hydrochloric acid is to us?

The short trip (eighteen hundred kilometres in forty-five minutes) left little time for Stephen to continue his musing. The plane landed and he followed the other passengers down the stairs to the blistering tarmac. He made his way to the RAAF building where a clerk was practicing his game of darts.

"Doctor Collingsworth, please take a seat, I'll see when the helicopter can take you."

"Aren't you going to check my ID?"

"Already done, your DNA matches our records."

"How did you get my DNA?"

"It was scanned the moment you walked in."

"Impressive."

The clerk turned around and said, "Smithy, got a customer for you."

A woman's voice answered, "Be there in an hour."

The clerk turned back to Stephen. "You have to leave your smartphone here, security you know."

Stephen handed it to the clerk who put it in a drawer and said, "There's some beer in the fridge if you wanna have a drink while you're waiting."

"Water will be fine."

The clerk turned a tap and filled a glass that he handed over to Stephen before going back to his game of darts.

The intense heat made Stephen drowsy. He closed his eyes, intending to pass the time snoozing, but his thoughts interfered. There were few, if any, facts to support his hypothesis. Just a novel he had written; a work of fiction, nothing else. His desperation to find out what had happened to his memory had led him to confuse his dreams with reality. It was distracting him from his work. Amanda, frustrated by the lack of progress, had asked Miguel and Sasha to work on his model, but he knew that he was the only man who could complete it.

"Hey wake up, your taxi's here!"

Stephen opened his eyes and saw a tall woman with short blond hair and ice-blue eyes. She looked at Stephen briefly and signalled him to follow her. A black helicopter was waiting for them outside. The woman climbed in the pilot's cabin and Stephen was directed to the passenger cabin. When Stephen saw that it had no windows, he protested that he suffered from claustrophobia, but the clerk pushed him inside and slid the door shut. Stephen pounded his fists on the front side of the cabin, but it was too late, the helicopter was lifting off. Stephen sat down and closed his eyes, but it only made his anxiety worse; his heart was pounding and he was trembling. He remembered the cognitive therapy sessions that the QPT administrators had offered the staff, but they had focussed on being in a large facility underground, not in a small helicopter. The feeble light inside the cabin gave him little comfort from the feeling of impending doom that gripped him. He puffed on his Ventolin inhaler, but was none the better. Damn, he should have stayed home, forgotten about his novel and tried to resume his work. Easier said than done, he had come here to prove a point—or disprove it if he wasn't lucky. He lost track of time; it seemed to stretch on forever until the helicopter landed and he was let out. He found himself inside a windowless hangar; a man in a white hazmat suit with a respirator tapped on his tablet and green, blue and red lights flashed in succession around Stephen.

"All clear sir, you may proceed," the man said.

Stephen showed him his Personal Health Assistant and said, "Wait a minute, my epinephrine levels are too high."

The man's blank stare prompted Stephen to add that epinephrine was the medical term for adrenaline. He stared at the display screen of the device until the level had dropped to what he considered an acceptable level, and said to the man, "OK, we can go now."

Stephen followed the man to a door at the back of the hangar and then along a white corridor. There were no clues as to where he was; it looked like a hospital, minus the smells. A middle-aged man stood in front of a door at the end of the corridor.

"Doctor Collingsworth, can you state the object of your business."

"I was wondering if any abnormal activity had been detected since the thirtieth of March."

"Did you see something on that day?"

Stephen hesitated before replying, but concluded he had no reason to hide the reason for his visit. "Since that date, three people, if not more, have lost parts of their memories; significant and valuable memories. It seems there's a sort of pattern to these memory losses; they are not random. The facts have led me to envisage the hypothesis of an alien intervention."

The man smiled. "Interesting, and where do these three people live?"

"Near Melbourne."

"I'll take you to the unit in charge of monitoring south-East Australia; we'll see if there's a correlation with their findings."

Stephen's hopes lifted; if something had been found, his trip here wasn't in vain.

The man opened the door and Stephen followed the man through another corridor. There were doors with foreign symbols painted in gold colour. The man opened a door with a more familiar symbol: an infinity sign inside a circle, traversed by a cross. Inside the room, a man studied a wall-sized monitor on which a series of graphs were displayed. The plotted lines moved continuously at different velocities, forming more or less regular wave patterns. He turned around and his sneer turned into a smile as his recognised his friend.

"Stevo, what brings you here? Have you finally decided to join the dark side?"

"Calogero, is that where you've been hiding? You bastard, disappearing overnight without saying anything. I couldn't figure out where you'd gone. Your sister thought you'd gone to a Tibetan monastery to start a new life, but I didn't believe her."

"Sorry about that, security's so tight here. We're not supposed to tell anyone where we've gone. I'm not a good liar, but she's so naïve she believed me. The thing is, once you join this place, you're here for the rest of your life. There's no shortage of candidates though, some people would give up both their kidneys to work here."

Stephen looked at him. "You haven't changed a bit since the last time I saw you!"

"I'm doing what I love best and I don't see time pass; I guess my body doesn't either. How long has it been anyway?"

"Fifteen years, give or take a few months."

"And what have you been up to during that time?"

"Oh, this, that and the other."

"Come on, I don't believe the years have made you become modest. It doesn't suit you."

"I'll tell you later; for now, I have a problem I need your help to resolve."

"And you've come all the way here? I'm sorry but I don't think I'm going to be of much help, unless it has something to do with aliens."

"I think it does, but I have no way of proving it, hence why I'm here. I was working on a theory of everything, and I made a critical adjustment to my model following a failed experiment to generate an acceleron, when I lost all memories of the past year."

"A whole year? How did it happen? You had such an amazing memory, how could you lose it?"

"My memory capacity is intact; I can clearly remember everything before and after that year. I did a brain scan and it revealed that my memories had been erased, like a computer file is deleted, but without a recycle bin."

"And you think aliens are involved?"

Stephen wasn't sure how to express how he had arrived at that conclusion. "It's a hypothesis, but I think that my memories were not just erased, but stolen."

Stephen's words wiped Calogero's smile from his face. "If that is the case, it means we're dealing with extraordinarily advanced beings. But why would they steal our memories? If they wanted to study humans, they could just scan them."

"Because if I succeed in mastering dark energy, it's going to give humans the means to travel anywhere, potentially to other galaxies. And they wouldn't want that to happen, it would mean that the chaos we have created on Earth would spread like a virus throughout the universe."

"So why not just erase them? What's the point in stealing them?"

"I'm not the only victim; there are two others."

Calogero pushed his blue-framed glasses up. "Other scientists?"

"No, one's an inspector; I suspect she saw something she shouldn't have. The other is a musician. These aliens are technologically more advanced than us, but suppose it's to the detriment of their artistic abilities. The beauty of music would be foreign to them and they would want to study it."

"Whilst I agree your reasoning has merit, it's not enough to form a definitive conclusion."

"That's why I'm here. If aliens are on planet Earth, you must have detected something."

"Something unusual did come up in the Melbourne area, but no conclusion has been reached on its nature. I am still analysing it."

"When was it?"

"Three weeks ago,"

"That's when I lost my memories. What was it?"

"A wave pattern unlike anything known on this planet." He turned to the monitors and tapped on his tablet. "All communications are monitored and analysed against known wave patterns. 99.9% of them are filtered out, leaving the outliers for my team to investigate. It's a rare occasion when that happens and I must say I've had a few sleepless nights because of this one." He pointed to a monitor. "See this signal here; to give you an idea of scale, I will put a 10+H network radio wave on the same axis."

The red line that had drawn a pattern that filled the monitor was now almost flat at the top of the graph, and a blue line was drawn at the bottom.

"As you can see, the strength of this signal was intense," Calogero continued. "If I extrapolate, this signal could carry nine hundred petabytes of data per minute."

"How long did it last?"

"About twelve minutes."

"Where exactly was it?"

"In Brighton, a suburb in the south-east of Melbourne."

"That's where I live!"

"Don't get carried away, there's nothing to say it's alien in nature, although I have sent it to other IETLIA bases and none have reported seeing anything like it. At first I thought there was a defect in one of our detectors, but two weeks ago there was another signal with the same wave pattern. It was closer to Melbourne, slightly weaker than the first one and lasted only six minutes."

"It could correspond to Inspector Ninoska. She lost six months of her memory. I'll check the date with her."

"Interesting, but it could be a coincidence. Didn't you say there was a third victim? There have only been two occurrences of a similar signal. Where was he?"

"In the Otway forest."

"Our detectors only monitor urban centres and villages."

"So you have no idea what this signal with a never-before seen wave pattern is?"

"No, it didn't travel far, which is strange. I've postulated several explanations, but none of them seem to hold up. Could the signal contain sound? Given the intensity, it would've travelled hundreds of kilometres. Could it contain light? It wouldn't have been unnoticed, although both times the signal occurred during the night."

"That correlates, the victims noticed the memory loss when they woke up."

"Hmm. I also asked myself if the signal could contain data."

"What if that data consisted of memories?"

"But why send it over such a short distance?"

"The memory thief must be close to its victim to extract its memory and store it in a container."

"If what you're thinking is true, I need to raise an alarm. But it's too speculative, I need facts."

"What more do you want? If you establish a correlation between the signals and the memory losses, isn't that enough?"

"I need something else, like an alien spaceship landing, or identification of a living being with non-Terran DNA. We've covered the planet with DNA scanners and communication monitors, and surrounded it with satellites that could spot a spaceship approaching Earth a hundred thousand kilometres away."

"But if they travelled through wormholes and imitated our DNA, the only way of detecting their presence would be unusual phenomenon, like people losing their memories."

"I hate to admit it, because it makes this whole place redundant, but you have a point. The next time someone loses their memory, call someone, anyone; it doesn't matter who, order a pizza for example. During the call, insert a message starting with IETLIA; follow it with the GPS coordinates of the victim, the time in twenty-four hour format and date in Julian format. Close the message with MS, that's MS for Memory Snatcher. I will configure a filter on the communication channel monitors to intercept your messages, and I will continue to monitor the occurrences of this new wave pattern."

"How will you communicate back to me?"

"I will do it in a way that cannot be traced back to this facility, it's too risky. This place was built not just to gather intelligence on extra-terrestrial activity, but if humankind was threatened, it would provide a shelter for its occupants. So we can't afford to let our location be detected by sending a message, except if our assessment of the situation concluded that Terrans had a chance of winning. It's only in that situation that we would call world leaders to summon their armies. So if we find that aliens are stealing our memories, they could very well grind human activity to a halt. Imagine what would happen if we all lost our memories, it would be chaos. I don't know how we would fight back."

Ninoska stood before her note board. She said, "Yoshimi, our time's up, we have to go back to the case of the serial killer. The first two victims were both wives of RAAF personnel who were at the same base as the pilot who bombed the Ishawar, and the date coincides. But in that same base, the abuse of women was being covered up by someone at the highest level and I stumbled on something that involved a senior politician. I don't know where that came from, but coincidentally one of my informers suddenly disappeared after giving me a tip. I wonder if the date of the murders was chosen to throw us off the trail. Now we know that one man was named as the perpetrator of the abuse, but what if he wasn't the only one?"

"You mean the Flight Sergeant and Squadron Leader would have taken part in the abuse? But why kill their wives? I can't imagine abused women killing other women to punish the man who abused them."

"The wives could have been blackmailing the abuser, in which case he would have had a motive for killing them."

"But the third victim didn't live at the base."

"The Chief of Defence Forces could be the culprit of both crimes; his mistress knew too much and she had to go. We'll have to pay him a visit."

Ninoska's phone rang; it was Stephen. He described his trip to the IETLIA facility.

"Although my hypothesis hasn't been refuted, I'm beginning to wonder if the Chinese could be behind this after all. This talk about research on teleportation is maybe a front to cover up the fact they've been working on a device to steal memories."

"Why would the Chinese steal my memory and Jimmy's?"

"I don't know. None of this is making sense; we're going round in circles. But I have another idea: when you saw Jimmy, he mentioned that he took a concoction called zook to enhance his creativity."

"That couldn't have caused the memory loss; he's the only one of us who's taken it."

"That's not what I was thinking. He said that it allowed him to see ideas that no one has had yet. I wonder if we could use it to find the answer to our questions."

"I'm not going back to ask him for a sample, forget it!"

"Give me his coordinates and I'll go."

"Alright, but don't count on me for anything else; I can't spend any more time on this. And before you go, change your appearance; he's blaming his memory loss on the Quantum Particle Transformer and he's probably seen you on TV."

After Stephen' call, Ninoska thought about the *babka*; although she hadn't used the word alien, she had said that the cause of the memory loss was unnatural and Stephen had been unequivocal about who was responsible for their memory losses. Ninoska's scepticism had begun to melt and she was almost disappointed that Stephen hadn't found the evidence he was looking for. There was nothing more Ninoska could do to find her memories, and the *babka* couldn't help her; she was going to have to trust this doctor. Was he the man with long hair that the *babka* had spoken about? He made her feel dumb with all his knowledge on particles that no one could see, but her instinct told her that he was worthy of her trust.

Stephen knocked on the door of the tree house. He had undone his pony tail, letting his hair flow freely around his face, and wore round sunglasses, a rainbow-coloured beanie and a T-shirt with the Eureka flag, a symbol of modern-day anti-establishment protest that was first used as the flag of the Eureka rebellion at Ballarat in 1854.

He heard a voice yell, "What do you want?"

"Hey there, I want to sign your petition against the black hole factory."

The voice softened. "Come in."

When Stephen entered, Jimmy had the petition in his hand, ready to be signed; he looked at Stephen for a minute—did he recognise him despite the disguise?

"Here it is, but how did you hear about it?"

"A friend of mine lost her memory; she came to see you and told me the same thing had happened to you."

Jimmy's nostrils flared. "If we don't stop it, that bloody machine will do more damage."

Stephen signed the petition. "You're right, you know. Those scientists really don't know what they're doing." He had struggled to say the last sentence and he hoped it didn't show. "My friend also told me you took a melange of herbs to see ideas that no one has had yet. It could be very useful for me; I'm a writer and I've got a case of writer's block." Stephen blurted out.

"A writer, eh? Not in the capitalist media, I hope."

"No, I write novels."

"Are you writing one now?"

"Yes, it's called the Memory Snatcher."

Evangelista had been listening intensely to the conversation before she joined in. "As a creative being, have you ever thought about where your ideas come from?"

The ideas Stephen got were solutions to problems he was trying to solve; they came through hard and long thinking. But if he *was* a writer, where would he get his ideas from?

"No, they just come to me as I write. But they're like Melbourne weather, not very reliable."

"Our ideas and our inspiration come from the noosphere. Do you know what it is?"

Stephen shook his head; he wanted to hear Evangelista's explanation.

"It's a network that links all of humanity's minds together. The interactions between them create ideas that our brain can tap into. Everything that has ever been created started off as an idea in the noosphere." Evangelista continued, noticing that she had Stephen's attention. "The way an idea materialises starts when the right side of your brain retrieves it in the noosphere, and that usually happens during sleep. Then the left side of brain transforms it into a painting, a song, a book, an invention or whatever."

"But does that mean that several people could come up with the same idea at the same time?"

"It happens occasionally, but not often because there are so many ideas out there. It doesn't work for everyone either; the right side of your brain has to be in harmony with the left

115

side, which isn't the case for most people. And you have to be looking for ideas; it's not as spontaneous as people think."

"There is a shortcut," Jimmy added. "If you take zook, you can travel to the noosphere without having to wait to be asleep. It gives you access to an endless stream of ideas."

"But if it links all human minds, can you see what people are thinking?" Stephen asked.

"No, you can only see ideas."

"Where did you get the recipe?"

"My father handed it down to me. He's an aborigine, so the effects on him are different; he sees the memories of his ancestors and visits the dreamtime. He's never said anything about seeing ideas, and when I take it, I can't see the dreamtime."

"Could you give me a sample?"

"No, my father and my ancestors would be furious; it's meant to stay in the family. I had to wait for our wedding to give some to Evangelista."

"Can't you make an exception? I promise I won't tell anyone, and I'll dedicate my next novel to you."

"What's it about anyway?"

"It's a science fiction novel about an alternative universe where the evils of capitalism haven't oppressed mankind."

"That's a great example of using creative avenues to disseminate our message against the system," Evangelista said.

"You're right babe, as always." Jimmy gave Stephen a bottle of yellow liquid. "This should be enough for you to finish your novel, so don't come back asking for more."

Stephen took the bottle and put it in his pocket; he had made up his mind.

As Stephen opened the front door of his house, doubts crept into his mind. As natural as it was, Zook was a mind-altering drug. Alcohol was natural, but that didn't make it less harmful. On the other hand, if the aborigines had used it since the dawn of time, they knew what they were doing. The idea of visiting the noosphere was too tempting, maybe he could find his lost memories, or find the value of eM_u. There was too much to gain, so little to lose. He felt like a teenager who was about to open his father's liquor cabinet during the week-end that his parents had gone on a romantic get-away. Not that he had ever done that; he had been more interested in amassing knowledge and solving problems than having fun. The frivolity of his peers irritated him; he wanted to take no part in it. A slight pinch of regret crept up in a remote corner of his mind; maybe he should have been adventurous. It was never too late, Stephen thought as he opened the bottle and poured a glass of the beverage that was the key to opening the door of the noosphere.

Stephen sat on the sofa; he sniffed the liquid, it reminded him of incense. He wished he could record what he was about to see. Could Trevor's scanner do that? Too late now, the zook had made its way down his oesophagus. He closed his eyes and waited, but nothing came. Jimmy hadn't told him how much to take; Stephen got up, filled another glass and went back to the sofa to drink it.

Stephen felt himself being sucked in through a tunnel with a yellow light at the end—the same yellow as the zook. It awoke a hidden memory inside him: his own birth, his journey from the darkness and warmth of the womb into the light of the cold world. It hurt, but he offered no resistance; even if he had wanted to, he knew he couldn't.

His mind was flooded with memories, just like his lungs had been swamped with air. They weren't his; they were the memories and thoughts of thousands of people. Stephen's mind was thrashing about, trying not to drown, reaching upwards, until he was floating above the psyches. That's when realised that there weren't thousands, but millions or billions of them and that the memories were those of people who had lived centuries ago. Without knowing why, he was attracted to one in particular: a room bathed in candlelight where a woman with a weather-beaten face, dressed in hessian cloth, was looking down. A loaf of coarse bread and a jug sat on a wooden table. There was neither joy nor sadness, just a quiet acceptance that there was no other possible life to be lived.

The vision fast-forwarded and became blurred; when it decelerated, Stephen saw a starry sky and heard a voice say, "You see this big star; now see the one on the left? Now then go to the right, there's another big one and a smaller one below slightly to the left and then go further below and to the left. See how they form a cross? It's the southern cross." It was his father's voice.

Then he saw himself as a little boy; he was sitting on the grass and he asked, "Can people who live in the northern hemisphere see it?"

The voice replied, "The ancient Greeks could see it, but then the precession of the equinoxes lowered the stars below the European horizon. Now you have to be below Latitude twenty-five North to see it."

He was looking through his father's eyes; they were his memories, and Stephen guessed that the scene he had seen before came from his father's ancestor's memory. Other memories rushed to Stephen's consciousness. He saw his father's research laboratory at the Commonwealth Scientific Institute of Research Organisation. He had been looking for a way to improve medical diagnostics by reading wirelessly all the information processed by the brain; as it was the central point that received signals from all the organs of a patient, it had all the information a doctor needed to make a diagnostic.

Stephen felt his father's excitement at the success of his first experiment where a patient's heart rate measured by his invention matched the measurement of a classic heart rate monitor.

At every successive experiment, his father was successful in measuring an additional signal: blood pressure, glucose, cholesterol, sodium, epinephrine and ACTH levels.

The next scene was at the laboratory director's office where he informed Geoff, Stephen's father, that JCN had filed an injunction for the CSIRO to stop their research. The corporation's Research and Development department had patented the same technology that Geoff had been working on under the name of Bio-Wi.

Geoff's thoughts came to Stephen's consciousness, as if he was hearing his father speak.

Bastards, how could they do that? I should have lodged the patent when I got the first positive results. But it can't be a coincidence, it must be industrial sabotage; that new assistant, I knew she was up to no good. Always on her smartphone, she must have sent the blueprints to JCN. There must be a way to prove it.

The next memories Stephen saw were thick, heavy and dark; the anger his father had felt metamorphosed into despair; it was suffocating.

Stephen remembered seeing his father, a man a superior intellect and integrity, become a wreck from the outside, now he saw it from the inside: the descent into alcoholism, the withdrawal from family and friends. He was dead to the world before he died. When he had caved in to his wife's insistence on seeking treatment, it was too late. The therapy and drugs did not overcome the death wish that proved to be too strong.

A sensation of unhindered movement and weightlessness followed, as if Stephen's father was floating; he saw his body on the hospital bed. He thought about his wife and he saw her weeping at home.

A funeral parlour, a coffin on a stand, sun light bursting through the narrow windows. In the assembly, Stephen saw himself, his mother, his father's friends...

Another tunnel, with a white light at the end, a bright, pure light pulsating with energy that had the power to cleanse, heal and restore. Now the light was everywhere. Wherever he turned, there was nothing but light. Out of the light appeared an ethereal being who radiated unconditional love.

The being asked Geoff what he had done with his life, but there was no judgement in that question.

Geoff's life flashed before his eyes.

Growing up in a farm, awarded a scholarship, studying in Melbourne, working at the CSIRO, meeting Janet and marrying her.

A life full of promises that had not been realised, but it could have been otherwise.

I wish I'd moved on from that setback and focussed on the essential things in life; if only I'd known, if only I'd believed my beloved Janet; she had faith that there was another life after our life on Earth, Geoff thought.

The being smiled, not that he had a face that could smile, but he glowed like he was smiling.

All is forgiven, he seemed to say.

A man appeared from nowhere—Richard, Stephen's grandfather whom he recognised from a photo that had been taken when Joseph was a young man. He smiled, welcomed Stephen's father, and other men and women came.

This was the tipping point for Stephen; he had been a spectator, viewing his father's memories like he was watching a movie. It should have ended, but it continued, challenging to his beliefs. Was the zook making him hallucinate? The noosphere, if that was really where he was, felt real and ethereal at the same time. How could a drug make him imagine the people and the events that he was seeing? Was there really life after death, as Stephen's mother had believed? He had always thought that religion was nothing but a crutch made my man to make his life on Earth more bearable.

Where are the memories of the living?

The question made Stephen jump out of his father's memories to another place in the noosphere, like clicking on a hyperlink could make you travel instantly to another place in the Web.

He saw an inscription on a tombstone:

Hubertus Janssen

2011-2041

Always in our hearts

What we keep in our memory is ours forever

Images, thoughts (they were in Russian, a language that Stephen had learnt when he was in Vladivostok} and emotions were clear and sharp, streaming in real-time. It wasn't like his father's memories, it felt like he was in a living person's consciousness and he knew that person. Thoughts in Russian, but a tombstone inscription in English; it must be the police inspector.

Other images overlaid the tombstone, hazier—Stephen guessed that Ninoska's mind was bringing up memories.

A handsome man in a suit smiled; a woman walked past behind him carrying an empty bucket.

A jolt of fear.

I knew it was a bad omen, but what could I do?

An old man blew his candles; behind him a white bird was pecking at the window.

A woman in an office; behind her, a windowsill where a white bird was pecking at the window.

Another jolt of fear.

Who is going to die next, Yoshimi or me?

A note board with pictures of three women and writing that Stephen could not decipher.

Lord, put me on the right path to find the serial killer. Show me a sign, any sign.

Stephen felt like an intruder, he wanted to stop.

Could the noosphere hold the clue to the case that Ninoska was trying to solve? How much time did Stephen have left? Jimmy and Evangelista said that they travelled to the noosphere to find their ideas, but so far all Stephen had seen were memories of his father and the consciousness of the inspector.

Stephen felt himself floating upwards through a void, a perfection of nothingness.

When his ascension stopped, Stephen saw a speck of light. It expanded to fill the emptiness, and the white light decomposed into millions of particles, each of a different colour, travelling in a different direction. They expanded one by one into spheres that contained men, women, houses, skyscrapers, mountains, oceans, planes, ships, animals or trees—anything that could be seen or imagined. Stephen was attracted to those that were filled with mathematical formulas, and he saw that the globes that were pulsating with light had music inside them.

When several spheres collided, they merged into one, combining the contents: a giraffe riding a bicycle, a dragon fighting an army, splashes of colours covering a canvas. The infinite imagination of Man was manifested here, but it wasn't what Stephen was seeking.

Stephen saw orbs that glowed; when Stephen focussed on one of them, he sensed the question that it carried inside.

"How can particles be transported from one point to another without traversing the space between them?"

"How can clouds be diverted to areas where water is desperately needed?"

"How can the contents of a human brain be stored?"

Each Orb was going in a different direction, but Stephen followed the last one. The orb collided with a multitude of spheres in a flash of light, and Stephen saw a man sitting comfortably in a sofa. He said, "Back up memory" and closed his eyes. The white cube that was in the middle of the coffee table shimmered and Stephen saw the man's life flashing inside the cube, from his birth to the moment just before he asked for the memory backup.

The cube returned to its original appearance and emitted a beep; the man opened his eyes, took the cube and put it on a shelf.

The vision became blurred and Stephen felt his head tingling.

He didn't want to go back, not now; he had so much to learn, but he couldn't resist the force that dragged him through the same tunnel that he had been through to enter the noosphere.

Chapter Seven

13th April 2046, Melbourne.

"Any luck with the friends and relatives of the Indonesian refugees?" Ninoska asked Alex.

"No, but when I was digging around Brunswick, I found one that didn't have a visa. I don't know how he got through, but I came back the next day and one of the guys there spat on the ground in front of me. He said I was a rotten swine for denouncing his friend. I swore to him I didn't, but this guy heard a car during the night, muffled cries and doors slamming; the next day his friend was gone."

Yoshimi came in and said, "Ninoska, doctor Collingsworth is here, he wants to speak to you."

Ninoska didn't want to speak to him in front of her team. "I'll be there in five minutes." She didn't like the way this investigation was going, but she had to keep her team busy. "Alex, Can you go back and ask if this has happened to other illegals, and see if you can find anything from the Border Protection Force."

"I don't reckon I'll get anywhere with them, they're worse than ASIO."

Ninoska went to reception where Stephen was waiting; he looked uncomfortable, like he didn't want to be there.

"Inspector, where can we talk?"

"There's a coffee place down the street."

They walked rapidly in silence, Stephen's eyes bloodshot eyes darting around him.

"Grab a table in the corner; what will you have? They make great cappuccinos here," Ninoska said.

"A tisane; ask them if they have lime verbena."

Ninoska placed the order and joined Stephen at the table.

"You look awful," Ninoska said.

"What I've seen in the noosphere has kept me up at night."

"The what?"

"The noosphere, it's a network that links all of humanity's minds together in the same way that Internet links computers together. I took some of that zook that Jimmy made and I saw what was inside the noosphere."

"Are you sure you weren't hallucinating?"

"I saw my father's memories and what I saw was accurate, although I'm not too sure about what I saw after his death."

Stephen described his father's memories of the after-life.

"But that means your father's soul lives on; he's in heaven with his family."

"I can't deny what I saw, but it means that all that religious nonsense is true, although I didn't see hell so I'll reserve my judgement on that one."

When a waitress brought their order, Ninoska couldn't refrain from showing her distaste. "Sorry, Stephen, I just can't stand the smell of tisane. My Babushka made us drink her concoctions every time we felt sick. We got so sick of them that we tried our best to hide our illnesses, even if it meant going to school in a blizzard. When I look back I wonder if she did that on purpose to toughen us."

Stephen sipped his tea. "I have another proof I was in the noosphere; I was in your consciousness."

Ninoska blushed. "What were you doing there?"

"It wasn't deliberate, and I didn't stay there for long; you were at the cemetery, at the tomb of Hubertus Janssen."

"He was my fiancé."

Stephen looked like he didn't how to respond. He had probably seen the emotions she had felt that day, and today they were still raw. If she could catch the *podonok* who did that, she would have no hesitation in killing him. She clenched her teeth and her hands as she pictured herself strangling him.

"The noosphere is also the place where creativity happens," Stephen said. "Painting, writing, jokes, inventions, they're all there, waiting for us to pick them like we would pick fruit from a tree."

He paused and looked at Ninoska. She nodded, appreciating the change of subject.

"To be creative, you have to let the left side of your brain listen to what the right side of your brain has found in the noosphere. Some of us do it better than others, but it means that anyone could be creative if they knew that. No need to attend a creativity workshop."

"Have you ever been to one?"

"Yes, but I have no memory of it; we all went, it was a bright idea of my boss. She figured it would help us get out of our rut. I don't know if there was anything about the noosphere though, it's a very marginal concept."

"Who ran the workshop?"

"Are you interested in going? I don't know if—"

"No, my boss had the same idea, but I don't remember going either. It was run by Tracy Van Der Berk."

"So was the one I went to, which means there could be a link. Consider this: all three victims were creative people. You and I are creative, in a different way to an artist, but we solve problems, elaborate hypotheses and test them in the field. We are always asking questions, bouncing ideas. Tracy makes a living by teaching people to be creative. What if she wanted to further her research by stealing creative people's memories?"

"Is that another theory of yours?"

"It's not a theory, it's a hypothesis."

"What's the difference?"

"A theory is a well-established principle that has been developed to explain some aspect of the natural; it has been tested and is generally accepted. A hypothesis is a specific testable prediction about the expected results of an experiment or a study. It's a speculative guess that has yet to be tested."

"Your hypothesis then is shaky: I went in February and I lost my memory in April. When did you attend the workshop?"

"In October."

"And why would Jimmy need to go to a creativity workshop? The zook gives him all the creativity he needs."

"Didn't you say Jimmy is married to Evangelista Chavez?"

"That's right; I saw her at his house."

"She worked with my wife."

"I remember reading that."

Ninoska took a serviette and wrote the names of the people involved in her investigation of the memory snatcher: Ninoska, Stephen, Tracy, Evangelista, Cécile and Jimmy. She linked the names that were linked by relationships, work and attendance of a creativity workshop: Tracy to Ninoska and Stephen, Stephen to Cécile, Cécile to Evangelista and Evangelista to Jimmy.

"You see, there are three degrees of separation between Jimmy and Tracy: Evangelista, Cécile and yourself. You can forget about your hypothesis. However, I just had an idea:

this zook could be a very useful in finding a criminal if it makes you see the memories of the dead."

"That's assuming the victims saw their killer, but I don't think Jimmy would agree to the zook being used that way."

"You don't have to tell him; he's given you some before, he won't suspect anything. If he finds out I'm a police inspector, there's no way he'll give me any."

"I haven't recovered yet."

"Doesn't matter, I'll take it." Ninoska feared what she would see, but it was the only way she was going to find the serial killer.

Ninoska tried not to look at the clock on the wall; it only made time go more slowly, but she couldn't concentrate on anything else. She had ignored her house's calls to be cleaned and her body's screams to be fed.

After the death of her fiancé, Ninoska had moved out of their apartment in Southbank and she had rented a house in Carlton. Her roller derby trophies sat on the fireplace mantle. A photo of Hubertus hung between two icons, one representing Jesus, the other Saint Nina, in whose honour Ninoska had been christened. Boxes full of Hubertus' belongings were stacked in the corner of the living room. Ninoska hadn't had the heart to give them away, and she had opened one of them to browse copies of the sport magazine for which he had worked as a photographer. Besides, how would he feel about someone else using his favourite camera?

Four P.M.

Stephen didn't go to Jimmy's tree house as early as she had wanted, fearing the singer's reaction if he dragged him out of bed. But he said he was going to be there at midday; asking Jimmy for the zook should take half an hour at the most, and driving back two hours. He should have been back at two thirty, unless he'd had to wait for Jimmy, or something else had happened.

She knew the victims' names by heart, by taking the zook she would be able to see their killer, or hear him, or smell him at least. She had seventeen days to stop the killer from striking again.

Ninoska sprang out of her chair to answer the knock on the door. Stephen looked like John Lennon with his round glasses and his long hair; Jimmy would have had no way of suspecting that the man to whom he gave the zook was responsible for the black hole he thought the Quantum Particle Transformer had created.

Ninoska asked Stephen to take off his shoes as he came in. He had a bottle of yellow liquid in his hand. "The good news is I got the zook, and it's fresh too. Jimmy was preparing it when I got there, that's why I'm late."

Ninoska took the bottle from Stephen; it looked like a urine sample.

"The bad news is unless you want to write a book or paint a picture, you won't get anything from it.

"Why not?"

"Consider this: Jimmy, Evangelista and I can use zook to tap into the creativity of mankind. When aborigines take zook, they see the dreamtime which I think is also in the noosphere, but on another level. I didn't try to see the dreamtime, but I think I could, because I have something in common with aborigines: we both have an extraordinary capacity to remember. And I saw the memories of deceased persons, which aborigines can also see. I also saw the consciousness of the living, which Jimmy and Evangelista can't. Even though Jimmy's half aborigine, he has a normal memory capacity, that's why he can only go to the creativity level, same for Evangelista. That means different people can go to different levels of the noosphere."

"So you're going to have to take it then."

"To solve your case? No way, I don't want to get involved in your investigation."

"You bloody *durak*! It's a matter of life and death; in seventeen days the killer is going to strike again."

Stephen stepped back and tipped a plate that was on the edge of a table; it crashed to the floor.

"*K schastya*, as we say. Don't worry, in my country breaking a plate brings good luck."

Stephen's moved away from the table; he twirled his ponytail while he thought about Ninoska's request. "Alright, I'll help you, but on one condition, that you help me to find the memory thief."

"What can I do?"

"You can help me to test my hypothesis about Tracy. I gathered some information when I got the zook that makes it more probable: Tracy Van Der Berk is a friend of Evangelista."

Stephen took the serviette where Ninoska had written the six names and drew a line between Evangelista and Tracy. "Now there's only one degree of separation; even if Jimmy didn't attend one of her workshops, she still had access to him."

"If that's the case, it's a strange way to treat your friends."

"After I've taken the zook, find out everything you can on Tracy."

Ninoska wasn't in a position to argue; Stephen was his only hope. After finding the serial killer, she'll have more freedom to look into Tracy's activities.

Stephen sat down on Ninoska's sofa and read the victim's file. Helen Giannikis was a pharmacist who cheated on her husband with the Chief of Defence Forces when he was in Melbourne. Her body was found in Albert Park Lake, tied with electrical cable; the autopsy had revealed that she had drowned, and that she had not suffered any sexual abuse.

Stephen drank the zook, repeating her name in his mind; he felt uncomfortable looking inside a stranger's memory, but less so than he had when he was inside Ninoska's mind. He was doing this for a good cause.

Stephen glimpsed Helen's anger at her husband Vincent for making her live a life of routine and boredom. There was nothing worth saving in her marriage, but she clung to the security it provided her. Her affair with Paul Battler made her feel alive, but after each encounter, guilt ravaged her.

Stephen fast forwarded to Helen's last day.

It seemed like an ordinary day, preparing scripts, serving customers, thinking about her last meeting with Paul Battler. Stephen skipped that part, wishing that the noosphere could have a safe filter like the Internet.

She was on duty until eight that evening, wishing for the day to end soon.

If only she knew.

She left the pharmacy and walked to the car park.

Stephen felt the pain on the back of the head as if he had been hit himself.

Consciousness returned with the pain; she opened her eyes but there was something blocking her vision. Her arms and legs were tied very tightly. She tried to scream, knowing the futility of it because of the thick sticky tape on her cheeks and mouth. She was lying down, and the floor was pitching lightly; she thought she was on a boat. Who had tied and gagged her? What was he going to do to her? Was it Vincent punishing her for her infidelity? She felt like shouting "I'm sorry, I regret it; I swear I will never do it again", but she had no way of communicating. No, it couldn't be; Vincent was too weak, and how would he have found out? Nothing interested him apart from his balance sheets and playing those stupid games. Once he was immersed in an artificial reality, there was no way of dragging him out. Could it be Paul, realising that if she was unhappy with their relationship and broke off, she could make noises that could damage his reputation? No, he had once joked that one of his former mistresses had realised that if she said anything, it was her word against his. Bloody pig, he thought he could get away with anything!

Panic submerged Helen's mind as she felt herself being lifted and thrown into the cold water. Her heart skipped a beat; she knew she was going to die without knowing why or by whom, without having said goodbye to her parents, her brother or even her husband, the man she had grown to despise. She tried to free herself from her bindings, knowing that it was in vain. Water entered her body through her ears and her nostrils.

Stephen quickly moved on; even if he hadn't known the outcome in advance, it was obvious and inevitable. No one was going to suddenly appear, dive in and rescue her, it only happened in films.

The last thought she'd had before being thrown in the water was for Paul Battler, the Chief of Defence Forces; Stephen jumped into his consciousness.

Three men in uniform and two men in plain clothes were sitting around an oval mahogany table. One of the men, a highly ranked officer spoke. "Vessel is approaching territorial waters, Sir. Submarine is positioned and ready to strike. It will look like the boat hit a reef and sunk."

"Very well Admiral, you may proceed."

Paul turned his head to the man who had spoken, Bob Fultrow.

A vessel entering territorial waters, was it a threat to the country that had been averted? Stephen didn't remember hearing about it.

He tried to access Paul's consciousness, but a barrier prevented him from entering, as if Paul had sensed an intrusion.

Stephen let his consciousness drift upwards and watched the whirlwind of ideas of the noosphere until the effects of the zook wore off.

Ninoska had been pacing the room while Stephen was exploring the noosphere; when she saw Stephen's face tense, she guessed that he was witnessing Helen's demise.

It was better for her that the zook wouldn't have had the effect that it was having on Stephen. If she could be inside a victim's head as she suffered at the hands of a murderer, Ninoska feared that she would get too involved emotionally.

Stephen's face gradually relaxed while Ninoska became more and more tense as she waited for him to come back to Earth.

"You're going to have to find someone else to help you next time, that was excruciating—imagine the horror of knowing that you're going to die in the next few minutes and that there's nothing that you can do; you're entirely powerless." Stephen drew in a long breath. "I witnessed it first-hand. It's not like watching a movie; when you're in the noosphere, you feel what the person is feeling."

Stephen shook his head. "And all that for nothing. The murderer knocked her unconscious from behind and when she woke up she was tied, gagged and blindfolded. The killer didn't say a single word. He knew where she parked her car which means that either he knew her or he had been watching her. She didn't think it was her husband or her lover."

"We've checked their alibi. Paul Battler was in Canberra until late that day, there was no way he could have flown to Melbourne, and Vincent was on a conference call with London that evening. You haven't found anything that we didn't know; you're going to have to go back and look into the other two victims' minds."

"What good is that going to do? We're dealing with a serial killer and by definition serial killers always operate in the same manner. So tell me, were the other victims tied, gagged and blindfolded?"

"Yes."

"Did they die from drowning?"

"Yes although in different places; the first one in her bath, the second one in her swimming pool."

"Were they hit on the back of the head?"

"Yes."

"So consider this, they were all hit from behind and when they regained consciousness they couldn't see their aggressor. If you knew all that, it wasn't hard to see that there was no way searching their minds would uncover anything. I could have avoided observing that poor woman's last moments."

"I was hoping there would be some kind of clue, a smell or a voice."

"He didn't say anything; as for the smell, I do remember a smell of filth, but it could've come from the boat she was in. Anyway you wouldn't be able to investigate all the filthy-smelling people in Melbourne, where would you start?"

Ninoska smelt the odour of defeat in the air.

"You're back to square one now; finding the memory thief is your only hope."

"Assuming the memories were stolen rather than erased. If you hadn't written that novel, we would never have imagined a theft."

"It's less conceivable, but you can't discount that possibility. Remember, you promised you would—"

"I haven't forgotten, but I'll have to do it when my boss isn't there. Meet me here tomorrow at six."

The message Ninoska was getting from her intuition about Tracy Van Der Berk was clear: she was getting warm. But she didn't want to admit it to Stephen; she didn't have the evidence to back up what her intuition was telling her.

When she saw the expectant look on Stephen's face, she knew he would be disappointed.

"I checked Tracy Van Der Berk thoroughly, but there are no irregularities. She has some very high profile clients in her portfolio and her business is booming. She lives on her own in a luxury apartment in Saint Kilda with her two Pomeranians, Nenette and Kekette. Her father was killed in the Afghan war, and she's a regular client of Crown casino. She does her grocery shopping online and consumes twenty-five kilos of dark chocolate a year. She barracks for the—"

"Is there anything more relevant?"

Ninoska smirked. "In my job, you learn that any detail could reveal something which will prove to be important, even to the point of solving the case."

Stephen bit his lip; Ninoska saw that he didn't like the situation he was in; he wasn't the expert in control, manipulating the variables used in a formula that only he could understand to prove the existence of particles that no one could see.

He regained his composure. "Do you have a list of her clients?"

Stephen read out loud the list that Ninoska handed him. "Immersion Gaming, Anderson and Johnson Architects, Fox Media, National Australia Bank, JCN. Aha, that doesn't surprise me." He looked at Ninoska. "Tracy has worked with this notorious idea stealer. If I was a gambling man, I would bet that they are behind this."

"Stop talking to yourself, you're not making any sense."

"My father discovered a way to read biological variables wirelessly: blood sugar levels, heart rate, hormones. He was going to use his invention to improve medical diagnostics, but he was forced to stop working on it when JCN claimed they invented it before him. Their lawyers filed an injunction for him to stop his research. I'm convinced that there was industrial espionage, but they were too clever and never left any traces. My father never recovered from it and when he saw his invention put to frivolous uses, it was the last straw."

"But when you went to the noosphere, you saw ideas and inventions floating there, ready for someone to use them. So it's likely that several people could get the same idea at the same time."

Ninoska's words pierced him like a dart, but he quickly recovered. "Yes, but they didn't have to stop him from using what they had discovered at the same time. He wasn't going to take away their market. He was advancing medical diagnostics; all they wanted to build was a device that knew you were hungry. They didn't even try to negotiate; they ruined his life with one stroke of a pen."

"And now you think they've invented a device to steal memories?"

"They've taken the concept of stealing ideas to the next level." Blood rushed to Stephen's face. "If they've stolen my

136

work on dark energy, they're going to reap all the benefits. I'm surprised I haven't received an injunction to stop my work. Actually, they don't need to; they know they're ahead of me now and that I can't win this race anymore."

"But why would they have stolen my memory and Jimmy's?"

"They could make some money from Jimmy's song; as for you I don't know."

"You're turning this into a personal issue because JCN wronged your father. JCN was one of Tracy's customers, so what?"

"They could be working together. Can you do some research on JCN like you did for Tracy?"

Ninoska ignored her intuition. "JCN is huge. I can't afford to spend time on this while the days are counting down until another woman is killed."

"If you're not going to help me, I'll deal with this on my own."

Stephen didn't have a plan, he knew that he was another victim of JCN, but how was he going to prove it? He felt lost on his own. When he had a hypothesis, he knew he could count on Andrew to devise an experiment, but what help would he be in solving a real-world problem?

The theory of everything, the unitron and dark energy seemed insignificant now. They were of no use to him, and yet they were the reason Stephen was fighting for the truth. If he could find the memory thief, Jimmy, Ninoska and he would retrieve their memories and resume their life. Could the stolen memories be loaded back into their brains, or would they have to view them on a monitor like the professor had viewed Stephen's memories? That was assuming they had been stolen rather than erased. If the latter was true, all the time he had spent chasing a hypothetical memory thief would have been for nothing.

What would happen to him if wasn't able to finish his work in time? Bob would be certain to lose the next election and it was very unlikely the opposition would continue funding the Quantum Particle Transformer. Maybe the Chinese Empire or the Russian Imperium would be interested in his work.

Stephen browsed JCN's web site at home, and soaked in torrents of information indiscriminately, without knowing what he was looking for.

Stephen's blood curdled; the company that was famous for their gadgets also had a medical division that made devices that monitored biological variables wirelessly just like the one his father had invented.

He continued, fuelled by his anger. Media, transport, power, biotechnologies—JCN was a conglomerate founded by Joseph Charles Nolan, who was estimated to be the richest man in Australia, and the fifth richest in the world. He was married to Claire Powell, a corporate lawyer. His father had made a fortune in the days when Australia was exporting its minerals and fossil fuels, and Joseph had invested his inheritance on high-technology firms. He was the sort of man who would stop at nothing to expand his business empire. He had to be behind the memory thefts.

The next day, Stephen went to go the JCN head office at number ninety-eight, Collins Street in the heart of the Melbourne Central District, not knowing what he was going to do when he got there.

Stephen looked at the gleaming two-hundred-storey JCN tower, the highest in the southern hemisphere. It had the colour and the shape of a tree; the bottom third was wide, the tubes on the side evoking roots. The middle was narrow and the top third was a globe with leaf-shaped windows and hundreds of bird houses that provided food and shelter to boisterous cockatoos and rosellas.

He considered the men and women streaming in and out of the building in a quiet hurry. He wondered how much they knew of their employer's activities; he was going to move towards one of the entrances, when he recognised a face amongst the multitude.

Tracy Van Der Berk; Stephen was sure it was her. He had lost the memory of the creativity workshop and his consultations with her, but he had seen her photo on her company's web site. Curvaceous, with long bright red hair, she stood out from the crowd.

A man walked up to her. He had olive-coloured skin that made his short hair and beard look whiter than they really were; anger was written on his face. Tracy spoke to him briefly; he replied frantically, looking around him with suspicious eyes. Was this a professional meeting or was there more between the two?

They walked hurriedly until they reached the Elephant and Wheelbarrow, a popular pub on the corner of Spring Street opposite the State parliament building, temple of ephemeral power.

Stephen untied his pony tail and fumbled in his pockets until he found his glasses and beanie. He followed them inside.

The pub was quiet, it was too early for the office workers who enjoyed having a liquid lunch there. Stephen went to the bar to order a drink, keeping his eye on his quarry.

Stephen buried his head in a newspaper when he saw Tracy getting up. She ordered a whisky on the rocks and an orange juice. Stephen peered at Tracy on the side of his newspaper. While the barman was pouring the drinks, she turned around to look at the man. If this meeting was of a professional nature, why go to a pub at this time of the day? Could they be lovers? She went back to the table with the drinks. Tracy put her hand in his, but it did little to calm him down. Stephen caught a few words. JCN ... Bastard ... Research.

I'm not the only one upset with JCN, Stephen thought.

Tracy nodded while he was talking. She said something that changed his mood. He asked a few questions, drank his whisky and they got up

Stephen took a hundred-dollar note from his wallet and gave it to the barman.

"That was my wife; she's cheating on me. I need the swine's glass to get his DNA."

The barman nodded.

Stephen grabbed the glass with a serviette and ran to the police station.

"I saw Tracy Van Der Berk with a man walking out of the JCN building. I got the glass he was drinking from. Can you get his DNA?"

"You've been watching too many cop shows," Ninoska said, "but yeah I can do that. You're lucky, my boss is out."

"But if he's not on your files, can you identify him?"

"These days, anyone who enters the Australian territory through a plane, a boat or a woman's womb gets his DNA registered. Stay here."

Ten minutes later, Ninoska was back. She picked up her tablet.

"Max Cochinery, 8 Dendy Street in Brighton."

The man's profile appeared on a monitor. Stephen read it at the same time as Ninoska and learned that he had a PhD in neurology at the University of Ballarat where he had worked as a researcher (he had published twenty-two papers on the functioning of memory) while he was practicing as a specialist in a Toorak clinic, until 2044 when he joined Incubatix, a private research laboratory."

"What was he doing at JCN head office?" Stephen asked.

She tapped on her tablet and looked at the monitor. "Incubatix is owned by Joseph Charles Nolan."

"And that's all the information you have on their activities?"

"Their secrets are well guarded. Incubatix has not filed any patents, JCN owns their intellectual property."

"Why not create a research and development department within JCN?"

"It must be Joseph's way of protecting his investment. Let's see what we can find about this Mr Nolan."

Every piece of information that was captured in electronic systems was listed: extracts from the civil registry (Joseph married Claire Powell, lawyer, in 2038; his parents died in a bushfire in 2040; his daughter Annalisa was born in 2041), tax returns (and audits), life insurance (paid a premium for racing Mach-speed vehicles in the Gibson Desert). Ninoska stopped at Joseph's Medicare record.

"Interesting, between 2041 and 2042, Claire Nolan consulted Doctor Cochinery six times. She was on Joseph's Medicare card, and although he didn't claim, the consultations were recorded by Medicare during their annual reconciliation. It looks like he was trying to hide the fact that his wife consulted a neurologist."

"Can we find out why she consulted?"

"Officially, I can only get access to the medical records in the context of a criminal investigation, and I can't open one on the memory thefts. Let's see what we can find on Claire." Ninoska looked at the results for Claire. "A corporate lawyer with an impeccable record it seems. Started working for JCN in 2035 and has not practiced since 2042. Whatever she had must've been pretty serious."

"So Joseph married his lawyer; she had a neurological condition that cut short her career. He consulted one of the best specialists to treat his wife, but the doctor didn't get any results so Joseph hired him, presumably to keep working on a cure."

"There's nothing wrong in that."

"Except that the doctor is Tracy Van der Berk's lover and she knows the three people who have lost their memories. Now don't tell me you don't see anything wrong there."

"I can't spend any more time on this. See that number on the wall there? Sixteen days until the killer's due to strike again."

But there was one detail that had caught her attention: Joseph Charles Nolan owned an unregistered white BMW sedan. Its registration had expired in November 2041. Why let a car gather dust in a garage? All the wealthy men Ninoska had known had one trait in common: they did not like wasting money. If an asset was not utilised or was not making money for its owner, it was sold.

Could Joseph be the man Ninoska was looking for?

Chapter Eight

16th April 2046, Melbourne.

Stephen stirred his tisane nervously; Cécile had called him when he had just woken up, panic in her voice. She said that something terrible had happened to her, and she wanted to talk to him about it because he was the only one who could understand. She asked to meet him at Flo's Coffee shop in Brighton. What could have happened that only he could understand?

He'd given up hope of seeing her again and had been surprised at the indifference he felt, as if his search for his lost memories was the only thing that mattered. But now that she'd called him, he felt like he was on a blind date, not knowing what to expect.

When she arrived, Stephen felt like he'd swallowed a brick. Cécile's hair was dishevelled, her eyes were bloodshot, and her clothes were crumpled. Something was definitely wrong, Cécile never went anywhere without doing her hair and putting her make-up, even if it was to go jogging.

"Thank God you got here before me," she said in a breathless voice. "I wouldn't have been able to wait for you even for one minute."

Cécile sat down and continued talking. "I don't understand what's happened to me, Stephen. Please tell me this is just a dream."

"Calm down," Stephen said in a firm voice, "and start from the beginning. I don't know what you're talking about."

Cécile took a deep breath and sipped Stephen's tisane.

"The last think I remember before going to bed last night is trying to calm you down and giving up. Something had happened at work, and you didn't want to talk about it. You were in a foul mood and you told me to mind my own business. I'd never seen you like this."

"What date was it?"

"Fifteenth of August I think."

The date of the failed experiment and his fight with Andrew. That could only mean one thing...

"And when you woke up, you found that eight months had passed?"

"Well yes, but I didn't know that at first. I was in a house I had never seen. You weren't there and I thought you'd carried me off and dumped me somewhere. I screamed as loud as I could, hoping I would wake up from my nightmare. Félicie came rushing in; my poor girl, she had no idea what was going on. I asked her where we were, and she explained that I'd had enough of you and had moved out of the house. Apparently I'm now living with a doctor named Richard, but I haven't seen him yet. I couldn't remember any of it, but she said that you'd lost your memories too. That's when I called you. I was hoping you'd be able to explain what the hell was going on."

"When I lost my memories, I didn't realise it straight away either; I thought you'd gone to work early and that the kids had a day off. I did notice a few unusual things in the house, but it wasn't until I got to work and was told the inauguration ceremony had been a year ago that I realised that I'd lost my memories. Then I had a brain scan, and it showed that I didn't have amnesia; my memories had been completely erased."

Stephen recollected his fruitless search for his lost memories and those of Ninoska and Jimmy.

"I'm sorry to be the one to disprove your grand theory, but I have never seen or heard of Tracy Van Der Berk. I'm the last person in this town that needs to go to a creativity workshop anyway."

"Oh really? You've never had a day where ideas didn't come and you were stuck?"

"Don't worry, I've had plenty. It doesn't bother me; I do something else like follow up my suppliers, and the next day I'm fine."

Stephen looked at his wife with new eyes. He admired her resourcefulness and her resilience.

"How can you be so sure that you didn't see her during those eight months? Perhaps moving out was harder than you thought; it affected your work so you sought help; there's nothing to be ashamed of."

The softness in her eyes evaporated, replaced by a steely resolution.

"You've always underestimated me, *Monsieur je-sais-tout*; you're the superior one, always with the answers. You think you know how the universe works when you've got no idea about the people you live with. We're not particles that you can play around with at your whim. *Merde alors!* You've lost your memories, but you haven't lost any of your pretentiousness, no wonder I moved out. I should've done that a long time ago."

Cécile got up and turned around.

"Cécile, wait, it's not like that. I admire you, I really do and I always have. You're talented, you're beautiful, you're—"

"It's too late for that. The kids told me you'd tried to contact me after your memory loss and I never called back, so just forget I called you, I'm sure you've got better things to do with your time. Go and find your *putain de* universal particle and be happy, if that's all that matters to you. You don't need me or the kids."

"But..."

Cécile walked out of the coffee shop, ignoring the disapproving stares from the other patrons.

Stephen felt like he'd wasted the second chance he'd been given with Cécile and that there wouldn't be a third. He thought about their marriage, the good times they had shared. He had set eyes on her for the first time at the Black Cat jazz club, where Mukassa's band was playing. Her husband had just left her for another woman, leaving her to look after their two young children. Her friends had taken her out, worried that she would not recover from this blow to her fragile self-confidence. Cécile wanted to turn the page as quickly as possible. Six months later, they were married.

Cécile knew that Stephen's work took a large place in his life and she accepted it as long as he left room for her, which he had done until the theory of everything had come into his life. It was a demanding mistress that needed exclusive attention and Cécile had been a collateral damage.

If there was one thing that could win Cécile back, maybe it was finding her lost memories. Another reason to find the memory snatcher.

Tracy Van Der Berk drew back one step. "Doctor Collingsworth, what a surprise, I was expecting another patient." Her lipstick matched the colour of her hair which was tied in a bun. She tugged her black jacket.

Stephen had called the day before to make an appointment, but the secretary had claimed that Tracy was booked out for the next two months. When he had called back with a different voice and a different name, Tracy's diary had suddenly cleared up.

"I had recommended you to a friend of mine, but at the last minute he couldn't come and he asked me if I was interested in taking his appointment. It was excellent timing you see, because I need your help."

Tracy's efforts to look relaxed didn't convince Stephen. She sat down at her desk and opened Stephen's file.

"The last time I saw you, I advised you to try your hand at writing."

"And I did, I started writing a novel."

"That's great, what's the story?"

"It's called 'The memory snatcher'."

Tracy swallowed hard. Stephen was enjoying her display of discomfort.

She cleared her throat. "Interesting, how is it going?"

"I have a case of writer's block; my main character has lost a year of his memories and he wants to get them back. But that's where I'm stuck; I just don't know where he should be looking. What do *you* think?"

Tracy reached for a glass of water and drank it in one mouthful.

"I don't know; it's a very unusual story, very creative. Well done, you've put my creativity program to good use. But as the writer, you must know who the memory snatcher is; you're the creator, the god of this universe. The words on the page are like the bricks of a house that you've put together."

"No, I didn't write the plot, I just started writing as the ideas came to me. I don't know where they came from. I feel like they were always there, waiting to be used; someone else could have written this story, but I feel a personal connection, like I was destined for it. But why me?"

Tracy looked at her notes. "You said that you had hyperthymesia, there's the link."

"And so has the main character."

Tracy curled her necklace around her fingers. "An autobiography disguised as a novel?"

"I hope not. I would hate to lose my memories. Imagine if the same thing happened to me as my main character. My work would grind to a halt and I can tell you I would do everything in my power to find the culprit."

Tracy chuckled. "You're lucky such a thing is purely fictitious."

Stephen stared at her. "Indeed, and so are the other characters. They've lost their memories too; the police inspector, the singer—"

"As you remember from the workshop," Tracy said deliberately, emphasising each word to give it the importance it deserved. "My program is based on the example of one of history's most prolific creative persons, Leonardo Da Vinci."

"Of course I remember very clearly, as if it was yesterday."

"He was multidisciplinary and excelled at many things like painting, drawing and inventing. I think it's time you moved on from your writing. You must exercise your creativity in different domains to fully realise your potential. There are creative pursuits you haven't explored yet."

"I was thinking of having a go at fashion design, like my wife. I don't think I mentioned her, Cécile Dubontant. Have you heard of her?"

"Yes, I love her designs."

"But would you say that she could benefit from your creativity program?"

"Of course, anyone can benefit by pushing the boundaries of their creativity." She emitted a brief but nervous laugh. "I'm sure even Leonardo would benefit."

"That's what I thought too. I noticed some changes in her behaviour recently and I thought she might have enrolled in your program without telling me. She's too proud to admit she could do with some help."

She tapped on her tablet. "No she hasn't, but perhaps she bought a copy of my book."

"I'll enquire, but discreetly of course."

Stephen switched on the kettle to make a tisane.

After his visit to Tracy, he had spent the rest of the day running simulations, but none of the values of eM_u had given the results he was looking for and he could not explain the variances.

Miguel and Sasha were not making any progress and Amanda was in a foul mood.

Had he really been as close to completing his model as he had assumed or was it inherently flawed?

If only he had written some notes, but his hyperthymesia enabled him to pick up his train of thought exactly where he had left it and it was infallible; why bother taking notes? If it wasn't for his rare condition, he would be in a better position.

His mind wasn't on his work anyway. He had thought about his visit to Tracy. She had seemed very nervous when he had made references to memories being stolen. She was a woman with something to hide, and she had a motive for stealing memories. But she would not have been able to do this on her own; she knew a neurologist, a man whose job was to understand the functioning of memory.

Stephen had called Professor Trevor Luong, who said that Max had worked with him on the development of the brain scanner, but he had been frustrated at the minimum funding that they received. He had left the university without notice and Trevor had thought he had gone to a country that was more generous towards scientific research.

Max lived a short distance away; Stephen put on his trench coat and walked to Max's house. The lights were out and no one answered the door.

He went to Max's neighbour's house. An old lady opened the door.

"I'm looking for Max Cochinery; have you seen him today?"

"I always do a bit of gardening in the morning; it's the best time of the day. I planted some pansies, but they're ruined. I'm sure some dogs peed on them; if I catch the foul creatures, I'll give them a kick in the backside."

"Does Mr Cochinery have a dog?"

"No, he lives alone and if he did, there would be no one to look after it. As I was saying, I do a bit of gardening in the morning and I usually see him leave for work. But I haven't seen him in two days, which is strange. I hope nothing's happened to him. He's a very quiet man, never causes any trouble, not like the family at number four; the children are always screaming like damned lunatics, and kicking their football or their tennis balls over the fence. They don't come to get them anymore since the time I sliced one in half with a knife."

Stephen had heard enough. He called Ninoska on his way home and filled her in on the events of the past two days. They reached the same conclusion; Max was with Tracy.

"I'm going to Tracy's house," Ninoska said to Stephen, "and you're coming with me."

"Are you hiring me?" Stephen said with a grin.

"Unofficially yes, as a scientific consultant. Besides, I need backup and I don't want anyone in my team to be involved."

Half an hour later, Max and Ninoska were in the leafy suburb of Kew where Tracy lived.

Ninoska had parked her car a hundred metres from Tracy's house. When they reached their destination, they saw that the lights were off and that the driveway was empty.

"I think we're too late," Stephen said.

"We'll just have to make our way in."

"Without a warrant?"

"I'm doing this in my spare time, remember?"

Ninoska took a box out of her leather jacket and pressed a series of buttons. A green light blinked. "That's the alarm neutralised, now for the door."

A minute later, they were inside and surveyed the house. In the dining room, two plates with decaying remnants of a meal were waiting to be taken off the table. Ninoska gave them a quick sniff.

"I'd say they left a couple of days ago," Ninoska said.

"That must have been after their meeting at the pub."

"Now what?"

"We need to visit the man who's in the middle of this web."

Stephen took out the serviette with the names, wrote 'JCN', 'Claire' and 'My father' and drew lines from JCN to Tracy, Claire, Max and his father. Then he linked Claire and Tracy to Max and his father to himself.

Ninoska smiled. "You're getting good at this."

"Tomorrow night?"

"No, we have to move faster; my intuition is telling me we're getting warm. Let's say tomorrow morning in his office."

"I thought you could only investigate the memory snatcher in your spare time."

"Yes but I have another case to take care of, and I need to check if Mr Nolan has anything to do with it."

Ninoska and Stephen didn't have to wait for an appointment to meet Joseph; he was very sensitive about his public image, and when his personal assistant announced the visit of two police inspectors, he asked her to let them in five minutes later.

His office was spread across the two-hundredth floor of the tower, giving him a panoramic view of Melbourne. He welcomed his guests wearing his self-confidence like a tailor-made suit.

"Inspector, I see you are in good company. I'm eagerly awaiting the results of your experiments, Doctor Collingsworth; the possibilities of a new energy source are mind-blowing."

Stephen stopped himself from saying that JCN was going to steal his discovery like he had his father's.

"Mister Nolan—"

"Please call me Jo."

"We are investigating a series of memory thefts and—"

"Oh dear, he's done it again."

"What?"

"How many?"

"There are four cases that we know of, including ourselves, but there could be many more."

Joseph led his guests to the African corner of his office, with its armchairs decorated with brightly coloured cushions and a mahogany coffee table. "I owe you an explanation and an apology, but please make yourself at ease. Would you care for a drink?"

"Short black for me," Ninoska said.

"I'll have a lemon squash," Stephen said.

Joseph gave the order to his assistant and sat down. "My wife Claire Powell was not only a brilliant lawyer, but a beautiful woman. And by that I mean not just on the outside, but she had a beautiful soul. She was a passionate woman, strong and fragile at the same time. She worked pro-bono for the less fortunate, and when I travelled to remote places to quench my thirst for adventures, she accompanied me and surveyed the local population's situation. By the time we came home, she had a detailed action plan: build a school here, install renewable power sources there. All I had to do was sign the cheque. She always got her way, using my role model's life as an example. Bill Gates was a self-made man like me and his foundation gave millions to eradicate diseases and improve living conditions in the third world."

He looked at his guests' reaction and said "You're probably wondering what my love story has to do with the matter at hand. I wanted to impart to you who this lovely person was before she lost all her memories. She suffered a cerebral haemorrhage after the delivery of our daughter Annalisa and went into a coma. When she woke up, she had no memory of who she was, let alone who I was or who her daughter was. She couldn't remember anything. Put yourself in her shoes for one minute. You don't recognise where you are or who you're with; you have no history, no sense of identity. I'll never forget the look of terror on her face."

Stephen nodded and saw that Ninoska was nodding too. He knew what it was like, although on a much smaller scale. He shuddered to think what it would have been like to lose all his memories.

"I consulted the most renowned neurologist in the country, Doctor Cochinery. He tried a number of treatments, but he warned me from the start that there was no cure for amnesia. All we could do was hope for a spontaneous recovery. I took her to her favourite places, to see if it would trigger a recollection. Then I thought, what would the woman

I fell in love with have wanted? To help others of course. I asked Doctor Cochinery if he could find a cure for amnesia if I poured some funding into his research. Even if it was too late for her, I'm sure she would have wanted to help others. I remember our conversation as if it was yesterday."

As Joseph spoke, an image sprang up in Ninoska and Stephen's minds of Max's eyes lighting up like a child opening a Christmas present, on hearing Joseph's offer.

He said, "Mister Nolan, I can do better than that. I have an idea that no one has had the guts to believe in. Until today—I'm sure that you're the man who's got the vision to do great things for humanity, and of course get rewarded in the process.

"Have you ever considered the fact that there are zettabytes of data that are backed up every day, and in that ocean of electrical impulses, there are photos and video recordings of our most treasured moments? Weddings, births, holidays, sport victories. But they can't capture the essence of those memories, the emotions that are attached to them. Joy, excitement, apprehension, hope. They are in our brains, alongside the other dimensions that cannot be stored, the taste of your grandma's apple pie, the smell of your lover's perfume, the touch of your baby's skin. The human brain is fascinating, so powerful and yet so fragile. Amnesia may be rare, but Alzheimer's disease isn't. What would those electronic memories be worth to you if you lost your memory? They are a pale imitation of the real thing and they are only a snapshot of selected moments. Now what would you say if our memories could be backed up, just like we back up our computers' memories?"

Joseph replied, "Our understanding of the human brain is way below what it would need to be to make this idea a reality."

154

Max smiled and said, "That's what everyone says, but Mister Nolan, you're like me, a man who thinks outside the proverbial box. Rather than waiting for our understanding to reach its climax, why not look at the brain at a more holistic level. In many ways, the brain works like a computer; it has memory, can perform processes, and the different parts of the brain are linked together by a neuronal network. The contents of the memory can be accessed in the same way as a computer memory. I have mapped the pathways to our memories; they form a web similar in many ways to the World Wide Web, and you can jump from one memory to another using mnemolinks that are similar in concept to hyperlinks. But I realised that reading the contents of our memories was impossible using existing technology. Brain scanners don't give satisfactory results; the signal received is too weak. The scanners require too much power and use radio wave technology from a bygone era. They can only read one memory at a time based on a trigger. Added to this limitation is the constraint that the dynamic nature of memory imposes. It's always processing new input or retrieving past storage units. I've applied quantum field theory to the functioning of the brain and I've concluded that by creating a quantum Geetha wave field, it should be possible to take a snapshot of the contents of the brain's memory at a given point in time. The next stage of my research is to build the Quantum Geetha wave transponder that will download a snapshot of a person's memory. The university's research board has denied me the funding; they think I'm crazy. They can't see the potential; they don't have any business sense. Imagine, JCN could be a pioneer in this domain; you would have the monopoly, the market is huge. Everyone will want to have their memories backed up. The possibilities are endless; once you have your memories downloaded, you'll be able to relive the most precious moments of your life. Knowing that their memories will outlive them will give your customers a feeling of immortality."

"But what media would you use to store the memory?"

"There's nothing better than DNA. It's easy to synthesize. It will also provide security: the DNA sequence of the patient will be used to generate the Quantum Geetha wave field and to convert the snapshot to human readable format."

"And how would you restore it?"

Max waved his hand dismissively. "Let me work out all the details. You provide the funding and the business plan, and I'll do the real work."

The sparkle in Joseph's voice was replaced by the bitter tone of regret. "That man certainly knew how to be persuasive. I was surprised he hadn't found someone to back his plan yet. I'm not a gullible man; if I were, I wouldn't be on the top level of this tower, directing an enterprise worth tens of billions of dollars. But my love for Claire had opened a breach in which he rushed in. I trusted him; I really thought he would succeed, and he nearly did. I created a research laboratory especially for Max's work; I called it Incubatix, thinking that it was going to be an incubator of ideas. I provided Max everything he needed; it was a researcher's dream come true. He called his invention Noogryth; when he was ready to test it, he asked for a volunteer. I didn't see the risk so I asked my mother to come to the laboratory. I thought it would allay her fears of getting Alzheimer's disease. Max assured me it would be painless and it was. It was done while she was sleeping to reduce interference in the snapshot. He said he would only back up a month of memories and he did. But he did much more than download my mother's memories, he erased them. She woke up terrified, wondering what she was doing in the laboratory. The shock precipitated the onset of the disease she feared above all."

Stephen looked at Ninoska; they had found the memory snatcher.

"I didn't want this accident to jeopardise the work Max had done. I had only myself to blame, letting him use my mother as a guinea pig. I told him to fix his machine, and to prove that it worked, to try it on himself. He continued his work, and as I saw my mother's condition deteriorate I began to have doubts about Max and his research. Had I unleashed a monster, or was it the price to pay for progress?

"Three days ago, I summoned him to my office. I bombarded him with questions on his progress, I asked him to implement safeguards, citing potential lawsuits that could sink JCN enterprises. What price would a judge put on the loss of a person's memories? What is more intangible and yet more precious? He didn't react very well, saying that he couldn't keep working if I interfered with his work. I reminded him that I had funded his work and therefore it belonged to me. I was the boss and I dictated my conditions. He stormed out, and I revoked his access to the laboratory. Max Cochinery is no longer an employee of JCN enterprises."

"Three days ago," Stephen said, "that was the sixteenth, the day I saw him walk out of the JCN tower and meet Tracy."

"The laboratory is secure," Joseph said. "He won't be able to cause any more damage. I'm really sorry about your lost memories; I'll bring you to the research facility where the Noogryth is stored. He said he had found a way to read the memories, but I don't know whether he was at a stage where he could restore them to their rightful owners."

Incubatix's research facility was hidden underneath a furniture warehouse in Port Melbourne, where no one could suspect its existence; the staff wore T-shirts with the 'Most Beautiful Interiors' logo and were indistinguishable from the real MBI employees.

Stephen and Ninoska followed Joseph to Max's laboratory; a man in his forties with a crooked nose and port-wine stains on his face said, "Mr Nolan, I'm glad you came; have you got the Noogryth?"

"Why would I have it?"

"I sent you a message yesterday, asking about the Noogryth."

"Isn't it here?"

"No, but when I came in and the Noogryth wasn't here, I thought Max had taken it to the meeting he was having with you. When I learnt he wasn't coming back, I thought that he had returned it to you. I waited a day and then I sent you a message to ask when you were going to send it back to the lab."

"He must have taken it home; I wonder if he knew what was coming."

"So now there's no stopping him from stealing more memories," Stephen said. "I hope you have a good lawyer for the four memory thefts that were carried out when he was your employee, using equipment developed with your company's funds. As you said to him, you're the owner, so you have to accept the responsibility."

Joseph's mask of guilt dissolved to reveal the CEO's look of authority and control.

"Don't worry about that, Doctor Collingsworth, I only hire the best."

"As you did when JCN filed an injunction to stop my father using his invention."

Joseph looked genuinely puzzled. "Which invention?"

"Bio-Wi was my father's invention. He was looking for a way to improve medical diagnostics, not to make a trivial gadget. He was a brilliant man who used his intelligence for the betterment of humanity, and you ruined his life."

"Inventors are like explorers in unchartered territories. They may think that their invention is their creation, but it was always *somewhere*, ready to be found."

Stephen wondered if Joseph knew about the noosphere.

"Explorers have a hard time these days, there's hardly a piece of land that hasn't been mapped, and even those that haven't are already part of a nation. You can't go somewhere, and plant the flag of your country like the British did when they landed on our shores. *Terra Nullius*, they claimed, ignoring that the great southern land had been occupied for tens of thousands of years by the aborigines. There are millions of inventions out there that we can't even imagine, but when we find one, we have to claim it as ours, plant our flag if you like. I invest a lot in my Research and Development department, and I have to get a return on my investment. It's simple economics really."

Joseph stroked his chin. "But I think we may be able to resolve this matter here and now. As I've explained, the Noogryth only works when the subject is asleep. Now I don't know how Max managed to come close enough to you to operate the Noogryth, but I'm willing to bet he did that during the night and that when you woke up the next morning, you realised that you'd lost your memories."

Stephen and Ninoska looked at Joseph, wondering what he was getting at.

"I'll take your silence as a yes."

"But how does this resolve the matter of the memory thefts?" Ninoska asked.

"It absolves me from any liability, inspector. I cannot be held responsible for the actions of my employees in their spare time. And if you want further proof, we can view the CCTV recordings of the nights when the memory thefts occurred, and see that Max took the Noogryth with him and returned it the next morning."

Stephen shrugged. "That won't be necessary. The inspector and I will deal with Max. I have an idea on how we can find him."

"Don't divide the pelt of a bear you haven't killed," Ninoska muttered, just loud enough for Stephen to hear.

"Before we go, I have one more question," Ninoska said.

"Why do you have an unregistered white BMW sedan in your possession?"

"It was Claire's car. As you can imagine, it's no longer safe for her to drive. I haven't renewed the registration because I don't drive it myself, but I've kept it in the hope that Claire would be cured one day."

"And where was your wife on the night of the 12th of April 2041?"

"What has this got to do with your memory loss?"

"A cold case of a hit-and-run driver."

"Claire would never have done such a thing," Joseph said indignantly. "Besides, she was eight months pregnant; it was a difficult pregnancy, she had contractions from the seventh month and was confined to her bed for the rest of her term."

Ninoska started the car.

"Take me to my house," Stephen said. "I'm going to take some zook and get into Max's mind. I should be able to pick up some clues as to where he is."

"It'll be night soon. You may not see much, why don't you wait for the morning?"

160

"On the contrary, the best time is when he's in Rapid Eye Movement sleep; it's the period when the memories of the day are being consolidated. The first REM sleep period occurs between ninety minutes and two hours after the onset of sleep, so I might have to wait."

Ninoska put her foot down on the accelerator.

Stephen felt like he was in one of those cop shows his wife, or should he say ex-wife, loved watching. Adrenaline flooded his bloodstream; now that they knew who the memory snatcher was, the chase felt real. Up until now, they had been formulating hypotheses, now they were in the real world. But the villain was no ordinary bad guy and his weapon was no ordinary weapon. Ninoska was one tough lady, but she was out of her depth; she needed Stephen and he needed her.

They stopped at a fish and chips place, but Stephen declined to partake in a greasy meal, afraid indigestion would create make it harder for him to rise into the noosphere. Ninoska devoured an enormous flake fillet and serving of chips. It must have been standard fare for her when she was on the road; he didn't envy her life for one minute.

Stephen yawned as they arrived at his house. The time was eleven PM.

"I'll wait until midnight; make yourself comfortable. I'm going to make a soup while we're waiting."

Stephen put some vegetables in the cuisinator; he whistled a tune he had heard while he was in Vladivostok.

"Stop that!" Ninoska ordered.

"Sorry, has it stirred a bad memory?"

"No, but if you whistle inside a house, it brings misfortune to the household."

Stephen's look of disbelief prompted Ninoska to reminisce about her childhood in Russia and the superstitions that were still part of her life, twenty years later and ten thousand kilometres away.

If a piece of cutlery falls from a table which has been set for dinner, it means that someone will come without an invitation.

If someone calls you on the phone and you don't recognise them, you can tell them they'll be rich.

You should never hand over a knife directly to another person, else the two will get in a fight.

If it's raining when you leave a place, it's a good omen and means you'll return.

If a bird shits on your property, it's good luck and will make you rich.

If one person steps on a person's foot, the person who was stepped on lightly steps over the person who stepped to avoid conflict.

If a chicken crows at you three times before noon, death to a close family member will occur in a fortnight.

Stephen hadn't heard of these superstitions while he was in Vladivostok; his colleagues were scientists, they had no room for irrational beliefs. But Ninoska wasn't so sure; she thought they would never admit to it but deep inside they were like everyone else.

At the appointed time, Stephen drank the zook. He jumped directly into Max's mind; he was no longer a novice in navigating the noosphere.

Max's memories flashed by in a seemingly random order.

Stephen had to endure the sight and sensations of Max making love to Tracy; he couldn't make it fast forward.

A brief blur was followed by Max looking at a monitor. "Tracy look, there's a new memory, one that I didn't take! How did it get in the Noogryth?"

Tracy joined him. "It must be a politician; he's making a speech in parliament. Listen to his voice—oh my God, you've got Bob Fultrow's memories!"

The monitor showed the reactions of the members of parliament as Bob was boasting about the success of his policy. Despite rising sea levels wiping out whole islands in the Pacific area, refugee boats had stopped coming; there hadn't been one approaching Australia since May 2041. An opposition member remarked that it the bombing of an Indonesian boat had been very convenient for the government. Bob ignored the insinuation and said in a sombre voice that it had been an unfortunate accident.

"I don't understand," Tracy said. "You've been nowhere near Canberra. Did you sneak out one night while I was asleep?"

"Of course I didn't! It must have found a way to relay the Geetha wave signals to Canberra to steal Bob's memories."

"But you didn't do program it to do that, did you?"

"No, I think it has developed a mind of its own."

"How could it do that?"

"Well, I remember when I downloaded Cécile's memories, there was some unusual activity. I saw the memories in the Noogryth shifting and rearranging. I thought it was a bug at the time, but I wonder if her memories merged with those of her husband."

"That makes sense; there would have been a mutual attraction between the two, just like in real life. Isn't that sweet, they can't bear to be separated," she said in a mocking tone.

"They are longer individual memories. They have fused into a single consciousness. Do you realise what it means Tracy, I've created a living brain!"

"I've scanned today's news. There's nothing about the PM losing his memory. Does it mean that the Noogryth can download memories without deleting them?"

"It's more likely he's keeping his memory loss under wraps; his campaign is in full swing, it wouldn't do his approval rating any good if voters knew about it.

"But why did it choose to download the PM's memories, of all people?"

"It's likely Stephen knew him; they seemed to be on very good terms at the inauguration of the QPT."

"Is the PM the only one?"

Max looked at the monitor. Images streamed continuously in a blur.

"Yes, but that's because it's full. I'm going to have to expand its storage capacity."

"Don't do that Max, it's dangerous. If it really has come alive, how are you going to control it?"

"Relax, we can just sit back and watch it evolve. You don't realise what a breakthrough this is."

"No Max, you're crazy."

Max pointed a black cone-shaped device towards her. Tracy took a step back and raised her hand. "Stop it Max!"

Max pressed a button. Tracy closed her eyes, grimaced and opened them again.

"Where are we? What's happening?"

"Sorry darling, I still need to work on the memory erasing part. But thanks to you, I know my modification has worked successfully; the target doesn't need to be asleep anymore."

"Inspector Ninoska Kristayeno, I'm Chief-Inspector Blake Wardes from the Australian Police Force. I believe you have some information which will be very valuable in a very sensitive case. Where can we talk?"

Ninoska's curiosity was in overdrive; could her investigation of a senior politician have attracted attention in high places? "The quiet room in the corner, over there."

"If word of this ever gets out, I'll know where it came from. There are only a handful of people in this country who know about this."

Ninoska's heart accelerated. She led the man with a square jaw, short grey hair and a pointy nose to the meeting room.

"Have you heard of Professor Trevor Luong?" He asked.

"Yes, I've consulted him."

"He mentioned that you were investigating a case of memory erasures."

"That's correct; I'm a victim and there are three others. I'm convinced that someone is behind this, although he seems to have contradictory motives."

"But it doesn't sound like you've made much progress. There's been another victim, and he's not your ordinary bloke."

"None of the others were."

"Yes, but the perpetrator has taken his activities to the next level. The Prime Minister has lost ten months of his memories. When he woke up two days ago, he thought that it was the eighteenth of July 2014. He went to a television studio for an interview, as politicians do when they are campaigning, and he stuffed up his answers big time. When he was asked about the fact that he hadn't delivered on his election promise to find a new source of energy, he replied that the Quantum Particle Transformer had been inaugurated only three months ago and that the scientists needed more time. Then he said he was going to ask the minister of the environment to stand down over his undisclosed ownership of shares in the company that got awarded the contracts for building levees around the capital cities, forgetting he had done that ten months ago. Zachary Windlesbow, his personal assistant put an end to the interview. It took an hour and calls to Bob's wife, his deputy and two of his trusted ministers to convince him that the date was indeed the sixteenth of April 2045, and there was no conspiracy to make him doubt his sanity. Zachary took him to the doctor who didn't find any traces of drugs; then he consulted Professor Trevor Luong, who performed a brain scan and found that Bob's memories had been erased. When asked if he had seen other cases, he replied that he had seen three, but that there could be more."

Blake pointed his finger at Ninoska. "I'm taking this case off you as at now. I'm going to get this wrapped up pronto. The Prime Minister's office is in damage control and asking for results. They're envisaging the worst: that the PM's memories were not simply erased, but stolen. If someone's got the PM's memories, there's no shortage of customers willing to pay top dollars for them: the opposition, leadership challengers in his own party, the media; they could ruin his chances at the next election. It's a lot of people to investigate, but we figured if we find the memory thief, he'll tell us who the buyer is. Personally, I find it difficult to believe that memories can be erased, let alone stolen. But even if they were just deleted, it gives the opposition an advantage. The PM's office is struggling as it is stopping anyone from finding out that Bob's lost some of his marbles. They're minimising his public appearances, but he's got an ear-piece so that Zachary can fill in the blanks when he does have to speak."

His voice became sharper. "I'm warning you now. You can either cooperate and tell me everything you know, or I'll make sure your career goes nowhere fast."

"I haven't found any pattern in the memory losses, or any common points between the victims. The serial killer I'm hunting would benefit simply from my memories being erased. In Stephen's case, other countries wanting to develop dark energy production could use his memories. You might want to get ASIO involved. Just suggesting if course, not telling you how to do your job. In Jimmy's case, hard to say— a jealous musician wanting to destroy Jimmy's career?"

"So you don't have any leads; I'm not wasting any more of my time here then. My guys are reviewing the footage from the surveillance cameras around the PM's residence. We'll get this memory snatcher, don't you worry."

Chapter Nine

20ᵗʰ April 2046, Beauharnois, Quebec Province, Federation of American Nations.

Marcel Bitoniaud poured maple syrup on his crêpe; he remembered opening the bottle yesterday and yet it was nearly empty. He looked out the window, and the sight of his garden painted in the yellow and white of dandelions and Carolina spring beauties aroused questions in his mind. How could they have grown overnight and in the wrong season? The leaves of the oak tree had been transformed too; they no longer looked like they were ready to fall and be swept away by the cold wind heralding the arrival of the long winter. His head throbbed and he wondered why. He hadn't drunk more than usual six cans of beer yesterday. He had invited his neighbour Jean-Yves to watch the football match between the Canadian wildcats and the bushland falcons—Forty-four to Forty-one, what a close match that was! He had cooked a *Truite aux amandes* with his catch of the morning. He ignored the signs warning of chemical pollution in the Saint-Louis River. If the trouts survived, there was no danger for humans.

He finished his *café au lait* and went to his neighbour's house. He knocked on the door. A plump woman with dishevelled hair he had never seen before opened the door.

"*Bonjour* Monsieur Bitoniaud, how are you this morning?"

"Who are you?"

"Why do you ask? You know me; I'm your neighbour, Arlette Bécasse."

"My neighbour, but where is Jean-Yves?"

The woman's jaw dropped. "*Oh la la*, you don't seem to be well today. I know it's hard for you, but you need to pull yourself together. You have to testify at the tribunal this morning, remember?"

"Testify at the tribunal, what are you talking about? What's happened to Jean-Yves? Are you a relative of his?"

"Calm down, Monsieur Bitoniaud. Come in and sit down; I'll explain everything to you and I'm sure it will come back."

Marcel did as he was told, looking around him. Jean-Yves' old sofa had been replaced by a bigger one with a flower pattern fabric. His collection of beer coasters was missing from the wall. How could this woman have moved in overnight? Jean-Yves would have said something to him if he was planning to move out.

"Five months ago, a burglar broke into this house; Jean-Yves woke up and threatened him with his hunting rifle. He shouldn't have done that, the burglar had a gun and he shot the poor man. You heard the noise and came out to see what was happening just as he ran out. You saw him and noted the number plate of his car; thanks to you, the police caught him and today you're testifying in court."

"How am I going to testify when I don't remember anything? Jean-Yves was still alive yesterday. We watched the football match together."

Vientiane, Laos, Chinese Empire.

Sen woke up with a headache; he had played *Derelict Doomsday Devastation* with his friends until two in the morning. Immersion games were getting more and more realistic; he had lost the last fight, lying dead on the battle field, and now he really felt dead. Today was Sunday; at least he could sleep in a little bit before doing his maths homework.

"Sen!" His mother called. "Get up, you're going to be late for your exam!"

"What exam?"

"Stop fooling around Sen!"

"I don't know what you're talking about; today's Sunday and my exams are in three months."

"Sen, you've worked hard for your exams, why are you backing out now?"

Sen didn't respond; it was clear his Mum had gone crazy. He was going to ask his dad to take her to the doctor tomorrow.

Bordeaux, European Union.

Gaëtan Mauberge had woken up with a feeling something bad was going to happen today. Was the *Guide Michelin* going to visit and find a reason to take away his second star? He had rejoiced when it had been awarded to his restaurant *Duc de Gascogne,* the consecration of years of hard work and intense rivalry with his brother François who had chosen molecular fusion cuisine, after dropping out of a Master of Quantum physics at the Jussieu university. But he knew that the hard work was not over, there was a quota of two-star restaurants and he had narrowly beaten his brother's *Délices Quantiques* restaurant for the last place. Every day had to be perfect, and today everything had to be more perfect than usual. He didn't want to end up like Quentin Montargis who had committed suicide after losing a star.

He walked around the dining room, inspecting every table with a measuring tape to make sure the layout of the plates, glasses and forks was irreproachable. He asked Sylvie Chattenfeu, the maître d', for the menu.

"*Bordel de merde!* I told you yesterday to add the fricassee of quail with porcini mushrooms and hazelnuts. What is this baby octopus on a bed of vermillion asparagus, I don't pay you to invent dishes. What—"

"But chef, the fricassee was seven months ago, and you asked me yesterday to add the baby octopus."

"Seven months ago, are you out of your mind?"

"No chef. How could we make this dish now anyway? It's not the season for mushrooms."

"And do you think it's the season for asparagus?"

Gaëtan stared at Sylvie who nodded with a barely suppressed grin. "So you think this is funny? We're inaugurating the autumnal menu today, there are people who would love to see me lose a star or even two, and you think I'm going to happily go to the market and buy some asparagus."

"Gaëtan," Yann the sous-chef called. "What are you arguing about now?"

"We'll settle this now so I can get on with my job. Yann, please tell Sylvie the date."

"Twentieth of April, 2046."

"So you see, autumn has...Did you say April? Please Yann, I'm not in the mood for jokes."

"What did you think the date was?"

"Twenty-third of September 2045."

"Gaëtan don't panic, you're going to be alright, but you need to see a doctor."

Gaëtan swallowed hard. "Just tell me one thing Yann, do we still have our two stars?"

Ouagadougou, Burkina Faso, United Republics of Africa.

Samira was woken up by the crying of a baby. The sound was very close; in fact it came from a cot next to her bed.

"Djamila's hungry, you better feed her," Yacouba, her husband, said.

"But whose baby is it, and what is it doing in our bedroom?"

"What do you mean whose baby is it? Is something wrong? Did you have a nightmare?"

She pinched her arm. "I think I'm having one now."

Yacouba took Djamila in his arms and looked at his wife. "It must've been something you ate. Hold her while I go to the pharmacy to get some baby milk."

Samira looked at her husband and started quivering. "Where did she come from? Did you get her from the orphanage without telling me? It's a lousy surprise, take her back right now!"

"No, she was born a month ago, remember?"

"No, I don't, I don't even remember being pregnant," she said in between sobs.

Yacouba made a sign of the cross. "Oh Lord, please help us. My dear Samira has been possessed by the evil one."

He recited the Lord's Prayer.

Australian IETLIA facility, Western Australia.

"There have been a large number of memory downloading signals," Calogero said.

Zachary Windlesbow, Bob Fultrow's personal assistant, had called Stephen and asked him to go to the IETLIA facility at once. When he had said that due to the nature of the matter, an Australian Police Force inspector would be accompanying him, Stephen had refused; he would go with inspector Ninoska Kristayeno or not at all. A lengthy discussion had ensued and it had been cut short when Bob intervened—he just wanted this problem resolved as quickly as possible.

"It's the same wave pattern as the signals we looked at when you were here, but there are differences." A map appeared on a monitor. "As you can see, they are no longer confined to Australia. There have been occurrences on the other four continents. But there seems to be a point of convergence in the little town of Kingston South East. Every time there's a signal in one part of the world, there is a corresponding signal there."

"How can you be sure they are memory downloads?" Ninoska asked.

"Our social media scanners have intercepted a number of conversations concerning people losing months of their memories. They have been swiftly erased; our directives are to avoid panic at all costs. If these memory thefts are caused by aliens—"

"Aliens have nothing to do with this. It's the work of a neurologist who's invented a machine called the Noogryth. It was supposed to enable people to back up their memories, but it's erasing them at the same time."

"How can you be sure he's not an alien?"

"I'm not, but does it matter?"

"It does, if we're dealing with a swarm of them stealing memories."

"But all the downloads converge to this little town in Australia. How could he be remotely downloading memories?"

"Could he be using the Internet?" Ninoska asked.

Calogero turned to a monitor. "Give me Internet traffic statistics for the hot spots." He looked at the numbers. "Spot on. The peaks match the time and location of the signals."

Ninoska gasped. "If the memory snatcher is using the Web, he's got access to memories all over the world. We have to get the Internet shut down."

Calogero gave her a condescending look. "The Web doesn't have an on/off switch. It's built for maximum availability, the world depends on it."

"Isn't possible to cut off the access where the Noogryth is?"

"No, that wouldn't work either; Kingston South East is a remote place, so it's connected to the Web by satellite."

"And a satellite can't be switched off either?"

"No it's impossible; and even if it was, all the nodes in the Web have been designed such that if one fails, another one takes over. All these safeguards were implemented during the great cyberwar."

"There's no time to lose," Stephen said. "We have to go to Kingston South East and find Max and the Noogryth."

"Give us the names of the latest victims, I'm curious to see if they have something in common. I have a feeling they weren't randomly chosen."

The monitor emitted a loud beep; a red light was flashing at the Australian capital city.

"A new signal," Calogero said. "It was forty times the size of the average."

Ninoska chortled. "It won't make much of a difference. Pollies have very short memories when it comes to their blunders, and they expect voters to have forgotten them."

Ninoska and Stephen went directly to the JCN tower on their return to Melbourne to see Joseph.

"The Noogryth is out of control," Stephen said. "It's stealing memories all over the world."

"But how is it doing that?" Joseph asked.

"Consider this: the Noogryth uses a person's DNA to generate the Quantum Geetha wave field and download the contents of the brain. What other device uses DNA to read signals from the brain wirelessly?"

"Bio-Wi smartphones."

"Max had access to Bio-Wi technology in your laboratory; he must have used it to adapt the Noogryth to download memories wirelessly. It was easy; he had our DNAs and our addresses. He must have come close enough to operate the Noogryth. When he got my wife's memories, they merged with mine and the Noogryth came alive. It connected itself to the Internet through Max's smartphone and then to other smartphones that were connected to the Internet at the time. The Noogryth generated Quantum Geetha Wave fields using the DNA in the smartphones that had Bio-Wi to download their owner's memories which travelled through the Web back to the Noogryth's storage module."

"How many Bio-Wi smartphones have you sold?" Ninoska asked.

"One hundred and sixty million, give or take a few," Joseph replied.

"That's a lot of potential victims."

"Would he have enough storage?" Stephen asked.

"The memories are stored in artificial DNA; as long as he has the ingredients, he could make as much as he wants."

"You're going to have to recall all the Bio-Wi smartphones," Ninoska said. "There's no other way to limit the damage."

"Are you serious? JCN would lose tens of millions, not to mention the damage to the brand."

"Is that all you care about?" Stephen said. "You wait and see what it feels like to lose a part of your memory."

Joseph looked at Stephen with wounded eyes.

"I'm sorry, I forgot about your wife, but I'm sure she would want you to do the right thing."

"Don't you dare bring her into this! She lost all her memory, you only lost a few months. You can still function, but she is an empty shell, dead to the world. The price is too high to pay. I would rather put the money JCN stands to lose to into her foundation. It could be used to free countless children from poverty."

Stephen saw that they weren't going to win the battle. He looked at Ninoska. "Even if Joseph agreed, it would take days to recall all the Bio-Wi smartphones, and the Noogryth would keep stealing memories. We have to neutralise it; how quickly can we get to Kingston South East?"

"A couple of hours; I can get a police plane to take us there."

Ninoska took her smartphone out of her pocket and handed it to Joseph. "You can have mine; I'm not taking any chances. It could come back and steal the rest of my memories, but I strongly advise you get rid of yours."

Stephen put a shoe-size box on the back seat of the police car.

"Is that the network neutraliser? It's very small; is it going to be powerful enough?" Ninoska asked.

176

"It's a prototype Andrew built for the Quantum Particle Transformer. He tested it on his house and its range was broader than he thought; the whole block was without access to mobile networks, and when his neighbours came knocking on his door asking if he had the same problem, he pretended to be as concerned as they were. He was lucky there were no emergencies. He called it the cone of silence, after a comedy show from the 1960s, 'Get Smart', I think it was called. Only in the show it never worked. He deserved a lot more recognition than he got, but in a way I understand why he didn't get publicly credited; the workers at the QPT hated being cut off from the outside world—no more web surfing while they were recovering from a hangover."

Ninoska switched on the siren and put her foot down. They reached the airport in fifteen minutes where the plane was waiting for them. Stephen and Ninoska got on, and soon they were flying above Melbourne's sprawling suburbs.

He looked through the window. "You should lift up your window shade, the view's great."

"No thanks, I'm not a great fan of heights."

Stephen realised that Ninoska was clenching her jaw and squeezing the arm rests of her seat. He took his phone out of his pocket. "I'm glad I never got the Bio-Wi model, but my son was pestering me to get him one. I bet my ex-wife bought him one after she left me."

He called Thibault and asked him if he had a Bio-Wi smartphone.

"I don't have time to explain everything, but you've got to trust me. The memory snatcher is using the Internet through the mobile network, but it only works for people who have a Bio-Wi smartphone. You have to switch yours off."

"But you don't have one, how did he get your memories?"

"The memory snatcher built a device that uses Bio-Wi to download memories. I suspect he went in my garden while I was sleeping and operated it from there."

"But how did he get your DNA?"

"The memory snatcher's lover is a creativity consultant; I went to one of her workshops and she must have got my DNA from a coffee cup or a hair."

"You're just finding excuses to stop me using JCN products. Nice try, but you'll have to think of something else."

Stephen put down his phone and shook his head. He looked at Ninoska. "It's no good."

"Why don't you call your wife and get her to switch off your son's phone?"

"We're not exactly on speaking terms any more. She left me last year."

"Oh, what happened?"

"She didn't tolerate my obsession with my work; she felt neglected and left me."

"And to think that if Max hadn't stolen her memories, the Noogryth wouldn't have come alive. What a mishmash: a separated couple, a police inspector, a rock star and a Prime Minister. A being with multiple personalities, how can they get along? It's worse than my family. "

"Bob has a way with people; he'll make the others do what he wants. He always has."

"Politicians are all the same. The way they carry on in parliament, it's a disgrace."

Stephen didn't contradict her, but he wondered how much politicians were conditioned to act the way they did by the political system. The party, the media, lobbyists, they all contributed to making Canberra the nest of vipers that it was. When Stephen had become friends with Bob at Scotch

College, one of Melbourne's most prestigious private schools, they'd had many discussions on how to solve the world's problems. Stephen believed in the power of science to make the world a better place, Bob had grand ambitions for his country and he was convinced that power could make them happen.

He didn't defend the actions of a man whose memories were intermingling with his own. Was it because Bob also had shared memories (although very small) with him that the Noogryth had chosen to steal Bob's memories? But that didn't explain all the other victims that neither him, Cécile, Jimmy or Bob knew.

He turned his attention to more urgent matters. "As soon as we get there, I'll activate the network neutraliser. I hope we won't be too late."

"While you do that, I'll go in with one of the local police guys; they're waiting for us at the landing strip. It was too difficult to explain the Noogryth. I just said we were going after a member of a Melbourne gang on the run."

"You'll have to be quick. If Max erases your memory, you won't even know why you're there."

"We have the element of surprise on our side, and the second local policeman will be posted outside. By the way, aren't you going to be hot with that trench coat?"

The bumpy landing took them by surprise. Ninoska and Stephen got off the plane and walked to what looked like an oversized garden shed. 'Welcome to Kingston SE' was painted in flaking yellow paint. A police car was parked nearby and two policemen were laughing at what could only be a salacious joke. They introduced themselves as Russell and Duncan; the latter hoped this wasn't going to take long, he was off-duty in one hour and he just had enough time to get changed to go to footy practice.

The GPS coordinates that Calogero had given him were those of a beach house. When they arrived, Stephen put the cone of silence on the ground and checked the power. There was three days' worth, enough time to disable the Noogryth. Ninoska had told Duncan and Russell that the man they were after had an electronic device with some precious information and they had to be careful to avoid damaging it in case of a clash. Stephen and Ninoska were hoping that they would be able to view the memories it contained.

Russell accompanied Ninoska while Duncan covered the beach side of the house. There was no alarm and the lock surrendered in less than a minute.

She heard Max's agitated voice.

"What's happened? The Noogryth is empty!"

"Don't blame me, I didn't touch it!"

"Unless there's something wrong with this damn monitor. I'll test it by getting a bit of your memory."

"No, you're not doing that again; no way!"

"Just a tiny bit darling, I promise. How about an hour; surely it won't matter if you lose an hour of your life."

"I've lost two days already; two days of my life I'm not getting back. Why don't you try it on yourself?"

Ninoska took position behind Max and pointed her gun at him. "Hands up, Max! You're not taking anyone's memories."

Max reached for the cone-shaped device that Ninoska recognised from Stephen's description. Ninoska took aim and shot the device which burst into small pieces. Max turned around put his hands up. Tracy looked at the two police officers with disbelief. Stephen and Duncan ran into the room.

"I heard a shot," Stephen said.

Ninoska put her gun back into her holster. "All under control."

"You fool," Max said, "you've destroyed the transponder."

"Max, you're under arrest for the thefts of the memories of Stephen Collingsworth, Ninoska Kristayeno, Jimmy Yarrawallah, Cécile Dubontant, Bob Fultrow—"

"I didn't steal Bob Fultrow's memory, the Noogryth became alive after I downloaded Cécile's memories."

"How did you get her memories?" Stephen asked. "You never saw her."

"I had coffee with her," Tracy replied, "to present my creativity program. I got her DNA from her cup."

"Just as I thought; you were the one behind the memory thefts."

"No, it was Max's idea. When Joseph asked him to test the Noogryth on himself, he wasn't keen on the idea. He was the one who convinced me to use my workshop participants as guinea pigs. I was reluctant at first, but when I saw the benefit I could gain by examining the memories of the most creative people in the city, I was sold. I was hoping that I could gain some insights into the creative process."

"Did your study of the memories lead to any discovery?"

"Not so far, it's very time consuming. A bit like mining, sorting through hours of mundane memories to find a nugget of interesting material. Because creativity isn't continuous, it occurs in bursts. Doctor Collingsworth for example, you're not particularly creative when it comes to choosing your clothes. And just when I started finding some interesting material, things got, how shall we say, out of control."

"Your study is over Tracy. Even if we can't upload our memories back, we're seizing the storage unit. There are some very important memories we need to access. I need to resume my work on dark—"

"You've got all the time in the world to do that," Ninoska said. "I've only got ten days to find the serial killer, and the clue is in my memories."

"No need to get excited," Max said. "There's been a malfunction, the Noogryth is empty."

"What do you mean, empty?" Stephen asked. "Have the memories been deleted?"

"I don't know what happened; they vanished just before you burst in."

"Are you sure there isn't a problem with the monitor?"

"If you allow me to put my hands down, I might have a chance to find out."

Ninoska nodded. "No funny business Max."

Stephen, Ninoska, Tracy, Russell and Duncan crowded around the monitor while Max keyed some commands into the console. A dashboard showed a number of parameters: storage capacity, processing activity, network traffic, as Max explained. He set the time back an hour to look through the history. Storage was at fifty per cent, processing at seventy per cent, network zero. As time sped forward, processing increased slowly while storage decreased quickly and network traffic increased to attain one hundred per cent. When storage reached the zero point, processing and network traffic went down to the same level.

"It escaped to the Web," Max said.

"Go back to the point just before storage reached zero," Stephen said.

The time showed four thirty.

"It was just before we arrived and I switched on the network neutraliser. If we'd arrived a few minutes earlier, it would have been trapped."

"It can't be a coincidence," Ninoska said. "It must have sensed what was going to happen."

"Is it going to survive in the Web?" Stephen asked Max.

"Not for long. Although the Internet has millions of servers, it's a completely different medium to the DNA it was living in."

"But it's used the Internet to capture memories."

"In that case it just used the Internet as a transport mechanism; the memories were downloaded into its storage module."

"You're forgetting something: it contains the memories of some extremely creative persons. It's got unparalleled problem solving abilities; it could have found a way to adapt."

"You're talking about it as if it was a living thing; is it dangerous?" Ninoska asked.

"What harm could it do?" Max replied. "I told you it won't survive; even if it did adapt to the digital medium, the defences that were built to protect the Internet during the great cyberwar will destroy it like a mere virus."

"This kind of threat was never imagined," Stephen said. "The Internet is going to give it limitless storage capacities, and who knows what it's going to do if it interferes with the Internet."

"But if it's in the Web, isn't there a way we can get our memories back?" Ninoska asked.

"The Noogryth could hide anywhere in the millions of servers that are part of the Web, and it could spread itself across thousands of them. It would be like finding a needle in a haystack. Even if we did find it in one of the servers, it could very quickly escape to another."

"I've got no bloody idea what you guys are talking about," Duncan said. "Can you take care of these guys so we can go home?"

Ninoska thought about what she was going to do with Max and Tracy. If she locked them up, what evidence was she going to produce before a court anyway? The memories were gone into the ether of the Web; it was all going to be too hard. "Max, if you cooperate, I'm ready to make some concessions."

Max shrugged. "What do you want from me?"

"You're going to help us clean up your mess."

Two days later, Stephen was back at the Quantum Particle Transformer.

He had searched the Internet for 'unitron', 'Stephen Collingsworth' and 'Theory of Everything', hoping to find his memories, but the search engines were not designed to index human memories.

He had made a change to his model and run more simulations. If the unitron was as unpredictable as the results of the simulations had shown, there were equal chances that experiment Goanna would create a photon, a gluon, a W/Z boson, a graviton or an acceleron. Stephen wasn't a gambling man, but Amanda hadn't given him a choice, he couldn't keep biding time.

Stephen nodded; Andrew pressed the button. A collective suspense gripped the personnel of the QPT.

Three minutes later, it was over.

At least the transformation chamber hadn't imploded like the last time.

All eyes were turned to the monitors displaying the results of the experiment. Monitor number three showed an image of a particle; Stephen's heart sank; it wasn't the acceleron he was hoping for, but a graviton, the particle that mediated gravity. What would happen if the experiment was run again? Would it produce a graviton again, or one of the other five particles? Was this going to be a game of roulette?

Stephen was going to have to wait for the Transformer to cool down to find out.

Ninoska had enlisted the help of the Police computer security unit, but her search of the Internet for her memories had been as fruitless as Stephen's.

"I've got the Chief of Defence Forces on my back," Claude said. He's given me a list of female partners of senior RAAF personnel and asked me to provide reinforcements to the RAAF police to guard them. The protection has to be discreet as well, because in that list, there are a number of unofficial partners, as he's put it."

"Didn't you explain to him the reason we believe the next victim was going to be related to the Minister of Defence?"

"Of course I did, but he doesn't want to take any chances. So I've had to request officers from other squads; it doesn't make us look good, I can tell you."

Their last hope was that the serial killer would be caught in time, but the Federal Police was in charge of the protection of the Minister of Defence and his family who lived in Canberra. Inspector Blake Wardes was going to get the credit for this; Ninoska felt little consolation in thinking that he wasn't going to resolve the loss of the Prime Minister's memories; she had little chance of doing that herself.

Thibault narrowly escaped the fire of the flame thrower the Helix Commando soldier had aimed at him. He felt his skin burn; he could not stop himself from touching it to assure himself that it was unscathed. Immersion games were getting better and better; his friend had pirated a copy of the latest version of *Derelict Doomsday Devastation*, and Thibault had waited for his mother to be asleep before starting to play.

He heard music; it sounded like *Flash Forward*, but Félicie usually put her headphones to listen to music.

Then he saw the band playing; the musicians were in what looked like a recording studio. It wasn't a video the band had produced; the singer stopped halfway through and scolded the keyboard player for a mistake he had made.

Thibault unplugged himself from the immersion console and went to Félicie's room; she was watching a video on her tablet.

"Félicie, you'll never believe what happened. I was playing my game, when suddenly I saw Flash Forward playing in a recording studio."

"Wow, what were they playing?"

"Something about the legends of the sparkling sea."

"It must be from their new album; I'm dying for it but Jimmy said it was delayed due to unforeseen circumstances. How did it get into your game?"

"Dunno. Some hacker must have inserted it into the game; but it was weird because you couldn't see the lead singer, it was like he had filmed the clip. I wonder how the hacker got hold of it though."

"I wonder if it's the same one who inserted a scene into Bella Canissima's latest video. It wasn't there yesterday and it doesn't have any music, it must've been hacked."

"What's in it? I wonder if he's taken it from *Derelict Doomsday Devastation.*"

"It's night time and you hear a gun shot. You see the light go on, clothes being put on and a hand picking up a torch. Then the camera goes outside to a house. The door's open. You hear a man's voice call 'Jean-Yves' but there's no answer. He goes inside, switches on the light and there's a man on the floor and a rifle next to him. He's bleeding; he looks like he's dead. It looked so realistic."

"Lemme have a look."

Félicie swiped her tablet and Bella Canissima, the diva, started singing.

Thibault cringed. "Ugh, fast forward!"

Félicie did that until the end of the song.

"That was quick, it's already been removed. Quick, let's go to your game and see if the song's still there."

Thibault and Félicie plugged themselves into the immersion console and resumed the game where Thibault had left it, but the clip was gone.

Alex selected the latest episode of the Purple Dynasties saga; he was hoping to find out who had betrayed King Leon. He had an idea of who it might be, but the writer excelled in giving false hints that threw fans of the series in the wrong direction.

A group of children were playing soccer in an ordinary suburban park; the setting was very far from the Kingdom of the Ayneels that Alex was expecting.

Damn, Alex thought, *what sort of joke is this?*

He swiped his tablet, but the movie, if that's what it was, kept playing.

"Hey guys, can I play with you?" The voice came from behind the camera.

"Piss off, Bob, we don't have room for midgets in our team." A boy with dark hair and an air of dominance said.

"And who says so?"

"We all do!" The boy turned to the other boys who nodded on cue.

"You can't do exclude me because of my height, that's discrimination."

"Oh yeah? What are you gonna do about it?" The boy laughed, joined by the others. "Come on guys, we've wasted enough time with this little prick."

187

The image darkened then blurred. The camera fast forwarded to the boy who fell down, no doubt surprised by the attack of the opponent whom Alex couldn't see.

Judging by the images of the next few minutes, the actor playing Bob must have had a mini camera strapped to his head, which made it hard for Alex to follow the action. At times, Graeme (Alex knew his name from the cries of the other boys encouraging him) was on the ground with Bob punching him as hard as he could, and then the situation was reversed, but only for a short time. Bob quickly gained the upper hand; he pinned Graeme to the ground and spat on him.

"Get off me!"

"Not before you let me join your team."

Graeme knew he had lost; he was bruised and his nose bled.

"Alright, you can be the striker."

"I wanna be captain."

"No way, I'm the captain."

The camera angle didn't allow Alex to see what Bob did, but it had the effect he was looking for.

"Ow! Captain if you want, just get off!"

"That's more like it."

Bob got up and saw the look of surprise on the other boys' faces.

Alex's satisfaction that Bob had won was mixed with remorse. A memory flashed in his mind: he was at high school, threatening an effeminate-looking new student for his lunch money. Despite the reprimand from the principal and his parents, Alex had felt no shame or regret at the time, but now he wondered if unconsciously he had chosen to serve in the police to make up for this petty crime. What was the boy's name? It came back to him, Bruce. Alex wondered what had been the impact of the bullying on Bruce's life; he remembered the tears running down Bruce's face, it had made him laugh at the time. Bruce had been too terrified to fight back like Bob had.

Alex felt that he knew Bob; he racked his brain but couldn't remember a boy named Bob in his class, and none of the other boys in the movie looked familiar either. Was it a movie or a real life video that Bob had posted on YouTube? How had he managed to substitute it for the episode of Purple Dynasties that Alex had looked forward to watching? Alex remembered something Ninoska had said about her memories being in the Web, along with those of Jimmy Yarrawallah, a quantum physicist and the PM.

Alex laughed at the conclusion that he just reached.

Fred Stoplegough called his girlfriend Gillian on her Skype account; he was in one of few remaining plots of the Amazon jungle to catch two of each of the animal species that still survived there for the Ark project.

There she was, naked on their bed.

"Honey, you're really making it difficult for me," he said. "When I see you like that, all I want to do is come home and make love to you."

Her image was replaced by that of a woman he had never seen. He tried to end the call but Skype wasn't responding.

The image of Fred on Gillian's wall screen was replaced by a man she had never seen before, and he certainly wasn't in the Amazon jungle. She covered herself, but the man didn't seem to see her.

"Stephen, we have to talk," the woman said.

"Talk about what?" the man asked.

"You haven't been yourself lately; you come home late, you hardly speak to me and when you do, you're rude to me. Is there another woman in your life?"

"No there isn't," the man snapped. "If you think I've got time to look at other women—"

"What do you mean? If you had the time you would look at other women?"

"No, stop distorting what I'm saying. All I meant was that my work is taking all my time. You know I still love you."

The woman raised her voice. "No I don't, you don't show it to me. If all that matters to you is your work, what are you doing in this house? You may as well sleep there and come back when you've finished whatever you're doing, but don't expect me to be there."

"You don't understand the pressure I'm under; I've got the Prime Minister on my back. If I don't deliver results, he's going to be in trouble, and so will I."

"That'll teach you to promise something you can't deliver; I told you it was a bad idea."

"I'm sure it can be done, but Andrew made a mistake in the parameters and the transformation chamber imploded."

"Typical, something goes wrong and you blame someone else."

The image of the woman faded and Fred was relieved to see Gillian.

"Looks like we intercepted someone else's Skype call; it's the first time it's done that."

"I hope we won't fight like that when we're married."

"Of course not, I'm crazy about you honey. You'll always be first in my life."

Gillian smiled. "About the wedding date, I was thinking about September 25th."

"No that won't be possible, I'll be in Alaska at that time; we need to get some bears before they hibernate."

It was the first time Fred heard his girlfriend use the F word; what did she have against bears anyway?

Ninoska answered a call from Stephen. "Have you seen the news? The unemployment rate on the ABS web site was modified by a hacker to an unheard-of low of two per cent, and the GDP growth rate to twenty-five per cent. The police are investigating, but unless it's a practical joke, the PM is the only person who would benefit from this. I have his personal number so I called him, but his Personal Assistant answered, saying Bob was unwell. It's just as I thought: Bob's mind has taken the lead of the amalgam of memories that has escaped to the Internet. It's as if Bob himself was living in the Internet; he's modified the statistics to make himself look good, and who knows what else."

"But it's very crude; how does he expect people to forget?"

"He would have to steal a lot of memories."

"Is Max making any progress?"

"No, and he's got an army of JCN technicians helping him. They haven't been able to trace the Noogryth yet, they have to analyse zettabytes of data travelling through the Web to detect unusual sequences of packets."

"Isn't that what the IETLA is for?"

"I've tried contacting Calogero, but I don't know if he got my message. If all Bob is doing is playing around with statistics, we don't have much to worry about."

Ninoska's intuition was telling her there was something to worry about, but she didn't know what it was. But even if she did, what could she do about it? She thought about the inspector from the Fed; he wasn't exactly her friend but he did know people in Canberra.

"Chief-Inspector Wardes, it's Ninoska. Are you still on the case of the disappearance of Bob's memories?"

"I'm getting the job done, that's all you need to know."

"I think you may struggle with this one; his memories are in the Internet."

"What are you talking about?"

"Haven't you heard the news about the ABS web site?"

"That's an easy one to solve; we've got the IP address of the culprit, he'll be behind bars before you know it."

Chiort ego poberi, Ninoska thought, let him go to the devil. Blake and his team of cowboys are probably going to lock up an innocent person. What did she expect anyway? It was hard enough for her to believe what was happening.

She joined Claude, Alex and Yoshimi, huddled around a monitor tuned to the ABC news channel.

"Hacking has been suspected in the destruction of a number of web sites; the list is growing every minute, but so far the web sites of the Labour party, the Green party, the Australian Council of Trade Unions, the Australian Workers Union, the Asylum Seeker Support Centre, the fusion music group Flash Forward, the Guardian newspaper, activist organisation GetUp and the Environment Militant Confederation have been hit. It's a similar story for each one of them: the hosts of the web sites have reported that the files were deleted from their servers. A few minutes after they restored the files from a backup, they were deleted again. Internet users trying the access the sites are getting the usual 404 error message. The Facebook accounts of these organisations have also been hacked. The same post is present on each one of them, a picture of a tombstone with the inscription Rest In Peace. Their email accounts are inaccessible, making communications very challenging."

The newsreader paused. "I've just had an update: so far three of the organisations that have lost their web site have also seen their bank accounts emptied. The Australian arm of the International Web Police is investigating and analysts are predicting another cyberwar. The All Ordinaries index has just lost five hundred points, with banks and technology firms the hardest hit. Over to sport now, India is five for two hundred..."

Claude scratched his bald head. "Sorry for not believing you before Ninoska, but you were right."

"None of us imagined what the Noogryth was going to do in the Web."

"But can't you do anything about it?" Alex asked. "It's not just Bob who's in it; your memories are there too."

"I'm outnumbered; there are only six months of my memories in the Web, and who knows how many years of Bob's."

"So couldn't you upload the rest of your memories to defeat Bob?"

Ninoska glowered at Alex. "That would be like committing suicide."

"But it's our duty to protect our country."

"Why don't you go in there then?"

"Leave the IWP deal with this," Claude said. "In case you forgot, you're supposed to find a serial killer."

The next day at seven AM, all Victoria Police officers were in video-conferencing rooms in their stations to listen to the Chief Commissioner, Jade Menores.

Ninoska settled herself in a chair next to her team.

Jade cleared her throat. "Thank you all for responding to my invitation at such short notice. Today is going to be a very busy day for us and we need to have all available officers ready to intervene. The situation on the hacked web sites has evolved rapidly and is evolving as I speak. Although the targets are all left-leaning organisation or opponents of the liberal party, investigations by the International Web Police have cleared all members of the party from wrong-doing. The only people in Australia that would have the necessary skills are currently serving jail sentences anyway. The IWP are currently looking for the hackers, but don't have any serious leads yet. We'll let them do their work, but we have to deal with the consequences. Massive demonstrations have been planned to occur today in all capital cities by the organisations that have had their web sites taken off-line. Yesterday they used phone chains to spread the word because that was the only means of communication they had left. There could be hundreds of thousands of people converging to the city today, and according to our monitoring of communications, it's going to be one angry mob. I'm not here to talk about politics, but as you all know Bob Fultrow's approval rating is at a historic low of five per cent and the contenders for his position in the liberal party are not faring any better. Despite assurances to the contrary by the IWP, people are convinced that the government is so desperate that it has tried to destroy all channels of opposition. They've had enough and as the hacking continues, the risk of violence occurring on the street increases. I trust you to do your best today, and bear in mind that if we are seen to be using excessive force, we could face a period of widespread civil unrest."

Ninoska felt powerless and she didn't like that one bit. The people on the street were right; Bob was the one behind this. Ninoska and Stephen knew it and surely that knowledge should give them the edge. But the Noogryth was an ethereal enemy. Ninoska wasn't used to fighting the intangible; she preferred flesh-and-bone criminals. They were driven by fear, anger or greed; once you understood that, they were predictable and that's how you could catch them. There was nothing she could do to fight this enemy. She thought about the *babka*'s words, she was right, this adversary was unnatural and Ninoska was experiencing many trials. The *babka* had advised to listen to the voice that was inside her. But that voice was silent today. As the *babka* had said, she would have to trust Stephen. He understood quantum particles and technology better than he understood men, unlike her. She smiled to herself, regaining confidence. The Noogryth was a hybrid of man and machine, with Stephen's help, she would overcome it.

Stephen was walking around the block; he found that when a tisane didn't clear his head, a walk usually did. *There must be a way to stop the Noogryth*, he thought, *but the risks of damaging the Internet in the process are real*. He answered a call from an unknown number.

"Doctor Collingsworth, I'm Zoltan Krakovitch from the International Web Police; Inspector Ninoska gave me your number; she's also on this conference call. She said something to Chief-Inspector Wardes about the PM's memories being in the Internet; I thought it was absurd, but I can't afford to discount any theory at this stage, no matter how crazy it may seem."

Stephen gave a summary of the events of the past month, leading to the realisation that the memories inside the Noogryth had taken on a life of their own and escaped to the Internet, led by Bob's memories who was using this opportunity to distort reality in a more blatant way than he usually did.

"What are you intending to do?" Stephen asked.

Zoltan didn't answer straight away; Stephen guessed that he was thinking about what he had just heard.

"This Noogryth must have a distinguish feature; it's not the IP address, it's different every time and it consists of random numbers. I'll figure it out, don't worry. And then I'll use BGP hijacking to destroy the Noogryth."

"What's BGP hijacking?" Ninoska asked.

Zoltan answered in a condescending tone. "BGP stands for Border Gateway Protocol, it's the core routing protocol of the Internet. BGP messages suggest the best route for specific packets of data to take to get to their destination. The results of your search may transit through several servers before reaching your computer. BGP hijacking is a technique that spoofs a BGP message that says the best place to send the packets is an IP address that specifies a host that isn't running or a host that hasn't been assigned. The packets would then just disappear into a black hole."

"I thought the routers had been upgraded after during the cyberwar to prevent BGP hijacking." Stephen said.

"There's a way to overcome this constraint, Doctor. Before the great cyberwar, I was one of the best hackers in the world. I was serving time when I accepted to join the International Web Police in exchange for my freedom. A closely monitored freedom, I might add, but the pay was good and I got access to the latest and greatest technology. I was on the team that developed the safeguards that were designed to prevent another cyberwar. So don't you worry, I know how to get around them."

"Wait, if you do that, our memories will be destroyed." Stephen said.

"Do you have a better idea?" Zoltan asked.

"Yes, we are going to set a trap."

"What are you going to use as a decoy?" Ninoska asked.

"A woman."

"But Bob never had a partner; I think he's more interested in politics than women." Zoltan said.

"No, that's not true," Stephen said.

"How would you know?" Zoltan asked.

"We were friends at high school, when Bob fell madly in love with a girl. He was obsessed with her, didn't stop talking about her. I was getting a bit tired of hearing him rave about how fabulous she was, so I asked him what he was waiting for to ask her out. He didn't say it, but I knew he was scared of being rejected because of his short height. He didn't want me to think he was a coward, so he asked her out and she accepted. I didn't see much of him after that, they were always together. I didn't mind, but I wondered how long their story would last; she was beautiful, she was smart, she could have had her pick any day. And sure enough, six months later she dumped him to go with the striker of the school soccer team. Bob was in shock; his worst fear had come true, but he continued to love her. He waited for her to come back to him. He thought she was going to get tired of the handsome but empty-headed Khaled Azhihar. And she did, but found another boyfriend. There was no way she was going back with Bob. He hasn't forgotten her; I'm sure he would do anything to have her. Her name's Wendy Butridge. Ninoska, find her DNA, I'll ask one of the JCN technicians to hook up a Bio-Wi smartphone with her DNA to a computer. Bob will try to get her memories, if he hasn't done so already. Let's hope she hasn't got a Bio-Wi Smartphone otherwise we may be too late."

"Assuming Bob takes the bait, what then?" Zoltan asked.

"Once the memories are in the computer, we neutralise all network access using the cone of silence. The Noogryth will be trapped inside and we can get our memories back."

"We can't afford to wait for your solution to work; people are starting to lose confidence in the Internet. If the Noogryth isn't neutralised one way or another, it'll be the world economy that falls into a black hole. By all means go ahead, but I'll keep working on my idea. If you manage to trap the memories before I figure out a way of destroying them, great."

"Stephen, I'll send you Wendy's DNA; call me if you have any success. Leave me a message if I don't answer, I'm on crowd control duty today."

Chapter Ten

26th April 2046, Melbourne, Australia

When Ninoska had come home last night, she had gone to bed with her clothes on. Dealing with the demonstrators had been more exhausting than any man-hunt she'd been on. It had been impossible to estimate the number of protesters, as they had spread across the main streets of Melbourne's Central Business District, but that number had fallen abruptly at four PM, when the gates of the Melbourne Cricket Ground had opened for the Collingwood-Carlton football match. The size of the gathering had fallen again at sunset, when Melbourne pubs had been swamped by crowds of thirsty protesters. There had been more arrests for drunken violence in the late hours of the night than there had been during the day.

Ninoska's dreams had been vivid: she saw her father's funeral, her brother's feeble attempts to explain why his father had wanted to leave everything to him and her argument with the prison manager.

She wondered if her memories had come back to her, but she could only remember her dream, and it had been interrupted just when it was getting interesting. There had been nothing about the lead that she had found just before she lost her memories. She still didn't know why she had tried to speak with the pilot of the plane that had bombed the refugee ship. What would he know about crimes that had been committed while he was behind bars? And what was the link with a senior politician? Could Bob, the man they were fighting with, have something to do with the crimes? But what? She just could not imagine what threat the victims could have been to Bob for him to want to eliminate them.

She checked her voicemail and her inbox; there was nothing from Stephen. She consulted the news to find out what damage the Noogryth had done overnight, as it was unlikely it needed to sleep.

The web site of the Guardian had been repaired; the headline was triumphant: "Freedom of speech restored following largest demonstration in Australia's history."

Ninoska read the article. All web sites of organisations critical of the PM's performance or opposed to his policies were now operational. The PM's office had continued to deny all involvement in the hacking of the ABS Web site and the closure of the Web sites. The prolonged absence of Bob Fultrow had fuelled speculation that he was in hiding, but John Aristopoulos, the deputy Prime Minister, had repeated that Bob Fultrow was in convalescence after an illness.

Zoltan must have been successful, Ninoska thought. *That's the last we'll hear of the Noogryth.*

She liked reading the comments section; she found the debates that went on between readers amusing, but she wasn't expecting what she was about to read:

TrueBeliever 2m ago

Hey you Bob worshippers, go to BobTheMessiah.com and make a donation, it's time we built a church where we can worship him.

Chiponhisshoulder 3m ago

I'm with you, JohnnyH. I prayed last night and Bob spoke to me. I couldn't believe it at first, but it was him. He showed me what life was going to be like if we followed his word. We will want for nothing and know no diseases. Unbelievers will be punished by water and fire. Now I understand why sea levels have risen and why Bob was so intent on keeping refugees from submerged islands out of Australia. It's clear that they're heathens and don't deserve to live.

BlabberMouth 15m ago

Thank God (or should that be thank Bob) I'm not the only one! I'm not a religious girl, on the contrary, but when I started hearing the voice of Bob inside my head, I thought I was going nuts! He told me I shouldn't have made fun of Gary when he asked me for a date because he was short. It's not the size that counts, he said. I've heard that one before!

CrackerJack165 15m ago

Now I understand why we don't see Bob anymore, but why is the liberal party hiding that their leader has risen and gone to heaven? They should be proud of him, but instead they hide the truth from us.

Reply

> **TrueBeliever** 10m ago
>
> That's because they don't recognise him for what He is. History repeats itself: who got Jesus crucified? The Jews themselves, his own people!

JohnnyH 30 m ago

I wish I had known before that Bob Fultrow was the son of God, but I can see it now. The economic crisis was a trial to test our faith, to show us that adoring and serving God was more important than our material comfort, that the poor would inherit the Earth. I've been unemployed for three years and I was mad at Bob when he stopped the job seeker allowance. I was sharing a twenty square metre apartment with five other job seekers and we all had to move out and live in the street. I didn't realise it at the time, but it was a blessing.

TrueBeliever 45m ago

I was praying for my mother's health; she was diagnosed with cancer and I can't afford the chemotherapy since Bob dismantled Medicare. And then I heard God talking to me, He said that Bob was His son and that my mother was blessed to be suffering, for who suffers like God suffered on the cross is with God. I asked him why I didn't have cancer and he replied that I wasn't one of the chosen ones. When he saw how upset I was, he said that all I had to do was to follow his word. I'm waiting now to hear what he wants me to do.

Vanda 1h ago

Comment was removed by the moderator

Zxc666 1h ago

It's so obvious Bob Fultrow was behind this; how can anyone believe what these guys are saying? They really must think we're f****ing morons. Well we showed them that they couldn't get away with it, and I'm surprised they backed down so quickly, I was ready to join the general strike. At the end of the day, it's not gonna change the fact they're gonna lose the next election. Good riddance!

Reply

> **NotaNaughtyBoy** 1h ago
>
> Zxc666, I was like you, I thought Bob Fultrow was evil and had to be defeated. I didn't march with you but I was with you in spirit, praying God, and He answered. All those years I've been speaking to God I knew he was listening, but I've never had such a clear answer. He told me that Jesus had come back under the name of Bob Fultrow and that he was now back with Him. I saw Bob; he was in heaven, smiling at me. I got on my knees and asked for mercy. He just said, 'All is forgiven my son' and I cried tears of relief and joy.
>
> **Zxc666** 1h ago
>
> What sort of drugs are you on?

Ninoska stopped reading. The Noogryth hadn't been destroyed, and now Bob was playing God, was he where she thought he was?

She called Stephen.

"The Noogryth must have escaped through the mind of a person with a Bio-Wi Smartphone while he or she was in the noosphere," Stephen said.

"But I thought the only way to get into the noosphere was by taking zook."

"Your mind also visits the noosphere while you're asleep, but I think that's less likely; Bio-Wi smartphones detect when their owner is asleep and they go in sleep mode themselves."

"That narrows down the list of suspects; the only people who know about zook are traditional aborigines and Jimmy."

"I don't know if he has a Bio-Wi Smartphone."

"I'll search the list JCN gave me."

The answer did not surprise them.

"Jimmy doesn't have one, but Evangelista does and she takes zook too," Ninoska said.

"Damn, I should've thought of it; if there was one person who should have switched off her Bio-Wi Smartphone, it was her."

"Should haves will not get us anywhere, except that now that Bob's in the noosphere, you can go after him."

"Why me?"

"Who else can go to the noosphere?"

"But the noosphere's huge, how will I find him?"

"I don't know, you're the noosphere expert. Unless you can think of something else, you're going there."

"Listen, you can't just boss me around like that, I'm not part of your team."

"But you are; remember I hired you as a scientific consultant."

"But a consultant is an expert who gives advice, not someone who's on the field chasing bad guys."

"What's wrong Stephen, are you scared?"

Ninoska waited a minute for his response and then said, "We'll continue this conversation at your place."

Thirty minutes later, Stephen opened the door to let Ninoska in; he lifted the bottle of zook he was holding and Ninoska smiled. He said, "Thanks for coming, boss."

"I don't know if I'll be much help, but at least I can give you moral support."

Stephen's hand was trembling, beads of sweat slid down his forehead and his eyes were blinking rapidly, but he was smiling, trying hard not to show his fear. He didn't want Ninoska to think he was a coward.

He poured the required dose of zook into a glass and sat down on the sofa.

"I've been thinking," Ninoska said. "We're dealing with a relatively unknown enemy. Make this trip to the noosphere a reconnaissance mission. Gather as much information as you can, but if there's an opportunity to attack, don't let it pass."

"I have no idea how I could do that, but I guess I'll know more once I see it. I'm going to go into Bob Fultrow's mind first to see what's left of it. I'm curious to see where he's hiding and whether he has any connection with the rest of his memories."

Ninoska nodded.

"Here goes."

Stephen drank the concoction and closed his eyes. He waited for the zook to take effect to jump into Bob's consciousness.

Judging by the bed frame and the colour of the walls, Bob was in a hospital. He had a toy Ferrari car in his hand, and he made engine noises, spinning the car around his bed, increasingly faster at every lap. Bob wasn't paying attention to the two men talking in the room, but Stephen could hear what they were saying.

"According to his parents, he doesn't remember anything past his sixth birthday," the first man said. Stephen identified him as Professor Trevor Luong. "He asked for news of his puppy Marley which he got when he was five and a half, but he thinks he's still at kindergarten. He was quite distraught when he saw his parents; he recognised their voice, but not their face. He thought something had happened to their skin and their head and that they were going to die."

"What are the odds of recovery?" the second man asked.

"I'm sorry, there's nothing we can do. I told you, his memories were stolen and even if we do find them, I don't know if we'll be able to restitute them."

"We must continue to hush this up. If word of this memory snatcher gets out, it's going to undermine voters' confidence."

"Unless we can show that we've got the situation under control," a third man said. "The sabotage of the Web has stopped, why can't we claim it as our victory?"

There was nothing to be gained by staying here; Stephen jumped out of Bob's consciousness.

In the sea of thoughts of the Noosphere, Stephen could see the prayers that desperate souls were sending to Bob.

"Forgive me Bob, for I have sinned."

"Dear Bob, please help me to find a parking spot."

"You are truly the son of God, come to restore justice to this wicked world."

"I'm sure my neighbour is an illegal refugee, should I denounce him to the authorities or deal with him myself? If I invite him and slip some rat poison in his coffee, I'm sure no one will mind."

Stephen heard his own voice calling him, "Over here Stephen, it's me!"

His lost memories were in the noosphere, along with the others. A part of him was here and it was calling him. He didn't quite know how to deal with this situation, and so he just replied the first thing that came to his mind. "Come back to me, I need to know why you changed my model."

"*My* model, you mean."

"It's the same thing, you're a part of me, remember?"

"But I'm trapped inside this amalgam; we're all fused together. You've got to find a way to free us."

"I wish I could, but can't you tell me what I need to know while I figure it out?"

Stephen heard a roaring voice. "Shut up!" It was Bob; he must have heard the two Stephens talking together.

Stephen saw a cloud of memories move across the noosphere: the experiments at the QPT, Cécile leaving him and the creativity workshop were his own. The others were seen through the eyes of their respective owners, but Stephen could distinguish many of them: Cécile moving into a new house, attending the Melbourne fashion festival and helping Félicie with her homework, Jimmy Yarrawallah rehearsing with his band, Ninoska interrogating suspects, Bob at university talking with Stephen, at parliament and on the campaign trail. There were many that Stephen didn't recognise; they formed a mosaic, constantly rearranging itself, pulsating with energy.

"Stephen, get me out of there!" Cécile's voice said.

Stephen felt himself freeze while the cloud moved above him. He wondered if it was going to engulf him, trapping him like his other memories, but he couldn't jump to another level of the noosphere. It was as if he was about to lose his life in an immersion game.

The cloud moved on in a blur and shortly after it was gone. Stephen felt free again, but he stayed where he was.

It was the first time that Stephen had felt his body while he was in the Noosphere. His heart was racing, he was queasy and his arms and legs were shaking. He wanted to leave the noosphere, but he was still under the effect of the zook. He could hear Ninoska asking him if he was alright. He felt like opening his eyes and yelling, "No I'm not, help me get out of here", but no sound came out of his mouth.

That was the last memory of his fourth trip to the noosphere.

When he opened his eyes, he saw Ninoska wiping his face with a damp face washer. His T-shirt and his trousers were wet and smelt of vomit.

"You scared me; I thought I was going to lose you. Do you want a tisane?"

Ninoska's question made the nausea come back.

"No, ice-cold water will be fine."

Ninoska went to the fridge to fill a glass half-way with ice and topped it with water. Stephen took the glass gratefully and drank slowly.

Stephen took his Personal Health Assistant out of his pocket and viewed the measurements: his epinephrine level was 745 ng/L, which wasn't surprising after the stress he had been subjected to.

He described to Ninoska what he had seen.

"There's nothing we can do now that Bob's in the noosphere and being worshipped as a god. He's getting really dangerous. His followers will do whatever he tells them."

"But not everyone follows him."

"That's even worse; it will trigger a religious war between his followers and infidels."

"I wouldn't go as far as predicting a war."

"When men worship different gods, it's a recipe for conflict; religion drives men to kill because they're so convinced their god is the right one and those who don't agree with them should be eliminated. History is full of wars fought over men's idea of who God is."

Ninoska raised her voice. "But religion isn't just about wars, look at all the people that have cared for the less fortunate because they were inspired by the teachings of their church."

Stephen was about to reply that non-religious men and women had done the same, but the last thing he wanted was a quarrel with Ninoska, even though the fact they were arguing proved his point about religion being a source of confrontation.

"Sorry Ninoska, I didn't mean to upset you; we're on edge and it's not getting us anywhere."

"You're right, we need to focus. Every adversary has a weak spot; I'm sure we can find it and use it to our advantage."

"Even a blob of memories wreaking havoc in the noosphere?"

"Don't forget these memories are human."

"Bob is the one we need to focus on, the others are his prisoners. We were good friends at uni, I think I might have something we could use, but I want to check what he's up to before I go any further with my idea." Stephen ordered his wall monitor to tune in to the news channel.

Joachim Stefanos, the president of the Federation of American Nations was speaking.

"I've had a revelation from God; he spoke to me through the intermediary of His son, the man who was known as Bob Fultrow when he was amongst us. I cannot hide anything from Him; he knows me and my past, including all of my unspeakable sins. He has revealed the plans He has for my future. They are indeed great plans, and I want to share them with you because they involve you, my fellow compatriots and the people of other countries, nations and empires if their leaders decide to do the right thing like I have and follow the word of God. Mankind is at a crossroads; humanity can either continue to follow the doctrines of evil men who have falsely professed that they were speaking on behalf of God, or follow the true word of God. Earth has been irrecoverably ruined by the sins of men, and it will soon be annihilated. That's the bad news. The good news is that God has prepared a new planet for the chosen ones, the followers of His son. He has showed it to me; it is a beautiful planet, where disease and pain no longer exist, where His people will live a life of joy and happiness. It is our promised land. When Moses led his people out of Egypt, they didn't go to anyone's idea of paradise, far from it. But this time, it's the real thing. I have seen it; you can trust me. I know that there are many questions in your head: how are we going to get to this new planet? Who are the chosen ones? I won't hide from you the fact that we're all going to make sacrifices because building the spaceship that will take us to the Promised Land will require a lot of money. As at today, I am cancelling all welfare payments; they are an unnecessary drain on our budget, because their recipients are doomed anyway. These funds will find a better use building the needle; that is what I am calling the spaceship, in honour of our Lord's words which have often been misconstrued. Wealthy people have been blessed by our Lord, and it is fitting that they will have their ticket to the promised land, provided of course that they demonstrate their generosity towards this worthy project. I will be shortly conversing with my fellow heads of state to bring them the good news."

"*Bohze moi*," Ninoska said, "this is a nightmare. You said you had an idea, what is it?"

"I don't know if it's going to work, but if it does, all our memories will be lost."

"It doesn't matter, we have to try it. We don't have time; can't you see the madness that's gripping the world?"

"We're going to trigger an amnesia in the Noogryth," Stephen said, as if it was the most obvious thing in the world. "Consider this: the Noogryth is made up of memories that have meshed together to form a sort of consciousness. An amnesia would therefore destroy it."

"How are we going to do that?"

"I've studied the different causes of amnesia. Alcohol can interfere with memory, but isn't practical in this case. Electroconvulsive therapy is out of the question as well, because it could destroy the noosphere. Same story with physical trauma. We're left with psychological trauma; intense shocks are a common cause of amnesia."

"What have you got in mind?"

"When I was in Bob's consciousness, I saw that he had lost his memories from his sixth birthday, and it correlated with the big signal we saw in Canberra when we were at the ETLIA base. I have a hypothesis that it was the Noogryth coming back to get the rest of Bob's memories. We can use that to our advantage.

"When he was at university, he joined the water-skiing club. The university had its own boat and they had a spot on the Edward River at Deniliquin. One week-end, he asked me to join him. I'm not a sports kind of person, so I said no. But he convinced me; he said I could just watch; it was more of a social kind of thing, with music, beer and lots of nice girls. I thought two out of three sounded good and I ended up going. I even had a go at water skiing and made an absolute fool of myself."

"Very interesting I'm sure but what's it got to do with—"

"I'm getting to it. He had left his wetsuit on the river bank to dry, and when his turn came up again, he went to pick it up and an enormous funnel-web spider crawled out of it. He turned as white as a sheet and collapsed. After he came to, he explained the reason for his arachnophobia. When he was five, a funnel-web spider crawled into his bed. As he was waking up, he felt something on his face and it bit him as he brushed it off. His father applied pressure immobilisation bandages and it probably saved his life, because the venom moved very quickly. He started vomiting, twitching and having trouble breathing. While he was in the ambulance, he passed out, and as soon as he arrived at the hospital he was given anti venom. He can't remember any of it; his father had to tell him what had happened, but his subconscious hasn't forgotten. He always gets someone to check his room wherever he's sleeping. He still has a scar on his face, but he doesn't like talking about it, he says he fell off his bike when he was a kid.

"If we can reproduce this on a bigger scale, the shock could trigger a bigger amnesia and therefore destroy the Noogryth. Imagine a giant man-eating spider running after him. He tries to run and finds himself caught in a giant web. He is trapped and the giant arachnid is approaching. Its jaws are clicking and it covers him in a sickening gooey substance which is going to start the digestive process."

"It sounds like a B-Series movie from the twentieth century, but how are you going to make Bob see it?"

"I'm going to take zook and imagine this monster to project it into the noosphere. I'll get Tanami to help me, he can spin the web."

"Who's Tanami?"

"A shaman I met when I was surveying the site of the Quantum Particle Transformer. What we call noosphere and what the aborigines call dreamtime are the same thing. It's a parallel dimension, home of their spirits. They're like quantum particles; they occupy simultaneous positions in our world and in the dreamtime."

"But if the spider is in the noosphere, everyone will see it, not just Bob. Think about the widespread panic it's going to cause. People will run away, there'll be massive stampedes, heart attacks, People will rather take their own lives than be eaten by a giant spider."

Stephen mulled over Ninoska's advice. "I'm sure Tanami will think of something."

Stephen parked at the foot of Mount Buninyong. Tanami was standing there, with a look of concern.

"I've been waiting for you," Tanami said. "Birrahgnooloo said you would come. I had a dream of a giant white fella sowing seeds of destruction in the Dreamtime, and I was very upset. White fellas have already tried to destroy our culture because they couldn't understand it. They can't control what they don't understand and they don't like that, so they destroy. But white fellas can't go to Dreamtime so they can't touch our spirits. When we want to commune with our spirits, we go to Dreamtime because that's where they come from. Dreamtime is sacred; we're the only ones who can go there."

"And to go there you take zook?"

Tanami nodded; he wasn't surprised Stephen knew about zook, or he didn't show it. "We also take it to visit our ancestors."

"I've taken zook to look for the truth; I visited my ancestors, I saw the consciousness of mankind, but not the Dreamtime."

His smile had a hint of condescendence. "Normal, you don't have a totem; you don't belong to any Dreamtime spirit."

"So what does Birrahgnooloo expect of me?"

"When I told her of my dream, she said Dreamtime was in big danger, but you have the answer, because you know how to defeat this evil man."

Stephen scratched his head. "She's right, I do know him, but I'm not sure I have the right answer. That's why I'm here, to ask you to help me."

Stephen told Tanami about Max, Tracy, the stolen memories, the Noogryth and what it had done. Tanami listened with the patience of a man who lived in harmony with the temporal rhythms of the land he belonged to, for his people did not own the land that nourished them, it owned them. It was their mother, the starting point where it all began, impregnated with the power of the ancestor spirits.

"We're going to have to wake up Thunpulthu Kurri-Kurri."

"Who is he?"

"It's a she, but let me tell you her story. Long, long ago there was an evil spider whose spirit could change into any animal she wanted to be, and she would trick the other animals into being her friend by being nice and kind to them.

213

Once she had gained their trust and the animals had their backs turned, she would turn back into the evil spider, trapping them and then eating them. Some spiders were nice and so the animals didn't know who to trust as they all looked the same. One day a very clever kangaroo was drinking from a waterhole, when he was approached by another kangaroo who wanted to be his friend. He was wary of the friendly kangaroo as he had not seen her before so he pretended to trust her, and they had a long talk together. After a while the clever kangaroo said he was thirsty after their long talk and needed another drink from the waterhole. He bent down and pretended to have a drink but while he was doing this, he was really looking at the reflection in the water of the kangaroo behind him and saw her beginning to change back into the evil spider. The clever kangaroo quickly turned around and with both feet kicked the evil spider with all his might. The spider went flying through the air and crashed into a red ochre rock wall. Her spirit was knocked from her body never to return, and the evil spider to this day still has the red markings from the ochre. She still eats anyone that enters her web, but now every animal knows by looking at the red marking on her back that she is evil."

"Just what we need, can she also take the form of a woman?"

"If the woman is still alive, yes."

"She is; her name is Wendy Butridge, childhood sweetheart of Bob Fultrow, the evil man in the Noogryth."

"I will consult Yurrundi; his totem is the kangaroo who defeated Thunpulthu Kurri-Kurri. The kangaroo will talk to her with the promise of a feast; I'm sure she will not resist. He will tell other spirits to hide because Thunpulthu Kurri-Kurri will call Bob into the dreamtime. Once he is there, he will be trapped and she will devour him."

"Sounds perfect."

"To you, yes. But there is a danger that Thunpulthu Kurri-Kurri will become strong by eating the spirit of Bob and other spirits won't be able to stop her doing evil."

"Don't worry; once Thunpulthu Kurri-Kurri reveals herself, the Noogryth will be destroyed by the shock and there won't be anything left for her to eat."

Tanami hesitated, lost in his thoughts. "Birrahgnooloo said you would have the answer; I trust her."

Bob didn't have to worry about opinion polls or elections any more, or even his party, the media or lobbyists. He had enough of these parasites who got in his way, asked for favours or wasted his time with their questions. He could do what he wanted and when he wanted.

If only he could silence the voices in his mind.

Once his mind was made up, they couldn't stop him, but they complained when they weren't happy, and that was more and more often. None of them had agreed with him pretending to be the son of God, but when he had heard prayers rising in the noosphere, it had been too tempting. What had started as a bit of fun had grown to an extent he hadn't expected.

The other memories got on his nerves with their moans and groans.

He had counted eight of them:

Stephen had been his friend and made him spend billions to build the Quantum Particle Transformer and had been unable to do anything with it. He shouldn't have listened to him; it had been a weakness and there was no room for weakness in his life any more. Stephen didn't say much and when he did, it was invariably tedious.

Ninoska the police inspector knew something she shouldn't. He should have gotten rid of her, but it didn't matter anymore. Even if she did find evidence against him, she would be accused of blasphemy. He should bring back the inquisition, no one would expect that.

Jimmy was the loudest whinger, the one who had the most hatred of the Prime Minister and indeed every form of authority. Bob had tried to silence him with threats but that had made him more vociferous.

Cécile had an opinion on everything, she couldn't shut up; Bob wondered how Stephen had put up with her. She often argued with him about anything. She didn't know her place, and was always going on about equal rights for women.

The only thing Marcel wanted was to go to the court to testify against the murderer of his friend Jean-Yves. A pain in the virtual backside.

Gaëtan was afraid of his own shadow, worrying about everything, and in particular about losing one of his stars. He didn't realise there were more important things in life than food. It was a pleasure Bob had to forgo when he had emptied his body of the rest of his memories, but he didn't regret it. Living in the Internet and the noosphere gave him outright freedom.

Sen was the least troublesome; he thought he was in a gigantic immersion game; his only complaint was that he didn't know where the controls were.

Samira often cried because she couldn't feel her baby anymore and couldn't see her husband.

Their voices were like flies buzzing around him in the Australian bush. As Prime Minister, he had avoided going to the outback as much as he could and delegated to his ministers whenever Canberra's presence was required there.

The few voters that lived in the bush were ignorant buggers and it was always scorching hot and dusty. The bush was mostly barren, but there were treasures underneath the soil, like uranium, opals and bauxite.

The voices of his other memories were the only inconvenience of his new life; a small price to pay for freedom and power. He had what he'd been seeking since his youth. He'd had more than his share of bullying and taunts, just because he wasn't as tall as the others. He had compensated for his short height by wearing heelpieces, but being in power didn't stop the mockery, on the contrary. There were many other short men who had risen to greatness: Napoleon Bonaparte, Mussolini, Stalin and even Nicolas Sarkozy.

From where he was, he could see every thought that was emanating from mankind; trivial stuff mostly. Hunger for wealth, love, power and recognition, and for many hunger for something to eat. Hunger was what made the world go round; if humans ceased to desire more than what they had, what would they do?

There was one thing he didn't have, he thought.

Wendy.

She had been his only love; Stephen had said there were plenty of fish in the sea, but he wasn't interested in other fish. He had looked at them, tasted a few, but none were a match for Wendy.

He heard a voice resonate. "Bob, my love come to me!"

Wendy? How could it be?

"I've been waiting for you to come to me. I've always loved you, Bob."

He looked in the direction of the voice. She was far away, but there was no doubt; it was definitely her. She was just as beautiful as she was when she was at high school. Voluptuous eyes, long wavy blond hair, generous breasts.

And to think she had always loved him. Why didn't she say so? They could have been happy together.

"Wendy, I'm so happy to see you! Stay where you are, I'm coming."

Wendy was in a place he had never explored because it was below the realm of the departed. But Bob didn't care what that place was. He was going to get her back, and together they were going to rule the noosphere.

As he approached, Wendy became hazier; the blur transformed into a more distinct shape, as though the autofocus of a camera lens was slowly honing in on its target.

It was too late.

A spider, a giant red-back spider, the red marking on its back glistening.

Like an electric discharge, fear radiated through Bob's mind and spread through the Noogryth, blazing through the memories.

The Noogryth burst into thousands of little bubbles, each containing fragments of a person's life.

The bubbles rose and scattered in the conscious level of the noosphere, where they burst one by one, the memories within them falling like autumn leaves to a place where they would find a new life.

Stephen clapped after Mukassa's band played their final note; the concert had made him feel that life was returning to normal.

The obvious conclusion to the news he had heard in the morning was that the Noogryth was no more, and with it all the memories it had gobbled up.

Millions of people who had been hearing Bob speak to them found that he was no longer answering their prayers. There were divided into two camps: there were those who thought that Bob was now too busy speaking with all of them. The silence had destabilised them, and schisms had appeared in the church of Bob, each claiming that they had the truth. The second camp thought that they had been victims of a mass hallucination and that it had been too good to be true anyway.

Ninoska and Stephen had each gone home to recover from the emotions of the past days, and when Stephen had cleared his voice mail, he'd had no hesitation in accepting his friend's invitation to see him play at the Black Cat jazz club. He needed to reconnect with the real world and real people.

Mukassa joined Stephen at his table. "You look exhausted."

Stephen wasn't in the mood to explain why. "Working late."

"Your memory loss still bothering you?"

"No, I've moved on."

"Talking about memory, something weird happened to me. I was watching TV last night, and all of a sudden, images of someone else's life flashed in my brain. It was overwhelming; I closed my eyes to stop them, but they kept coming. I thought I was going nuts, but I hadn't taken anything. I swear I was as sober as you are."

Stephen nodded; he believed his friend, why wouldn't he?

"And now, I can remember this person's life like it was my own, like I had lived what she had lived. It felt so real."

"A woman, how interesting..."

"Oh yeah, but a tough one; a police inspector. She was on the case of that serial killer who kills someone every year on the first of May."

Stephen spluttered his drink. Could Ninoska's memories have survived and uploaded themselves in his friend's mind?

"I happen to know this inspector, her name's Ninoska Kristayeno."

"Sounds like a Russian name; explains why I couldn't understand everything."

"Her memories were stolen, like mine. We found the memory snatcher, but we didn't get our memories back, we thought they were lost. I don't know where mine are now, but it looks like Ninoska's memories were uploaded into your mind."

Mukassa's eyes widened, but he didn't say anything. He looked like he was trying to make sense of what he was hearing.

"Just before her memories were stolen, she found a lead that could have taken her to the killer. She's only got a few hours until the killer strikes again. You said you remember her memories like your own. You're her only hope."

"What do you want me to do, call her and tell her I've got her lost memories?"

"No, tell me know. I don't want to take any chances. If anything happened to either of us, the other one can still give her the information. Skip the bits that have nothing to do with the case."

"She found a link with the bombing of an Indonesian refugee boat by an RAAF plane on the first of May. The RAAF made a statement that the pilot did not act on orders, and an investigation subsequently revealed that he was a member of The White Australia Resistance gang. He was sentenced to life imprisonment for manslaughter. She went to the Sunbury high security jail to see the pilot of the plane, but she was denied access because of the security risk. She argued with the prison manager. She was so pissed off, she threatened him and he called his security guards to calm her down. It was an obstruction of justice and she asked her boss Claude to do something about it. He called the minister of justice, but that didn't work, and his request to the high court for a warrant wasn't a success either.

"But she didn't let go. She thought that authorities at the highest level were hiding something. She had no access to the pilot's file; he had been arrested by the military police and tried by a military court. It was a dead end and she knew it, but she was convinced she was on the right trail.

"She searched the news archives, following the fate of the pilot from the trial to his transfer to the Sunbury prison, looking for irregularities. Then she turned to her informants; there are some ugly faces you wouldn't want to come across in a dark alley."

Mukassa stopped. "All this talking's making me thirsty."

Stephen stood up. "I'll get you a lemon squash." He saw in Mukassa's eyes that he was expecting something else. "You have no idea how precious those memories are, there's a life at stake, it's Ninoska's only chance to catch the killer before he strikes again. So I'm not letting you drink one drop of booze until you've told me everything."

Stephen came back to the table with two glasses; Mukassa gulped half his glass and continued his story.

"None of them knew the pilot, he wasn't one of them. They despised The White Australia Resistance gang above all. But there was one informer who overheard a conversation in a pub. I think his name was Fingers or something like that. He's a barman at the Burning Cross where the members of The White Australia Resistance gang were having a drink. They were boasting about houses burned, cars sabotaged and that sort of thing. The most gruesome was their leader, Brutus Maximus. He said that he kidnapped an illegal immigrant, filmed himself torturing him, gouging out his eyes and eating them. The gang members congratulated him and asked to see the video clip. Ninoska knew that his ideal targets were illegal immigrants because if they disappeared, no one dared to say anything. She had never been able to convict him because of the lack of evidence. Fingers heard them talking about the pilot of the plane. No member of their gang was able to claim as many victims on their score board. Brutus said the RAAF had done a great job fabricating evidence that he was a member of their gang. It was great publicity.

Ninoska wondered why the RAAF had claimed that the pilot had been a member of The WAR gang; was it to cover up their bungle? Did it mean that the pilot acted on orders from his hierarchy? But why would the RAAF order the bombing of a refugee boat? Did the order come from even higher? Ninoska felt that she was onto something big, but she didn't speak to her team about it. She just said that she suspected a link to a senior politician but she needed to be sure. She was scared if her boss got wind of it, he would ask her to stop."

Stephen listened to his friend; there was something familiar about what he had just said, but he brushed it aside. He would deal with it later.

"But what did it have to do with the serial killer? It couldn't be the pilot, he was in jail."

"Exactly the question Ninoska asked herself. Could it be a relative or a friend of the pilot seeking revenge? But if that was the case, why was she denied access to the pilot? It didn't make sense. She investigated the pilot, but there was nothing interesting—just mundane stuff like bank accounts and bills. Then she called a man called Fred, an RAAF police officer. She asked him for the pilot's file. He said he couldn't access it because it was classified top secret, but Ninoska was very convincing, if you know what I mean. Before he came to her apartment to seal the deal, she prayed to a man called Hubertus. She asked for his forgiveness, said that her love for him was eternal, and that there was no love in what she was about to do, only the desire to find the truth. She thought about the day they would be reunited and said that she would never rest until she found his killer.

"I'll skip the details of what happened next. When Ninoska opened the file, the first thing she saw was a photo of the pilot. She remembered that his face had never been shown in the media; he had always appeared with a hoodie. His face was familiar, but where had she seen him before? She racked her brain but she couldn't remember. She got up to get a coffee and saw the face of the pilot on a 'Wanted' poster. It was him, there was no doubt about it; she remembered the first time she had seen his photo added to the wanted list, it was four years ago. The same year as the trial of the pilot. It couldn't be a coincidence; the pilot's escape had been covered up and he was in hiding."

Stephen listened to his friend describe how Ninoska had imagined the life of the pilot.

He had been ordered to destroy a refugee boat, killing all its occupants. Innocent people who were fleeing the destruction of their homes by rising sea levels. They had nowhere else to go; in desperation they sought asylum, as they were entitled to do under the refugee convention. They knew the risks they faced: typhoons, pirates, but not being bombed by an RAAF plane.

The pilot didn't question orders; he did as he was told. He wasn't responsible for the act he committed, someone in his hierarchy was.

It was a convenient way of getting rid of a problem that refused to go away. The RAAF personnel were sworn to secrecy, no one would know about it. It would have been a perfect plan if a drone hadn't been there filming the scene. The 360 degree camera filmed the plane and the whole world knew an RAAF plane had killed innocent men, women and children. The government didn't have a choice; they manufactured evidence that the pilot was a member of The White Australia Resistance gang and had committed an atrocity using the weapons that were supposed to defend his country. The RAAF made up a recording of the controller asking the plane to turn back.

The trial of the pilot was swift, but gave the world a sense that justice had been rendered. When the pilot escaped, the minister of Justice was asked to cover it up, knowing that the pilot would have to go into hiding. He was a public enemy; who would believe his version of the facts if he spoke up?

The pilot fought against the urge to take his own life. His rage against those who had betrayed him kept him alive.

Burning with hate, but alive.

They had made him kill innocent men, women and children who haunted him in his dreams, burning, drowning, and screaming for mercy.

He wasn't going to kill the men who had made him an instrument of death; he wanted them to suffer for the rest of their lives by taking away the women they loved.

A memory stirred in Stephen's mind, an admiral informing Paul Battler and Bob Fultrow that a vessel was approaching territorial waters and that a submarine was ready to strike. Bob Fultrow was the one who had ordered the bombing of the refugee boat four years ago and he was continuing to sink the boats, from below rather than from above. Stephen felt sick. This man who he had been friends with in his youth was a monster. Stephen had never thought he was a saint, no politicians were, but he would never have imagined that Bob would be capable of mass murder.

"It was Sunday and she thought she would tell her team the next day to look for the pilot. She was confident that she would get him and close the case. That's where the memories stop."

Mukassa stopped and stroked his chin. "You said her memories were stolen, like yours were. Does that mean she forgot about the pilot?"

Stephen nodded and got up. "I have to go and tell her straight away."

But Stephen wanted to do better than repeat to her what he had just heard; he drove back to his house and went straight to the fridge where he stored the zook. There was half a bottle left.

Stephen breathed in and breathed out slowly; it did little to calm his nerves. He didn't want the excitement of helping Ninoska find the serial killer to interfere with his trip to the noosphere. He pictured himself proudly announcing to her the address of the man she had been pursuing for years.

It was well past midnight; Stephen forced himself to drink the zook slowly, despite its bitter taste and pronounced the name of the pilot distinctly, wondering what would happen if there were several people with the same name; would the noosphere 'know' which Leonard Camdron he was after?

A wall in a badly lit house; there were four photos of women, three of them had a red cross across their face. The fourth one was middle-aged, her auburn hair flowed down her face. Other photos scattered on the wall showed houses, cars, dogs, cats, and children. A calendar was opened at April and the man picked up a red marker and crossed the thirty-first.

Stephen knew he was in the killer's mind; he waited to see something that would enable him to locate him or identify his next victim. The photo he had seen wasn't enough. There were hundreds of thousands of middle-aged women in Melbourne with auburn hair.

The next images were blurry; Stephen guessed that Leonard was reviewing his own memories.

He pressed a button on a black box. A panel prompted to enter the date and time. He entered 01/05/2015 7:00 AM; an error message informed him that the date was in the past. He entered 05/01/2015 7:00 AM, cursing the Americans for their date format. He touched the screen to validate.

Leonard blinked, and the next images showed a black four-wheel drive in a car park. They were too blurry for Stephen to decipher the registration number, but the colour of the number plate informed him that the vehicle was registered in Victoria. Leonard looked around him; at that time of day the car park was bereft of life. He went to the right side of the car, knelt down and placed the black box underneath the chassis. He checked that it was securely placed, got up and walked out. He looked at his watch: two-thirty.

Leonard blinked again. The images were clear now.

He looked at a monitor showing a mansion in a quiet suburban street at night time. The number of the house was twenty. He made an adjustment to focus the view on the driveway. All good, he thought. There was a feverish anticipation in his mind, like a child waiting for Christmas morning to come faster.

Leonard had placed a bomb underneath the car of a middle-aged woman who drove to work in a black four-wheel drive, presumably leaving her house before seven, and who lived in a mansion in a suburb of Melbourne. It wasn't much to go with, but it was a lot more than Ninoska ever had. It was Stephen's turn to be impatient, waiting for the effects of the zook to wear off so he could call her.

Stephen banged on Ninoska's door. Ninoska hadn't answered her phone, and he had taken a taxi to her house.

Ninoska opened the door. "Have you seen the time? This better be worth it," Ninoska slurred. She was struggling to open her eyes.

Stephen walked in. An empty bottle of vodka laid on the floor.

"Sober up Ninoska." Stephen looked at his watch. "We've got five hours to find out who the next victim is."

"It's all under control. There are about twenty feds guarding the spouses and relatives of the Minister of Defence, the Prime Minister and the Governor-General."

"Do any of them have auburn hair and drive a four-wheel drive registered in Victoria to work that they leave in a car park during the day?"

Stephen summarised what he had seen in the noosphere.

"The killer's changed his modus operandi; the first three victims died in water, like the refugees."

"But it's not inconsistent; many of them would have died from the explosion of the bomb."

Ninoska called Blake and asked him to check the ladies' cars. She put the phone down with a vexed look on her face. She was fully awake now; her fists were clenched.

"He was furious at being woken up; when I asked him about the cars, he thought I was telling him how to do his job. The Federal Police dogs have already checked and they haven't found any explosives inside or around the houses."

"But how did you figure out the potential next victims?"

Ninoska turned to her wall screen and cleared her throat. "Browser, show me the RAAF ranks," she said with a husky voice.

"The pilot has been working his way up the hierarchy: he was a Leading Aircraftman, and his first victim was the wife of his Flight Sergeant. Between him and the Flight Sergeant, there's the Corporal and the Sergeant, so he skipped two rungs in the ladder. His second victim was the wife of his Squadron Leader; between Flight Sergeant and Squadron Leader, there are three ranks. His third victim was the mistress of the Chief of Defence Forces. Between Squadron Leader and Chief of Defence Forces there are four ranks. If he was following a sequence, he would be skipping five ranks this time. The Chief of Defence Forces reports directly to the Minister of Defence, who reports to the Prime Minister who doesn't really report to anyone, but he's appointed by the Governor-General who is appointed by the Queen. The hierarchy stops there; if we discount the Queen because she's not in Australia, it leaves us with the Minister of Defence, the Prime Minister and the Governor-General. Browser, find photos of spouses and female relatives of Frank Dibbly, Bob Fultrow and Evan Abercrombie."

Stephen looked at the screen. "No, I don't recognise any of them." His ears twitched. "What if he was targeting someone else who was responsible for his conviction?"

"Criminals who seek reprisals often target the inspector who arrested them. I can find out his name; I've got the pilot's file from an... acquaintance at the RAAF security police." The last words were spoken rapidly, as if she didn't want Stephen to hear them.

Ninoska searched through a pile of papers on a desk in her room. "Phone, call Lewis Hansu, loudspeaker on." He answered after ten rings. "Inspector Hansu; I'm inspector

Kristayeno; Do you remember Leonard Camdron? He has killed three women and he's about to kill another one in less than five hours. Tell me, do you have a wife or partner with auburn hair who drives a black four-wheel drive to work and leaves it in a public car park during the day?"

"Yes, my wife Karen—is she in danger?"

"Quick, look underneath the chassis and tell me if you see a black box, but don't touch it."

Ninoska's question was answered five minutes later.

"Nothing, I've checked everywhere. But I'll get one of our dogs to check it again. I'll call you back if we find anything."

"Criminals also target the judge who convicted them," Ninoska said. "Leonard was tried by the military court." She searched through Leonard's file again.

"Browser, display Judge Brian Pulzow's details and those of wife and relatives."

Ninoska scrolled through the results.

"No photos?" Stephen asked.

"He must've invoked privacy restrictions that I can't override with my police access, but he does live at a number twenty. Browser, display street view of twenty Bell Street, Canterbury."

"Can't see anything with that brick wall in front."

Ninoska swivelled the controls to obtain a view from above.

"That's the one; it was dark, but I recognise it."

"Phone, call Brian Pulzow."

There was no answer.

"Let's go."

Ninoska and Stephen ran to Ninoska's car; she switched on the ignition and drove well above the speed limit, calling a SWAT team with an explosives expert to join them at the address.

"Tell them not to park in front of the house and not even to drive in front of it," Stephen said. "If he's monitoring the camera and sees the police, he could remotely override the timer and detonate the bomb; I don't know how powerful it is, but it could do a lot of damage."

Ninoska called back to give the order.

She parked the car a hundred metres from the mansion. Stephen looked at his watch. Five AM.

A two-metre high brick wall with barbed wire on the top, a thick steel gate and security cameras protected the mansion.

"Looks like the judge isn't taking any chances," Ninoska said. She tried calling again, but there was no answer. "He must've switched off his phone."

Ninoska pressed the intercom buzzer. Stephen turned around and looked at the light pole across the road where he thought the camera was, hoping that it didn't have a microphone sensitive enough to pick up what Ninoska was about to say.

A minute that seemed like an hour passed. Ninoska pressed the button again. A light turned on, blinding the inspector and the doctor.

"If you don't stop pressing the buzzer, I'll call the police." A voice coming from the intercom said. It could be the judge or his butler—he was wealthy enough to afford one—or his security guard—he was the sort of person who needed one.

"I am the police," Ninoska said in a quiet voice. She showed her police card. "Inspector Ninoska Kristayeno, and her assistant Doctor Stephen Collingsworth."

Stephen straightened himself. Police inspector's assistant—he never expected to be able to put that in his résumé.

"Assuming that you are who you say you are, what do you want in the middle of the night? If you want a search warrant you have to follow the procedure and contact my office."

"Sir, your wife's car's been booby-trapped."

"What on earth are you talking about? I'm going to call the Chief Commissioner."

"Please sir, we don't have time, the bomb has been set to explode in less than two hours."

"But why would anyone want to do that?"

"Remember Leonard Camdron, the pilot of the plane who—"

"Of course I remember him, but he's in jail."

"Sir, he's escaped and he's already killed three women, all related to RAAF hierarchy. He's seeking revenge because he was framed."

"I've never heard such nonsense."

"Sir, Leonard's put a camera across the road," Stephen said. "He's probably watching us and if you don't let us in soon, he's going to get suspicious and trigger the bomb."

The judge hesitated. "Two hours did you say? I've got time to call the Chief Commissioner. Come back in fifteen minutes."

The lights switched off.

Ninoska and Stephen walked away slowly and deliberately.

"Have you informed your hierarchy?" Stephen asked.

"I didn't have time. But I'll get a call after the judge speaks to the Chief Commissioner, don't you worry about that."

"Once the judge lets us in, what do we do? If Leonard sees him and his wife walking out of the house, he won't hesitate to trigger the bomb."

"Did you see how broad the range of the camera was?"

"It was focussed on the driveway leading up to the garage, but I could see part of the house, the gate and the street just in front."

Ninoska stopped walking. "Are we out of range now?"

"Yes."

"And was the neighbour's house visible?"

Stephen shook his head.

"Good, because we need to evacuate them now. The judge and his wife can escape on the left hand side."

"Leonard won't see them, but how are they going to do that? The house is worse than a prison."

"I'll get the SWAT team to go to his neighbour's front yard, cut through the barbed wire and throw a ladder down."

Ninoska's phone rang; she summarised the situation to the Chief Commissioner and answered his questions. The succinct responses she gave to save time prompted more questions. When the interrogation was over, she called the SWAT team to give them their orders.

Her phone rang again, it was the judge. She gave him his instructions.

Stephen watched the men of the SWAT team climb over the front fence of the neighbour's house. Fifteen minutes later, a woman that Stephen recognised as the next victim walked out of the neighbour's front yard with her husband Brian Pulzow. They were followed by another couple with two teenagers that Stephen assumed to be the neighbours and their children.

"I've left the back door open as you asked so they can enter without being seen," the judge said. "Can they neutralise the bomb? There are some priceless paintings in the house."

"Sir, in theory we've got ninety minutes left until the bomb explodes; the SWAT team is going to use a remote-controlled vehicle to neutralise the bomb. But there's always a risk that tampering with the bomb will set it off. I'm sure your insurance will cover the damage, but safety is the priority. The fire brigade is on stand-by; I'm going to check that the neighbours have been evacuated."

Stephen watched the judge and Ninoska; one was concerned about his possessions, the other about her colleagues for whom risking their lives was part of their job. It was the first time in his life Stephen had been in a life-threatening situation. The bomb could have gone off when he was at the gate with Ninoska or worse, if the judge *had* let them in, it could have gone off when they approached the garage which was near the front door.

Ninoska picked up her radio.

"In the garage. Bomb located. RCV is positioned and ready to operate. Retreating now. Over."

"Wait for go-ahead to operate RCV."

Ninoska glanced at her watch: six zero five. "Ninoska to all units: explosive device can explode any moment now. Confirm all neighbours in a perimeter of one hundred metres have been evacuated."

"Unit Alpha—confirmed. Over."

"Unit Bravo—confirmed. Over.

"Unit Charlie—confirmed. Over."

"Delta unit. Commence IEDD RSP. Over."

"Roger."

"Explosive device located; held to the chassis with super magnetic charge. Starting analysis now. Over"

Ninoska saw the puzzled look on Stephen's face. "IEDD RSP stands for Improvised Explosive Device Disposal Render Safe Procedure. RCV is the Remote controlled Vehicle; it's outfitted with cameras, microphones, sensors for chemical, biological and nuclear agents and an X-Ray camera. It will determine what type of bomb it's dealing with, how powerful it is, and what tools to use to neutralise it."

Stephen couldn't help holding his breath while he was listening to Ninoska, as if he could trigger the bomb by exhaling.

"Analysis completed. Attempt to demagnetise explosive device has sixty-seven per cent probability of provoking detonation. Need to remove the whole vehicle. Over."

"Too dangerous. Criminal is monitoring area; he could detonate the bomb remotely. Any other options? Over."

"Trepanation has forty-eight per cent probability of detonation in the initial stage. Over."

"Start trepanation now. Over." She turned to Stephen. "Trepanation is a technique in which a bore is cut into the side and the explosive contents are extracted through a combination of steam and acid bath liquefaction of bomb contents."

Stephen didn't appreciate Ninoska's effort to keep him informed. His mind was blank, he couldn't think about anything.

The silence was broken by the radio. "Trepanation completed. RCV will now demagnetise device and proceed with disposal. Over."

Ninoska breathed out loudly. "Evacuate RCV through the same way it came in. Don't want killer to know we're here. Over."

"Roger."

"Ninoska to all units. Explosive device neutralised. Expecting killer to make his way here when he realises bomb hasn't detonated. Don't know how far away he is, he could be here any time after seven. Keep all residents and marked police cars well clear of the area and activate honey fly trap. Over."

"If he turns up and sees the police, he'll just turn back," Stephen said.

"A honey fly trap is when two police squads position themselves on either side of the house, disguised as road maintenance workers. They'll have a sign marked 'Local traffic only' and won't let in anyone other than the killer. Once he's in, he's trapped. I'll position myself in the house across the road, and you join Yoshimi with the other residents over there."

Stephen refrained from saying that he preferred staying with her; the curious side of him wanted to, but the cautious side of him wanted to run to safety. It was thanks to him that a crime had been averted, but Ninoska had a job to do and unless the killer did something desperate, he would be caught alive, no one would get hurt and justice would be done.

Stephen opened the fridge which offered nothing to satisfy his hunger. He had gone home after the killer had been caught and the residents of Bell Street had returned to their homes. Ninoska hadn't had the luxury of resting; she had to debrief the chief inspector, file her report and attend a media conference. Stephen had gone to bed with his clothes on and had woken up ravenous. On the bottom shelf stood the bottle of zook which was one third full. Stephen thought about the man that Ninoska had prayed to. Hubertus, her fiancé, killed by a person that Ninoska hadn't been able to catch.

Why hadn't she asked Stephen to take some zook to find her fiancé's killer? Was it because of the way Hubertus had been killed, he wouldn't have been able to see his killer? Had

Hubertus served in the police force? Did Ninoska feel responsible for his death and want to take the matter into her own hands rather than ask someone for help?

Stephen had thought about using the rest of the zook to explore Hugh Everett's memories, to see what had gone on in his head when he formulated the many-worlds interpretation of quantum physics, but he preferred helping Ninoska to find closure. He thought about Cécile; she was still alive, but he had lost her and he could only blame himself. Finding love again wasn't high on his list of priorities. He didn't know what was on top of that list—the memory snatcher had been caught, his memory was probably in someone's head, and if that someone could do something with it—a very unlikely scenario, there were only a handful of quantum physicists on earth, one thousand at most out of a population of twelve billion—then good for him, or her. It didn't matter anymore if he wasn't the one to discover how to generate dark energy.

If Ninoska did find closure, would it set her free to love another man, or would she remain faithful to the end?

He had grown to like her but he couldn't imagine falling in love with her, although she was attractive and he did enjoy the way she rolled her r's.

Stephen stopped a train of thought was going nowhere. He swigged down the zook and waited for the familiar feeling of being sucked in through a tunnel with a yellow light at the end. Travelling to the noosphere had become as mundane as going from sleep to consciousness, or even going from one side of the road to the other.

He thought about Hubertus and Ninoska.

The hand of a man attaching a telephoto lens as long as a forearm to a camera body.

He turned the camera and looked at the display panel on the back; he turned a dial and a number flickered. Four thousand.

Stephen was no expert in photography, but it was a tool of Cécile's trade and she had taught him the basics. A number in the thousands could be the ISO sensitivity (beware of the grain!) or the shutter speed (a high value is ideal for capturing fast movement).

Hubertus slung his camera on his shoulder and took his smartphone from his pocket.

I better check out how this game's played before it starts.

He read the information displayed on his smartphone:

Roller derby is a contact sport played by two teams of five members roller skating in the same direction around a track. Game play consists of a series of short matchups (jams) in which both teams designate a scoring player (the jammer) who scores points by lapping members of the opposing team. The teams attempt to assist their own jammer while hindering the opposing jammer.

Scoring

Point scoring occurs during "jams": plays that last up to two minutes. During a jam, points are scored when a jammer on a scoring pass (every pass a jammer makes through the pack after the initial pass) laps members of the opposing team. Each team's blockers use body contact, changing positions, and other tactics to assist its jammer to score while hindering the opposing team's jammer.

Blocking

Roller derby athletes may attempt to knock their opponents out of bounds or impede their movements by blocking (actions which are not solely within the prerogative of the official blockers). Legal blocks follow certain rules. Contact by hands, elbows, head and feet are prohibited, as is contact above the shoulders, below mid-thigh or from the rear.

Equipment

Players skate on four-wheeled ("quad") roller skates, and are required to wear protective equipment, including a helmet, wrist guards, elbow pads, knee pads, and mouth guards. Additional gear that is acceptable though subject to individual team rules include padded knee length pants and gender specific gear such as a hard case sports bra for female players and protective cups for males.

Safety concerns

Since roller derby is a contact sport, there is a risk of injury. Injuries range from common bruises and sprains to broken bones and concussions and beyond.

Hubertus raised his head and looked at the two teams taking their positions. Tattoos seemed to be part of the uniform, whilst some players wore tutus or fishnet stockings.

This sure beats cricket.

Hubertus thought about the cricket games he'd covered. He still didn't get the Australians' enthusiasm for a game where a match could last for days. He had been in Australia since he was ten when his parents emigrated from the Netherlands and he felt as Australian as anyone, except for the fact that he found cricket as boring as watching tulips grow, as they said in the old country.

"Ladies and gentlemen, welcome to tonight's semi-final match of the Great Southern Slam. The Titanic Terminatresses are playing on their home ground,"

Loud cheers and whistles.

"Against the South Sea Slimy Sirens."

The cheers scattered throughout the crowd were drowned by the boos.

Stephen watched the match through the lens of Hubertus' camera; Ninoska was the most photographed player. Stephen didn't know the game anymore than Hubertus, but he could tell that Ninoska was a remarkable player. She was fast and controlled her strength, never receiving a penalty.

"And with the score at two hundred and forty points to one hundred and eighty-four, the winner is the Titanic Terminatresses."

Hubertus' job was finished, but he felt lucky that night. He followed the winning team to the Camel's back, a pub in King Street.

The drinking at the winners' table was as fast and relentless as the game; Hubertus didn't have to wait long at the counter for Ninoska to buy her round.

"Fantastic game."

"Yeah, we gave'em a good thrashing."

"I'm a photographer for The Age; give me your email and I'll send you some of my shots. Unofficially of course."

"Yeah, that'll be great."

Hubertus gave her a business card and she wrote her email address.

Stephen didn't want to see anything he would regret seeing, so he fast forwarded by thinking about Hubertus' last day.

A blur was followed by a view of Hubertus shaving.

In the dining room, he joined Ninoska who was having breakfast.

The mood was leisurely; they weren't in a hurry.

Stephen deduced that it was Saturday or Sunday. An ordinary day in the life of an ordinary couple. Except that for one of them it was his last day, and he didn't know it. *Live today as though it was your last day.* How many times had

Stephen heard that, but what would he do if today was his last day? He hadn't even tried to think about it, his research was a long-term occupation, dying was not an option until he had found what he was looking for. How pretentious he had been, thinking that his work was so important that death would have left him alone.

Later that day Hubertus took his bag and checked that his cameras and lenses were where they were supposed to be.

"I'll probably be home after ten; I'll be covering a basketball game."

He kissed Ninoska on the lips and left.

Stephen wondered why anyone would want to kill Hubertus—unless someone that Ninoska had arrested was seeking revenge. But surely Ninoska would have thought of that; the men and women she had put behind bars would have been the first suspects.

Stephen jumped to the end of the game. Melbourne beat Sydney 129 to 92. Hubertus didn't leave at the end of the game; he waited outside the basketball court. A woman walked towards him; Stephen recognised her as the forward of the Melbourne team, the biggest scorer of the match; she cupped his head in her hands and kissed him.

She whispered in his ear, "I don't want anyone to see us together. Go to my place now and I'll see you shortly; I'm just going to have a quick drink with the girls."

Hubertus watched her join the rest of the team; he switched off his smartphone.

Ninoska knows I usually have a drink after the game, so she won't try to call me, but if she does I'll say that I hadn't heard it because the pub was too noisy.

The pedestrian light was green; Hubertus crossed the road, thinking about the moment of bliss he was going to live with his mistress. He only saw the white car just before it hit him.

A tunnel with a white light at the end.

An ethereal being welcomed Hubertus and embraced him.

Hubertus' life flashed before his eyes, in its totality from birth to death. He had cheated Ninoska with more than the basketball player; indeed it could be said that he had sampled players of every game. The being did not express judgement; Hubertus was the only judge of his own behaviour and he saw for the first time the repercussions of his actions.

Stephen had seen enough.

"Wait, don't go yet."

Stephen hadn't heard the words, they were formed in his mind, but they didn't come from his mind.

"Please tell her I'm sorry."

"Sorry for what?"

"For cheating on her."

"But she doesn't know you cheated."

"You have to tell her; I owe her the truth. She's never stopped loving me; she was faithful when I was alive and she stayed faithful after my death. But her love for me wasn't enough; I always had to get more than what I had. I want her to be happy with another man now. She's got her life in front of her and she deserves to be happy."

"But how is she going to react when I tell her that the man she is grieving for cheated on her?"

"You're a good man, you care about her. But trust me, truth is more important than anything. It will set her free and will prepare her for the day we are reunited. I apologise about asking you to be the bearer of such news, but please do it for her. Tell her that I love her and I long for the day when we'll be reunited."

Stephen said goodbye to Hubertus. This time there was no doubt about it; there *was* life after death, and the consciousness of the deceased was as much a part of the noosphere as the consciousness of the living. It was a different sort of consciousness, because every second of the life the deceased had lived on earth was in the noosphere. They could not even try to forget the moments of their lives they were the least proud of.

Stephen knew what it was like to remember everything, but he had never thought his memories would live on after his death.

Whoever had said that eternity was very long, especially towards the end must have been right.

Stephen rose to the creative level of the noosphere.

He glimpsed the answers to his question before the effects of the zook wore off.

Dark energy was a misfit; it could not be explained by the same model as gravitation, electromagnetism, strong interaction and weak interaction. The first conclusion was that it was impossible to convert one of those forms of energy to dark energy. The second was that there was no theory that could explain all physical aspects of the universe.

Stephen was not disappointed; he had found something much more interesting: dark energy could be *harnessed* like the wind, and it would take mankind to the edges of the universe.

Or as close as possible, because by the time a spaceship would get there, the universe would have expanded.

But who would be bold enough to believe in Stephen's vision?

There was one man who had believed that our memories could be backed up (and according to the noosphere, he *was* right), and it was thanks to him, albeit indirectly, that Stephen had made this discovery.

The man that Stephen had hated with all his heart because he had been responsible for his father's downfall had become Stephen's friend.

And somehow he knew that his father wouldn't mind.

Epilogue

30th April 2046, Garmisch-Partenkirchen, Bavaria, European Union

The cuckoo clock marked the eighth hour. Frau Wichter put the *spätzle* in boiling water; she stirred, watching the noodles spin around. She drained them, covered them with cream, cheese and onions. She served Dieter's plate first and then hers.

Dieter was late; he had started milking the cows at six, like he did seven days of each week that the good Lord made. He should have come back at eight, like he did every day.

Perhaps Yvonne had gone into labour; she had started to spring this morning. She was swollen and a liquid was dripping from her tail end, sure signs that she was close to calving. But if that was the case, why hadn't Dieter called her?

Frau Wichter decided to go to the milking barn when Dieter rushed in the kitchen.

"*Liebling*, are you alright?" she asked.

Dieter sat down and poured himself a glass of *Himbeergeist* which he gulped down.

"I thought I had gone crazy down there."

"What happened?"

"I was removing the milking cups from Suzie when all of a sudden I saw images of a man's life."

"Whose life? Was it your father?"

"No, it was someone who spoke English, I couldn't understand anything. He was entering numbers and formulas into a computer, lots of them. All I know is that he was happy about finding something he had been looking for."

"The numbers, do you remember them?"

Frau Wichter memorised the numbers Dieter recited; it was a gift from above. She was going to give them to her youngest son Peter who played lotto every week. If he won, he could realise his dream of sailing around the world. She had never been outside her beloved mountains; she had everything she needed here, why go somewhere else? But Peter was adventurous; he would never be satisfied living the life that his father, his grandfather and his ancestors since time immemorial had lived.

Frau Wichter watched Dieter eat his *spätzle;* she sighed, daydreaming about her son sailing on a yacht. They would be able to communicate with that smartphone Peter had offered his Dad for Christmas. Dieter wasn't a fan of technology, but he took it with him when he was milking to play music to the cows.

She would love to go with her son, but who would look after Dieter?

It was an adventure she would have to live vicariously, but it was better than not at all.

Connect with Pascal Inard

If you've enjoyed reading The Memory Snatcher, please leave a review at your retailer and/or book cataloguing website (Goodreads, for example). Thank you in advance.

If you want to keep in touch, here's how you can connect with Pascal.

- Email: inard@internode.on.net
- Facebook: www.facebook.com/Pascal.Inard.Writer

About Pascal Inard

Pascal Inard has published novels, non-fiction books and short stories, as well as articles in online magazines. He writes mostly in English, but sometimes in French or in both languages.

He lives a creative life in Cheltenham, a suburb of Melbourne in Australia with his illustrator and crafter wife Isabella and their three children. When he's not writing or photographing, he manages IT projects for an Australian bank.

Also by Pascal Inard

Web of Destinies - a time travel mystery like no other:

Guillaume Chambon, a French doctor has inherited a mysterious typewriter that can change the past. He doesn't have to travel in time; the past comes to him through a vision of anterior events that he describes using the typewriter. When he sees those events leading to a tragic end, he types a different continuation. Reality is thus modified, but there are consequences that he didn't foresee.

To use the typewriter to stop his sister from losing her life twenty years ago, he is going to have to remove the safeguards put by the inventor, a friend of Jules Verne who found crystals with extraordinary properties. As Guillaume tries to unravel the mysteries of the typewriter, assisted by his friend Sylvie who has secrets of her own, he is confronted with a secret agent who wants to use it to make a major change to history, and a Buddhist monk who is trying to stop him because if he succeeds, the fabric of the universe is in danger of collapsing.

Available in print and eBook at Amazon and other major online retailers

Pushing up the digits - a collection of short stories on the digital afterlife.

Have you ever wondered what was going to happen to your digital self when you pass away?

Your 'likes', your connections with friends and family, your photos, your purchases, the web sites you visited, your tax return, your curriculum vitae and job applications, the films you watched, the music you listened to, the books you read and rated, the meals you ate, the events you attended and (almost) everything else you experienced. There are few aspects of our lives that aren't stored as binary digits on a server somewhere in the web.

But does your digital self die like you do, or does it take on a life of its own? Has heaven kept up with technology to offer its inhabitants their own social network?

Jason, Vince and Stephanie, the characters of the short stories in this collection are confronted with these questions, and the answers will change the way they use their connected devices forever.

Available on eBook at Amazon.

Dear France, sweet country of my childhood – Chère France, doux pays de mon enfance:

A tribute to France with beautiful photos, delicious recipes, vintage postcards and posters, stories from the authors' childhood and interesting facts on French places and traditions. A must for anyone wanting to learn more about France or who is learning French, as it is entirely written in both English and French.

Read about it on www.dearfrance.net

Available in print at Amazon and other major online retailers.

Un dernier roman pour la route (novel in French)

The story of a bestselling author with writer's block who travels the world in a quest for his inspiration.

Available in print and eBook at Amazon and other major online retailers.

Thank You

I am deeply grateful for the following persons and organisations that helped me to write The Memory Snatcher, knowingly or unintentionally:

- My wife Isabella.
- Oxana, who provided invaluable insights on Russian culture.
- My beta readers for their valuable feedback.
- Metro Trains Melbourne: The Memory Snatcher was written in the carriages of the Frankston line, and I was one of the rare commuters who enjoyed the times when my train slowed down or stopped unexpectedly because it gave me more time to write.